She smiled up at him, winding her arms tightly about his neck so he could not fly away from her.

His hair was like warm satin against her skin, his body so warm and solid and delicious against hers. How she yearned to stay here in his embrace all night—forever! To kiss him, *feel* him, and forget about thieves and ghosts and families and everything.

His eyes widened in surprise, but before he could answer she went up on tiptoe to kiss him, pressing one swift caress to his lips, then another and another, teasing him until he groaned and pulled her even closer, until there was not even a breath between them. He deepened the kiss, his tongue seeking hers, and she was lost in him.

It wasn't like their first kiss, soft and tentative as they learned the taste of each other. It was fast and hungry, filled with the yearnings of their time together, the drive to be close and know that this was real.

* * *

To Catch a Rogue
Harlequin® Historical #989—April 2010

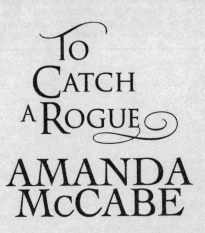

To Catch a Rogue

Amanda McCabe

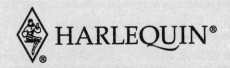

HARLEQUIN®

TORONTO • NEW YORK • LONDON
AMSTERDAM • PARIS • SYDNEY • HAMBURG
STOCKHOLM • ATHENS • TOKYO • MILAN • MADRID
PRAGUE • WARSAW • BUDAPEST • AUCKLAND

Recycling programs
for this product may
not exist in your area.

ISBN-13: 978-0-373-29589-0

TO CATCH A ROGUE

Copyright © 2008 by Ammanda McCabe

First North American Publication 2010

To Laura Kay Gauldin, who has been brave enough to be my friend since we were teenagers! If not for the three Gauldin sisters there never could have been three Chase sisters.

Prologue

"Where'er we tread 'tis haunted, holy ground;
No earth of thine is lost in vulgar mould
But one vast plain of wonder spreads around,
And all the Muses' tales seem truly told
Till the sense aches with gazing to behold
The scenes our earliest dreams have dwelt upon...

Lord Byron

Never had a night been as dark as this one.

The moon was a mere sliver high over the crooked rooftops of London, nearly obscured by scudding clouds. There were no stars at all, not even a tiny, bead-like sparkle, and an infamous London fog was creeping inward over the sluggish Thames. Heavy and greasy, a noxious grey-green, it would soon blanket the city, cutting off even the dull shimmer of that tiny moon.

But all the guests at the Marchioness of Tenbray's ball—and that was nearly everyone in the *ton* who mattered at all—cared not a whit for the ominous night outside the brilliantly lit mansion. They were far too busy moving through the crush of the ballroom, laughing, dancing, trading the latest *on dits* behind silken fans, drinking champagne, stealing kisses under concealment of the terrace's potted palms. All the world seemed compressed into this one marble-and-gilt room, a swirl of music and chatter and clinking crystal rising up and up with no care for the dark chill outside.

Not one of them—not even the marchioness herself, deeply preoccupied by a sudden shortage of lobster tarts—noticed a window in the library sliding silently open.

Someone else was taking full advantage of the darkness, and not for surreptitious caresses on the terrace. No, this person had something far more important, far more devious, in mind.

As the window swung all the way open, this person, tall and slim, muffled and masked all in black, climbed inside and hopped lightly to the Aubusson carpet laid over polished parquet. The figure made no sound, as soft as cat's paws on the silken weave. It went automatically down into a low crouch, breath held as bright eyes, revealed through the slits of the satin mask, darted from left to right. The library, as expected, was deserted, lit by only one small Colza lamp on the polished desk. It cast a circle of golden glow, flickering, sweetly scented, and all the far corners were deep in gloom. Bookshelves rose to the ceiling, crowded with leather-bound volumes that looked scarcely touched, let alone read and loved.

Well, thought the intruder. *Old Lady Tenbray is scarcely renowned for her brains, is she?*

Yet the late Lord Tenbray *had* been renowned for his passion for Italian antiquities, and this was what drew the black-clad figure's interest. Once assured of being alone, the intruder rose from that crouch and moved stealthily across the room. The shadows were no deterrent—the library's layout had been carefully studied, every chair and table mapped. This person knew what they sought.

At the far end of the space, on either side of the carved fireplace, were glass-topped cases, each one filled to the brim with the marquess's ill-gotten gains. In his youth, long ago, he had served as a diplomat to the kingdom of Naples. From there, he sent home crates full of statuary, jewellery, frescoes, vases. Only a small part of the collection resided in this library.

The very best part.

"Ah, yes," the intruder whispered. "There you are."

From a pocket tied around the waist came a thin piece of metal, which was carefully inserted into the case's lock. One upward twist, and the mechanism popped free.

"Lax, lax," the person murmured, lifting up the lid. Really, people who could not take care of their possessions did not deserve them.

The object of desire lay in the very centre of the display, an Etruscan diadem of gold hammered very thin and formed into the shape of delicate leaves and vines. Once, it had graced the head of a queen. Now it satisfied an old Englishwoman's vanity.

But not for long.

The figure reached for it with black-gloved hands. Even in the shadows the diadem glowed like the Italian sky, so light and perfect. It seemed so fragile, yet had survived so much for these thousands of years.

"You will soon be safe," came the reassuring whisper, as the diadem disappeared into the pocket.

As its glow vanished, there was a loud thump outside the library door. The figure's masked head whipped around, eyes wide, heart pounding.

"No, Agnes, we shouldn't!" a man groaned, his words slurred, overly loud in the quiet room.

"Oh, but we really must!" a woman answered. "We haven't got very long. My husband will soon leave the card room and be looking for me."

There was another thump, then a click of the door handle as someone, either Agnes or her drunken companion, groped for the entrance.

Time to be gone. One more object emerged from that pocket, a perfect white lily that was carefully placed in the diadem's abandoned spot. Then the figure sprinted lightly across the floor, jumping up on to the window ledge. Just as the door flew open, the thief was gone, disappearing into the gloomy night.

The Lily Thief had struck again.

Chapter One

"I call this meeting of the Ladies Artistic Society to order," announced Calliope Chase, sounding her gavel on the table in front of her. "Our secretary, Miss Clio Chase, will take the minutes."

Slowly, all the teacups and plates of cakes were lowered to laps and tabletops, and the members of the Society turned their attention to their founder and president. Bright sunlight flowed from the tall windows of the drawing room of the Chases' townhouse, warm and bright after the chilly misery of the night before, casting pastel spencers and muslin gowns in a brilliant light. Everything in the fashionably appointed room was just as expected—the ladies seated in pretty groupings of chairs and settees, china tea sets, silver services, hovering housemaids, the soft sound of Mozart from the pianoforte in the corner.

All expected and proper. Except for one thing. Behind Calliope, set high on its pedestal, was a marble statue of Apollo. An anatomically correct, completely naked statue of Apollo.

But then, what else could be looked for in a house belonging to the famous scholar of Greek history, Sir Walter Chase? A house where his nine daughters, named after the Greek Muses, resided and pursued their own, not always completely ladylike, interests.

Calliope, the eldest of the Chase Muses at age twenty-one, was also not all that was expected. She was quite attractive, taking after her late mother's French family with her black hair and brown eyes, her flawless fair skin; and those good looks—with the Chase fortune—had attracted more than a few offers from very eligible *partis*. Yet she had turned them all down. "They just don't care about history and antiquities," she told her father, and he immediately agreed that those young men would never do for one of the Chase Muses.

She also cared little for fashion or for dancing or cards, preferring to spend her time in study, or in conversation *about* her studies with like-minded people.

That was why she founded the Ladies Artistic Society in the first place, so that she and her sisters could reach out to other females with more on their minds than hemlines and hats. "Surely there must be others like us here in London," she told her sister Clio. "You know—ladies who wish they could take books with them to pass the dull hours at Almack's."

And so there were. Their membership now included two of their friends, along with the three eldest Chase daughters (the other six still being in the schoolroom, and therefore members-in-waiting). There was also a waiting list, though Calliope suspected that many of those just wanted a glimpse of Apollo. They met once a week during the Season to talk about history, literature, art, music. Often a guest lecturer, provided by the Muses' father, would speak, or a painter would give a demonstration. Sometimes they would just discuss amongst themselves a book read or an opera seen, or Thalia, the third Chase sister and an ardent musician, would perform a scandalous, passionate Beethoven piece.

Not today, though. Today there was very serious business to discuss, and obviously everyone discerned that from the stiff set of Calliope's shoulders in her white muslin day dress. A hush fell over the bright room, all clinkings and rustlings stilled. Even Thalia ceased playing the pianoforte, swivelling around to face her sister.

Calliope lifted up a copy of the *Post*, pointing at a black, shrieking headline: *The Lily Thief Returns!*

"It has been many weeks since this criminal struck," Calliope said softly. Her voice was quiet, but she felt her cheeks burn with the force of her inner anger. Many weeks—and she had thought the Lily Thief gone, vanished like so many other ephemeral sensations in Society. A two-day scandal, and then something else, an elopement or divorce, or other such harmless trifle. "I suppose he realised that attention was drifting from his foul deeds."

Her sister Clio glanced up from the minutes, her auburn brow arched above the gilt frames of her spectacles. Clio said nothing, though. Merely went back to her note-taking. It was Lady Emmeline Saunders who spoke. "Perhaps the Lily Thief has very good reasons for what he does."

"Reasons such as profit and riches?" Thalia cried from her piano. Her golden curls, so shiny and pretty, trembled with indignation. Thalia might look like a china shepherdess, but she had the heart of a gladiator. And that accounted for the many scrapes she always found herself in. "I am sure he saw a pretty penny from the sale of Lord Egermont's Euphronios krater and the Clives' Bastet statue."

"Antiquities have more than a monetary value, you

know," Clio said quietly. "Something their previous owners seemed to have lost sight of."

"Of course they do," Calliope said. "And that is what makes the exploits of this Lily Thief so heinous. Who knows where these objects have gone, or if they will ever be seen again? We will have no access to the lessons they could teach us. It is a terrible loss to scholarship."

Clio bent her head back over her notes, murmuring low enough for only Calliope to hear, "As if there was much *scholarship* going on in Lady Tenbray's library."

"The Lily Thief does not just steal money or jewels, as a common burglar would. Objects that could easily be replaced," Calliope said. "He steals history."

The other Society members glanced at each other. Finally, Emmeline raised her hand again. "What must we do about this, Calliope? Perhaps engage a don from Cambridge to speak on cultural thefts?"

"Or tomb-raiding!" cried Miss Charlotte Price, the youngest and most excitable of the Society. She had an unfortunate predilection for reading horrid novels, but her father was a friend of Sir Walter Chase. He hoped the Society would help her expand her horizons. So far the hope was in vain, but one never knew. "I did read about a cursed tomb robber in *The Baron's Revenge*—"

"Yes, indeed," Calliope said, interrupting smoothly before Lotty could be carried off into a rambling synopsis. "But I have something rather more—personal in mind."

"Personal?" the others chorused.

"Yes." Calliope placed her palms flat on the table before her, leaning towards her audience. "We are going to catch the Lily Thief ourselves."

A great sigh went up, floating to the plaster-ceiling medallion in a wave of exclamation.

"Oh, how very thrilling!" trilled Charlotte. "Just like *The Curse of Lady Arabella*—"

"We are to turn amateur sleuths?" Thalia said, clapping her hands. "What a marvellous idea!"

"Indeed," agreed Emmeline. "Scholastic inquiry is all very well, but sometimes we need to *move*."

Clio's pen stilled, her brows drawn down in a puzzled vee. "How do you propose we go about this task, Calliope? If even the Bow Street Runners could not find the Lily Thief…"

Honestly, Calliope had not thought quite that far ahead. The idea of taking action themselves had only occurred to her at breakfast that morning, as she read the papers in mounting anger over the harmful exploits of that show-off Lily Thief. She had some vague notion that, as ladies of the *ton*, they could move about more freely and with far more stealth than those Runners. They could listen and observe with no one being the wiser, and perhaps catch the villain at a vulnerable moment.

For she was sure of one thing—the Lily Thief was a member of the *ton*. He had to be, to possess such knowledge of the houses and schedules of lords and ladies. But she was *not* entirely sure how to begin catching him in their net.

"I suggest," she said slowly, "that we begin with last night's theft of the Etruscan diadem. Was anyone at Lady Tenbray's rout?" Calliope herself had not been, turning down the invitation to what was sure to be a dull crush to attend the theatre with her father. *Macbeth*, she had thought, was sure to be more exciting. If only she had known the Lily Thief was to strike again!

Clio and Thalia were of no help, having chosen to stay home with their studies. There must have been *someone* there whose observations she could trust!

Finally, Emmeline raised her hand again. "I was there, but I noticed nothing untoward, I fear."

"No one behaving oddly at all?" Calliope asked hopefully.

"Just Freddie Mountbank," Emmeline answered. "But then, what does one expect of him? I would have been suspicious if he behaved *normally*."

The ladies all giggled. Poor Mr Mountbank—he was so earnest, so very much in love with Emmeline, yet he had the unfortunate tendency to lose his temper and blurt out curses when he was nervous in a lady's presence (which was always). He had launched more than one dance set into disarray by knocking down all the participants. Unless Mr Mountbank was very clever indeed—and, judging by his parents, that was not likely—he was not the Lily Thief.

"Nothing else?" Calliope asked.

Emmeline shook her head regretfully. "I fear not. It was so very crowded. And my mother insisted I dance with Mr Mountbank, so I was rather distracted in dodging him."

More giggles rippled around the room, and even Calliope had to laugh at the vision of her rather tall friend ducking behind curtains and potted palms to hide from her persistent suitor.

"I'm sorry," Emmeline said. "If I had known…"

"Yes." Calliope sighed. "If only we all knew."

"What shall we do now?" asked Thalia, her tone suggesting that *she* would prefer to armour up like a Valkyrie and go marching out into Mayfair to destroy all villains in her path.

"I am not entirely sure," Calliope admitted. "But I think I *do* have an idea where the Lily Thief will strike next."

"Really?"

"Where?"

"Oh, do tell us!"

Calliope had not completely worked out all this in her mind. Yet sometimes, she thought, intuition was the best guide. "The Duke of Averton's ball."

"Oh!"

"Of course."

"The Alabaster Goddess," Thalia said. "Lud, but that is clever of you, Cal."

"I'm surprised the Lily Thief hasn't made a move towards it yet," Emmeline said.

"He is obviously growing in audacity," Calliope said, gesturing towards the newspaper. "To snatch the diadem in plain sight indicates confidence."

The Alabaster Goddess was a rather small, perfectly preserved statue of Artemis with her bow, taken only a few years ago from a ruined Greek temple on the island of Delos and purchased by the Duke of Averton (or Duke of Avarice, as he was known in certain circles) for his famous collection. She was quite unblemished for being thousands of years old, and the duke loved to show her off, strangely enough, for he was a well-known recluse. The goddess had even sparked quite a fashion in society for "Artemis" hairstyles and "Artemis" sandals. The duke had made it known she would soon be moved to his heavily fortified castle in Yorkshire. But next week she could be seen at a grand masked ball the duke was hosting. His first ball in years.

The ball had a Grecian theme, of course.

Yes, Calliope thought, suddenly sure. The Lily Thief would strike there.

"We must all go to the ball, and there we will—"

"Oh!" Calliope's instructions were cut off by a sudden cry from Lotty, who sat closest to the window. She pressed her nose to the glass, leaning forward precariously. "Oh, it is Lord Westwood! And your beau Mr Mountbank, Emmeline."

Those words, of course—Lord Westwood—caused a
great rush to the windows, silks and ribbons furiously
a-rustle. More noses and fingers pressed to the glass, un-
heeding of smudges and dignity.

"Oh!" cried Thalia. "He is in his beautiful phaeton. I
wish Father would buy one for me, I'm sure I would be a
rare hand at the reins. But Westwood appears to be in some
sort of altercation with Mr Mountbank. How fascinating."

Oh, what a great surprise, Calliope thought sarcasti-
cally. Where Cameron de Vere, the Earl of Westwood went,
"altercations" were sure to follow.

"Cal, Clio, come, you must see this. It's too amusing,"
Thalia said.

Clio left off her scratching of pens and joined the others,
peering down as if observing some scientific demonstration.

Calliope did not *want* to go and gawk with her friends,
as if they were all silly schoolgirls who had never before
seen a man rather than the intelligent, rational women they
were. She did not want to give Lord Westwood the satisfaction of yet more attention. Yet, somehow, she could not
help herself. It was as if a thick cord suddenly tightened
around her waist, pulling her inexorably towards the
window. Towards *him*.

Calliope dropped the newspaper and strolled reluctantly
towards the others, peering past Thalia's shoulder to the
scene below. It was indeed Lord Westwood, his bright
yellow and gleaming black phaeton wedged into traffic, at
a complete standstill. His matched bay horses snorted and
pranced restlessly, as Mr Mountbank, in his own conveyance, blocked Westwood's way, shouting and gesticulating,
as he was wont to do. Mr Mountbank's face was an
alarming shade of purple above his overly starched cravat,
yet Westwood looked on with an expression of amused

boredom on his ridiculously gorgeous face, as if the quarrel had nothing at all to do with him, and he merely watched the action at Drury Lane.

"Really," Calliope muttered. "Our street is hardly Gentleman Jackson's saloon."

"Oh!" Thalia exclaimed. "Do you really think they might come to blows? How terribly interesting."

"How very handsome he is," sighed Lotty. "Just like the comte in *Mademoiselle Marguerites's Fatal Secret.*"

Handsome—well, yes. Even Calliope had to admit that, albeit grudgingly. Westwood was sometimes called "the Greek God" in more florid circles, and strictly from an aesthetic viewpoint it was all too true. He could have been their Ladies Society Apollo statue come to warm, vivid, breathing life, if he were to shed his buckskin breeches and exquisite bottle-green coat. He was hatless now, despite the sunny skies, his glossy, sable-dark curls tossed by the wind until they fell in artistic disarray over his brow. His skin was always a golden-bronze, his eyes dark and maddeningly unreadable.

No, Calliope thought as she watched him now, trying to reason with Mr Mountbank with a half-grin on his lips. He was not so much a god, as a young Greek fisherman, virile, earthbound, as secret as the deepest sea. Surely he got that sense of *otherness* from his mother. Like the Chases' own mother, the late countess had hailed from more exotic climes. She came from where else but Athens, the daughter of a famous Greek scholar.

For an instant, it seemed as if Westwood would actually alight from his phaeton and face the apoplectic wrath of Mr Mountbank. The ladies at the window held their collective breath, but, alas, fisticuffs—and shirtsleeves—in Mayfair were not to be. Mountbank, faced with an opponent potentially closer than several feet away, backed off and hurried on his way, steering his carriage precariously around the corner.

The ladies, disappointed, also backed away, leaving the view to return to their seats. The drawing room was soon filled with the mingling of chatter, music, tea being poured into delicate cups. Calliope, though, could not yet leave with them. Could not break that cord. Something tightened, binding her there, staring down at Cameron de Vere.

He laughed aloud at Mountbank's precipitous retreat, his head thrown back with the unbridled freedom of his humour. His hair fell away from his chiseled face, the sharp angles of his cheekbones and nose. He leaned back easily on the cushioned seat, free as a corsair at the helm of his ship. Passers-by paused to stare at him, as if drawn by the sheer *life* of him, yet he noticed not at all, so comfortable in his own skin, his own world.

Blast him, anyway, Calliope thought wryly. Blast for being—*him*. For being all she was not. For being so free. Not bound to family responsibilities.

Calliope leaned her forehead against the cool glass, watching as Lord Westwood's laughter faded and he once again collected the loosened reins. Even his casual movements were filled with a smooth, unstudied grace.

She watched him, and remembered their first meeting, at the beginning of the Season. Was that only weeks ago? It felt a lifetime. Or mere moments. That night when…

No! No, that didn't bear thinking of. Not now. She was in the middle of a Ladies Society meeting! Her friends were nearby. Thinking of Cameron de Vere, seeing him, fantasising about him as some Greek fisherman on a beach, would only discompose her. Her friends were sure to ask questions, and that would never do. She was always col-

lected and calm. Always in control. She had to be, her
family relied on her.

Why, then, did she tremble so much, just from watching
him down on the street? It was ridiculous!

Calliope reached up for the fringed edge of the satin
drape, clutching at it to draw it over the window. Before
she could do so, concealing herself and all her unruly
emotions, Lord Westwood glanced up and saw her there.
Saw her staring at him.

For an instant, it was as if a cloud passed over the Grecian
sun. He frowned, his velvety brown eyes narrowing. Then,
as swiftly as it came, the cloud vanished. He smiled, a wide,
white Corsair grin, and gave her a jaunty salute.

Calliope gasped involuntarily, and yanked the curtain
closed. *The rogue!*

She spun away from the window, wrapping her
cashmere shawl tighter around her shoulders—only to find
Clio observing her closely.

Calliope adored her sister, the closest to her in age and
in artistic inclination, but sometimes, just sometimes, she
was a bit uneasy to be faced with those unerring, unwavering green eyes.

"You should stay out of the sun, Cal," Clio said quietly.
"It makes your cheeks so flushed."

Calliope Chase.

Cameron frowned as she thrust the draperies shut, as if
to block out a demon from her home. To bar all laughter
from the premises. To bar *him*.

He shouldn't care. He *didn't* care. Calliope Chase was
beautiful, it was true. Yet London was filled with lovely
ladies, most of them far less prickly and mysterious than
Miss Chase. Yet somehow, ever since their first meeting—

or first clash, as he thought of it—he couldn't get her out of his mind. Was he becoming like his rather bizarre cousin Gerald, who paid lightskirts hefty sums to whip his bare backside with a riding crop, pain and aggravation equalling pleasure?

Cam laughed aloud as he guided his horses back into the flow of traffic, picturing Calliope Chase wielding a leather whip with fire in her brown eyes. It was not an unlikely vision. She was named after the wrong mythological figure, surely. She was not a Muse, changeable and capricious and seductive. She was Athena, goddess of war, marching into battle to defend what she believed in, right or wrong.

An Athena with such an intriguing sadness behind her gaze.

Cam glanced over his shoulder before he turned the corner of the street, but the Chases' house was closed up tight. There was no flash of shining raven curls, no glimpse of fair skin and sparkling eyes. Yet he knew she was in there. Could still see her in his mind.

As he headed off into the park, a shortcut to his own home, he let his horses have their head a bit. He saw Mountbank far ahead. Such a silly puppy, getting so upset because Cam had danced with Lady Emmeline Saunders! Anyone could see he was no rival for her affections. She was a pretty girl, and full of interesting conversation (unlike most of the society chits mothers were always pushing his way!). She had a quick humour, too, despite being bosom friends with Miss Chase. But there was something missing when he talked to Lady Emmeline, looked at her.

There was *always* something missing. Something so empty and hollow at the centre of his life, something that was not filled by all his pursuits—his clubs, his horses, women, even his studies. It was a cold and echoing spot, always with him. He only really forgot it, felt a new warmth spark on that ice, when he crossed swords with Calliope Chase.

Curious. Very curious indeed. And not something he cared to think about too deeply.

His horses were now a bit winded after their gallop through the park, so he eased them out of the gates towards home and their own mews. But they were blocked by an unexpected traffic obstruction, a tangled knot of vehicles and horses and pedestrians that brought all movement to a temporary standstill.

"Blast!" Cam muttered, craning his neck to try to peer past a lumbering barouche. He was meant to attend a musical evening later, one he was rather looking forward to as it featured a speculative reconstruction of ancient Greek theatrical music. "What is it now?"

Then the barouche lurched to one side, and he understood. A great crowd had gathered in front of the Marchioness of Tenbray's home, gawking up at the window where the infamous Lily Thief had climbed in to snatch away her ladyship's Etruscan diadem. The thief had been gone from society for a while; his reappearance was the latest sensation.

Cam chuckled, and sat back on the seat to wait for the crowd to clear enough for him to pass. The Lily Thief— how dramatic the moniker was! And how amusing his exploits were, tweaking the noses of some of the *ton*'s most misguided collectors. If only...

If only it was not so dangerous, and destructive. Cam was usually the first to applaud daring, to laud independence, even eccentricity. Look at his own family! Eccentrics one and all. But some things were simply too important to trifle with, including objects of immense cultural heritage. Like that diadem, or the other antiquities that fell into the Lily Thief's hands. Who knew where those precious pieces had gone? What would become of them?

And then there were objects that had not yet fallen to the Lily Thief. Objects whose fate was even more vile. Averton's Artemis, for instance.

Cam's gloved hands fisted on the reins, causing the horses to toss their heads restlessly. He forced himself to relax, murmuring to them soothingly, but by damn, there was nothing that made him more furious than the Duke of "Avarice"!

That Artemis was snatched from her home on Delos, the place where she had belonged for thousands of years. She was *Greek*, and now she was merely an object of greed for an English lord. A vile man who had no care for her true worth.

"You know of Artemis?" Cam could almost hear his mother whisper so long ago, her accent as warm and musical as her Athenian home. *"Zeus' favourite child, the goddess of the moon and the hunt, the Maiden of the Silver Bow. She races through the forest in her silver chariot, always free, never the possession of any man. Once she shot an arrow into a vast city of unjust men, and the arrow pierced all of them, never ceasing in its flight until justice was served…"*

And now she was a prisoner, locked away from the Greek moonlight for ever.

What would the learned Miss Chase say about that? For Cameron was certain she had an opinion about the Duke of "Avarice" and his newest prize, his famed Alabaster Goddess. But would she tell that opinion to *him*?

The traffic snarl finally eased a bit, letting him guide the horses through on their way home. Yes, indeed. Calliope Chase was sure to have something to say about it all. And he very much looked forward to hearing it.

Chapter Two

Calliope watched in her dressing table mirror, distracted, as her maid brushed out her hair in preparation for the evening ahead. A *musicale*, featuring not the usual young and untalented misses with their harps and pianofortes, but a recreation of music that might have been performed at plays by Aeschylus and Euripides at the great festivals of ancient times. She had been very much looking forward to it, it was just the sort of thing that most fascinated her. But now her thoughts were scattered and hazy, scudding here and there like springtime clouds.

She couldn't stop thinking about Lord Westwood. He just kept popping into her mind, the vision of him outside her window, laughing and windblown and carefree.

"Pfft," she sighed impatiently, reaching for one of the small white roses on the table and tearing at the soft petals. It was ever thus when she saw Cameron de Vere. He unsettled her, made her feel so ridiculously flustered and foolish. His smiles, so mocking, made her angry and impatient. So *disordered*.

He was an impossible man, with such incorrect ideas. But why didn't he like her?

"Miss Chase!" her maid protested. "There will be no flowers left for your hair."

Calliope glanced down, startled to see that she had destroyed two roses. "Sorry, Mary," she muttered, dropping the denuded stem.

"Shall I try that new Artemis style, miss? It's ever so popular!"

"No, thank you," Calliope said, shuddering at the thought of appearing at the party with the same coiffure as everyone else. "Just my usual."

Mary pouted a bit. She had surely long thought her talents were wasted on Calliope and her conservative tastes! But Calliope could not help it. She knew what suited her, what she liked.

And she had even dared fantasise once that Cameron de Vere would "suit her". When he first arrived back in London, after a very long voyage to Italy and Greece, rumours raced through the drawing rooms of how handsome he was, how dashing, how scandalous. But that was not what fascinated her. She was interested in the fact that he was a student of art and history, as she was. She longed to hear tales of his travels, to see the beautiful antiquities he had surely brought back with him for study and preservation.

It seemed they were destined to be friends, as their fathers had once been many years ago. Sir Walter Chase and the late Earl of Westwood were both scholars and collectors, great rivals as well as friends. The earl finally pulled the trump card in their collecting race, a bride who was actually Greek, not just French as Lady Chase was. Calliope and Cameron both grew up surrounded by the glories of the ancient world, though they never met after the de Veres departed for their incessant travels when their son was small.

When he came back to London, a grown man, the earl in his own right now, Calliope listened to the whispers about him and dared to let a tiny hope grow in her heart. Could this, then, finally be a man who could understand her? Share her passions, as none of her suitors could?

Those hopes were blighted when they at last met in person, at a reception he gave at his parents' townhouse, his house now.

From her earliest childhood, Calliope remembered an antiquity she had adored, a bust of Hermes that once graced the foyer of that house. Her father had tried to buy it, but the old earl refused all offers, much to Calliope's sadness. She loved Hermes' mischievous smile, carved to be almost lifelike in the cold marble, loved his winged helmet and the swirls of his curling hair. She was so very excited the night of that reception, so looking forward to seeing Hermes again.

But he was not there! His niche was empty, as were all the others that had once held exquisite vases and goblets. Stunned, Calliope stayed there in the foyer as her father and sisters joined the gathering in the drawing room. She stood below that empty niche, staring up as if she could *make* her Hermes appear. Her plans for this reception—seeing all the lovely antiquities, meeting the new earl, talking with him about those cherished objects and perhaps forming a bond—were completely thrown awry.

Calliope did not much like having her plans upset.

"Well," she heard a voice say, deep and velvety, faintly amused "you must be the missing Miss Chase."

Calliope glanced over her shoulder to find a man standing a few feet away, a faint half-smile on his lips, as sensual as that of her lost Hermes. He was dressed most properly, in buff breeches, a dark blue coat, and a pale grey brocade waistcoat, his cravat simply tied and skewered with a cameo pin. Yet he seemed an alien creature dropped into the sumptuous foyer, a man of bronzed skin and too-long, glossy dark curls. Of flashing, familiar brown eyes.

"The Greek god," she remembered Lotty sighing. *"Oh, Calliope, he is a veritable Greek god!"*

"And you must be Lord Westwood," she answered coolly, disconcerted by her reaction to him, to that smile of his. This was not how she pictured their meeting!

"I am indeed," he said, moving closer, graceful as a cat. He stopped close to her side, so close she could smell the faint lemony scent of his cologne, feel the heat of his skin, reaching towards her enticingly. She stepped away, closer to the reassuring chill of the marble wall.

"There used to be a bust of Hermes here," she said, swallowing hard to still the sudden tremor of her voice. "A most beautiful piece."

"Most beautiful," he answered, gazing not at the niche, but at her. Steadily. "I returned it to Greece. Where it belongs."

And *that* was when she knew they could never be friends...

"Miss Chase? What do you think?"

Calliope jumped a bit in her seat, startled out of her memories by the sudden sound of Mary's voice. She glanced into the mirror, only to find that her cheeks were flushed, her eyes too bright. As if that scene in the de Vere foyer, weeks in the past now, had only just happened.

But her hair was tidy, swept back in her usual braided knot and decorated with the remaining white roses, her curls perfectly smooth.

"It's lovely, Mary. As usual," Calliope said breathlessly.

Mary nodded, satisfied, and went about finding Calliope's shawl and slippers. Calliope reached for her pearl drop earrings, trying to forget that past evening, to focus on the soirée ahead. Cameron de Vere did not matter in the least! He was merely a misguided individual. Albeit a handsome one.

As she clasped on the earrings, there was a knock at her chamber door. "The carriage is waiting, Miss Chase," the butler announced.

"Thank you," Calliope answered. She took a deep breath, and rose slowly from her seat. It was time for the show to begin.

"If Lady Russell's plumes were any higher, I fear she would launch up into the sky like some demented parrot and leave us quite without a hostess," Clio whispered, leaning close to Calliope's ear.

Calliope pressed her gloved fingertips to her lips, trying not to laugh aloud. The hostess of the *musicale* did indeed look a bit like a bizarre parrot, with towering, multi-coloured feathers spraying forth from a purple-and-green satin turban. Clio always did this; she was so very quiet that everyone believed she had nothing to add to any conversation and thus ignored her. This was a great mistake, for her sharp green eyes observed everything, and she sometimes broke forth with startling—and acerbic—insights. Comparisons to jungle parrots were quite mild for her.

"But what of Miss Pratt-Beckworth?" Calliope whispered back. "I'm afraid someone told the poor girl that orange stripes were all the rage this season and she believed them."

"Indeed. It is better than that chartreuse creation she wore to the opera last week. Perhaps the Ladies Society needs to take her under its wing?" Clio shook her head sadly.

Calliope joined her in perusing the room, turning away from the mediocre painting of a stormy sea she and Clio had been pretending to admire. An evening of ancient Greek music would surely not sound too jolly to most of the *ton*, but Lady Russell was popular, turban or no, and tended to attract around her those of a more philosophical bent. So the room was quickly filling up, people milling about between the rows of gilt chairs, chatting and sipping lemonade—and stronger beverages—before the music began. It was not a "dreadful crush" by any means. There was no danger of overheating, or fainting, or having one's train trodden on. But the colours were vivid against Lady Russell's collection of bad paintings and very good antique statuary, a swirl of pastels, blues, greens, reds—and one orange—mingling with the hum of conversation. Talk of music and history were *de rigeur* tonight, exactly what Calliope usually loved.

But she could not entirely concentrate on the classical world. She still felt so restless. Unfocused.

Next to Calliope, Clio removed her spectacles, squinting out at the crowd as she rubbed the bridge of her nose. Unlike Calliope, who usually wore Grecian white muslin because it was the simplest choice, Clio was clad in emerald-green silk embroidered with a gold-key pattern, her auburn hair bound back by a gilded bandeau. A parrot of a far more subtle sort.

"What do you think, Cal?" she asked quietly. "Is the Lily Thief among us tonight?"

Calliope stiffened. *The Lily Thief*—how could she forget? Her gaze quickly scanned the gathering, jumping lightly from one young man to the next. There were so many there, tall, short, plain, handsome. Yet not the one she sought.

Could that possibly be the cause of her strange restlessness?

Certainly not! Calliope shrugged that away. The doings of Cameron de Vere were none of her concern. Just because she had been certain a Greek evening would appeal to him…

"I don't believe so," she said.

"Then you *do* suspect his identity?" Clio asked. "You know?"

"I don't *know*," Calliope answered impatiently. "How could I? I simply have an idea."

"Yet he is not here, your suspect?"

Calliope shook her head.

"But then how…?" Clio could not say more, though. Thalia called to her from across the room, where she was closely examining the musicians' instruments—much to their chagrin. Clio wandered away, leaving Calliope alone.

There were several friends she could join—indeed, a few people she really ought to speak to. She feared she would not be good company at the moment, not with such wild thoughts of de Vere and the Lily Thief whirling through her mind. She placed her half-empty glass on the nearest table and drifted away from the crowd towards the doors of Lady Russell's conservatory.

The glassed-in space was invitingly warm, scented with the rich, green fragrance of geraniums, lavender, mint, the earthiness of the damp soil. The room was empty now, though softly lit and furnished with scattered wrought-iron settees for visitors. Calliope welcomed the silence, the moment to collect her thoughts and become her usual calm self again.

At the far end of the conservatory was a cluster of antique statues, a stone Aphrodite and her scantily clad acolytes. They watched all the horticulture with expressions of impassive, scornful beauty. They were quite stunning, and their cold perfection drew Calliope closer.

"If only I could be like you," she whispered to the disdainful Aphrodite. "So very—certain. So unchanging. No doubts or fears."

"How very dull *that* would be," Westwood said.

"Did you follow me in here?' she asked, not surprised, glancing over at him.

"On the contrary, Miss Chase," he said, giving her one of his too-charming smiles. "I was in here enjoying a quiet moment to finish my wine…" He displayed a half-empty glass. "And here you came, talking to yourself. One couldn't help but overhear."

Calliope reached behind her to plant her palms on the cold stone base, trying to hold herself upright, to maintain some dignity. His cognac-coloured eyes, so deep and opaque, seemed to see far too much. She didn't know where to look, where to turn.

"I, too, was looking for a quiet moment," she said finally. "Before the music begins."

He nodded understandingly. "Sometimes people ask for too much. The only recourse is solitude." He took a step closer, then another. Calliope shivered in her thin gown, yet he no longer watched her. He gazed up at the statue.

"You chose a fine confidante," he said. "She looks so very—knowing. As if she has seen everything in the long years of her life."

Calliope, too, glanced up at Aphrodite, her pointed, cracked white chin, the clusters of her rippling hair. She did seem knowing, mocking even. Just as Westwood himself was. "I wonder what she makes of Lady Russell's routs? How they compare to the revels of Greece."

He laughed, that rich, rough sound that touched her to her very core. "I am sure she thinks them very tame affairs indeed! For did she not come from the inner sanctum of a temple to Aphrodite, where there were, er…"

"Orgies?"

He glanced towards her, his brow arched in sudden amusement. "Miss Chase. How very shocking."

Calliope could feel her cheeks heat under his regard, but she forced the horrid blush away. A scholar did not always have time for niceties. "My father possesses an extensive library on the ancient world. I have read much of it, including John Galt's *Letters from the Levant*. And Lady Mary Wortley Montague's narratives of her travels."

"Of course. Well, after the *orgies*, she must find musical evenings a bit tedious. I'm sure she was most happy you chose to converse with her."

Calliope reached out to touch Aphrodite's sandaled foot, the stone cold through the thin kid of her glove. This *was* the best sort of confidante—the mute sort. "If it was up to you, she would surely be sent back to moulder in the ruins of her erstwhile temple, with no one to talk to at all."

"Ah, Miss Chase." He leaned even closer to murmur in her ear, his warm breath lightly stirring the curls at her temple. "Who says all the orgies have ended?"

Calliope stared up at him, captured by his voice, his breath, his gaze—everything. It was as if she was suddenly paralysed and could not move, could not turn away. All time was suspended, and there was only *him*.

He, too, seemed startled by whatever this moment was. He watched her, his lips parted, the glass in his hand perfectly still.

"Miss Chase," he murmured. "I…"

Outside their green sanctuary, the sound of music tuning up began, and it was as if the prosaic noise burst some enchantment, some spell. He shifted back, and she turned her head away, sucking in a deep breath. She felt as though she had just run a long distance, all achy and airless.

"Shall we go in?" he said, his voice taut, even deeper.

"Of course," Calliope whispered. She spun around and marched back along the flagstone walkway, smoothing her palms over her warm cheeks. He was behind her. She could hear his steps, the soft rustle of his superfine coat, but mercifully he did not offer his arm or touch her.

She wasn't sure what she would do if he *did*.

Chapter Three

Calliope slipped into the empty chair next to Clio just as the musicians finished tuning their instruments. Her throat ached as she tried to draw in a calm, normal breath, tried to still the clamorous beating of her heart.

Clio gave her a sidelong glance as she slid a handwritten programme into Calliope's hand. "Where were you, Cal?" she whispered.

"Just in the conservatory," Calliope whispered back, resisting the urge to fan herself with the thin parchment. Why did Lady Russell insist on keeping her room so warm? "Looking at the Aphrodite statue."

Clio's expression was unreadable as she glanced at her own programme, her lips pursed. "Oh? Did you suspect she would be the next victim of the dreaded Lily Thief? Spirited away into the night for nefarious purposes?"

Calliope bit her tongue to keep from laughing aloud. "Certainly not. Aphrodite is solid marble and at least six feet tall. Unless the Lily Thief is the reincarnation of Hercules."

"One never knows. He could then lift the statue up through the skylights and…" Her words trailed away as

Lord Westwood appeared in the room, leaning carelessly against a pillar at the very periphery of the audience. His gaze met Calliope's as she watched him warily, and then, slowly, audaciously, he *winked* at her.

Blast him! Calliope's stare shot back to the front of the room, her face burning. Where was the cold marble of Aphrodite when it was truly needed?

"Were you quite alone in the conservatory, Cal?" Clio murmured.

"Lord Westwood might have wandered in just as I was leaving," Calliope answered reluctantly.

"And did you two quarrel again?"

"I never *quarrel* with people!"

"Never? With anyone?"

"You and Thalia are different. You are my sisters; I'm allowed to quarrel with you in the privacy of our home. But not with people at parties. Lord Westwood and I merely discuss our artistic differences."

"Hmm," Clio said, very non-committally. "I do believe our hostess is about to say a few words."

Calliope had seldom been more grateful to anyone than she was to Lady Russell for her timely interruption. Usually she felt she could tell Clio anything, and her sister's quiet understanding could soothe any hurt or trouble. There was no use in trying to articulate what a meeting with Cameron de Vere made her feel, though. It was a tangle of temper that could never be unwound.

Calliope hated—*hated*—to be so discomposed! The solution would be never to see him again. Yet he always popped up wherever she was! If only he would go back to Greece, and carry on with his misguided, dangerous work far away from her...

Calliope folded her gloved hands tightly in her lap to

still their trembling, staring straight ahead at Lady Russell's multi-coloured plumes, now even more lopsided than before.

"Good evening, my dear friends," Lady Russell said, holding up her hands so she did indeed seem to be a parrot about to be borne aloft. "I am so glad you could join me on this very special occasion. We will hear for the first time in centuries the strains of music last heard in ancient Greece. Using a fragment of measures copied from a work by Terence, fortunately preserved during the Renaissance and hidden away in an Italian monastery, we have reproduced a 'Delphic Hymn to Apollo'. The instruments used tonight greatly resemble the lyres, aulos and citharas seen here."

She waved her hands, and two servants appeared carrying a large blackwork krater. A gasp rose in the room. This was one of Lady Russell's greatest treasures, borne out of Greece decades ago by her grandfather. She seldom displayed the vase; it was rumoured she kept it locked up in her own bedchamber where only she could view it. It was exquisitely lovely, completely intact except for some thin cracks and a missing handle. The decoration was a party scene, graceful dancers, musicians, reclining drinkers. The ancient instruments they held did indeed resemble the gleaming new ones held by the musicians seated now in Lady Russell's drawing room.

That vase would make a prime target for the Lily Thief, Calliope thought, examining its gleaming elegance.

"Now, my dear guests," Lady Russell said. "Close your eyes and imagine you are sitting in a Grecian amphitheatre thousands of years ago…"

"I'm surprised she didn't make us all wear chitons and sandals tonight," Clio muttered. "What a sight we'd make then. Especially old Lord Erring. The poor man must weigh three hundred pounds. I doubt there would be enough white muslin in London."

Calliope laughed behind her programme. She could think of *one* man who could do a short chiton justice, and it wasn't poor old Lord Erring. She peeked at Lord Westwood over the gilded edge of the parchment. He was also watching the krater, a small frown etched across his brow. An unhappy Apollo.

What could he be thinking of?

Cameron's gaze followed the krater as it was carried from the room. How lovely it was, and how tragic it was so seldom seen. Seldom loved. Like Lady Tenbray's Etruscan diadem, it had been snatched from its home and locked away for the selfish delectation of a tiny group, its true purpose long forgotten. Lost in time. That krater was made for parties and merriment.

Yet at this moment it was not the vase's sad fate that pre-occupied him. It was the carefully etched figure of a woman along one polished curve of the krater. Her slender body, draped in the fluid, graceful folds of her robe, was bent over her lyre. Dark curls, bound by a bandeau across her forehead, sprang free around her oval face. Her expression was serious, pensive, in contrast to the merrymaking dancers gambolling around her. She seemed to hear only her own music, lost in her own thoughts and feelings.

The image was ancient, and yet the artist's model could have been Calliope Chase. The slim, dark beauty, the seriousness, the single-minded purpose—it was all Calliope.

As the music, a strange, discordant, haunting tune, filled the room, he glanced from the disappearing krater to its living embodiment. Calliope had been giggling with her sister, but now she stared raptly at the musicians, her pink

lips parted and dark eyes shining as if she, too, could see
things that were long dead living again, bright and vibrant.
When Cameron saw ancient temples and theatres on his
journeys, he saw not just the broken, silent ruins they were
now, but the centres of life they once were. Places where
people gathered, where they talked and laughed and loved,
where they created art and beauty that were the greatest
heritage of flawed mortals.

Calliope Chase shared this ability to see the vibrancy
of the past, the living arc of history. He could see that in
her eyes as she gazed at a sculpture or vase—as she listened
to lost music roused to life again. But he could never understand her despite what they shared. If she could sense what
he did, sense the true value of the heritage left to them by
their ancestors, how could she advocate that these objects
be locked away, unseen, far from their homes?

She *was* beautiful, just like that ancient woman with her
lyre. Beautiful and intelligent and spirited. But as stubborn
as a wild horse in the valleys of Greece.

Seeming to sense his regard, she glanced towards him.
For a fleeting moment, she lacked the protective veil she
usually drew around herself. Her gaze was open, vulnerable, gleaming with unshed tears. The eerie beauty of
the music had moved her, as it did him, and for an instant
they were bound together by the enchantment of the past.

Then the veil fell again, and she turned away so that he
saw only her black curls, the pale curve of her neck and
bare shoulder. But the magic was still there, a shimmering
web of connection that urged him to press his lips to that
white hollow at the nape of her neck, to trail kisses along
her spine, breathing in the warm scent of her. Feeling her
tremble under his touch until she cried out and that maddening veil vanished for ever, and he could see her true self.

Yet what would that true self be? A beautiful muse in truth—or a gorgon of destruction? Only a madman would take on one of the Chase Muses, and Cameron wanted to hold on to his tenuous sanity for as long as he could.

Suddenly, the music, the overheated room, the strange allure of Calliope Chase were too much for that thread of sanity. The old wildness was rising up in him like a fever. He spun around and left the room, the strains of music trailing behind him. In the foyer, the servants were placing the krater on a high pedestal where it could be viewed in distant safety after the performance.

It was too high to be touched without the stepstool the servants took when they left, yet from his vantage point Cam could clearly see the lyre player. The jewels in her headband, the delicate sandal peeking from the hem of her robe. From here she was even more like Calliope Chase. Beautiful and untouchable.

"Are you trying to decide how to steal it?" Calliope asked.

Cameron glanced back to find her standing in the drawing-room doorway, watching him with those steady brown eyes. Her face was a smooth and unreadable piece of marble, yet he could feel her tense wariness.

He should not be surprised at her suspicion. They had been at odds ever since that reception at his house, when she found Hermes missing from his niche. Their arguments only grew with every meeting after that. Yet still it hurt, like the sharp pinpricks of a tiny but fatal poisoned arrow. As he listened to the ancient music, as those strange, intimate thoughts of her neck and skin bombarded his mind, he felt so bound to her. So close to discovering the mystery of her.

But she seemed to think him a thief. The connection was not there for her. Not a muse then, or a gorgon either. Just a cold judge. The cool Athena he had once thought her.

He buried that hurt, shoving it down deep and piling other emotions on top of it—carelessness, insouciance. A chill to match her own.

"Perhaps you would care to come closer, Miss Chase, and ascertain for yourself if I carry a fresh lily in my pocket," he said lightly, as if he did not care one whit for her suspicions. He stepped forward, holding out the edges of his coat so she saw the smoothness of the silk lining.

She did not move away, but her shoulders stiffened. "I am not a fool, Lord Westwood."

"Indeed not, Miss Chase. 'Foolish' is the last word anyone could use to describe you. 'Misguided', perhaps."

Something flared deep in those unreadable eyes, a flash of some black fire. But still she did not rise to his bait. She seldom did. "I am not the one so *misguided* as to turn to crime in order to prove a point! I am not the one who holds the honour of my family or the claims of scholarship so cheap. Those of us with the advantages of education and travel have a duty—"

"And who are you, Calliope Chase, to lecture *me* on duty? Or honour?" His temper, tamped down so carefully for so long, burst out in a veritable Catherine wheel of sparks. His desire for her, her beauty and stubbornness, his frustration—it would all drive him mad, in truth!

He stalked closer to her, so close he could smell the summer scent of the roses in her hair, see the delicate blue tracery of veins under her ivory skin, the throb of her life pulse at the base of her throat. That wild urge to grab her and kiss her until her chilly frostiness thawed and flowed away, leaving only her, *them*, was nigh undeniable.

She did not turn away, just stared up at him, still and wide-eyed, that pulse beating until he swore he could hear it. Hear her heartbeat. He even reached for her, his fingers aching to clasp the smooth, bare inch of skin above her kid gloves, but some last flicker of sanity made him drop his hands, back away from her.

"How can you know me so little, Miss Chase?" he said hoarsely.

Her lips parted, yet she said nothing. For a second, a whisper of doubt floated across her face. A hint of puzzlement. Then it was gone, hidden again.

"What else am I to think?" she said. "How can I know you at all?"

Cameron could bear it no longer. He spun away from her and left the house, storming past the startled footman who appeared at the front door. The night air was chilly and clammy as he strode along the quiet street, leaving the lights and music of Lady Russell's house behind him. He could not quite leave Calliope Chase behind, though. Her quiet, accusing ghost seemed to follow him as he turned the corner.

"Infernal woman," he muttered. There was only one place he could exorcise her—the most raucous, most disreputable gaming hell he knew, far from these genteel squares and solemn prosperity. The Devil's Dice. There not even Calliope Chase's ghost could survive.

As Lady Russell's front door slammed behind Lord Westwood, Calliope sagged against the base of the krater's pillar. Every ounce of willpower that held her upright, that kept her from fleeing, flooded away in a cold rush, leaving her weak and trembling. Why did she feel this way every time she saw him? Why did they always quarrel so?

Behind her, she heard the click of the drawing room door opening and closing, the rise and fall of music, the patter of slippers against the parquet floor.

"Cal?" Clio whispered. Her steady arm went around Calliope's waist, and Calliope turned into her gratefully. "What is wrong? Are you ill?"

"No, no. I just—needed some air," Calliope answered.

"So you came out here alone?"

"I was not quite alone. But then I said something wrong, as I always do with him, and he left. Just ran out the front door into the street rather than be here with me!" Calliope realised she was not making any sense. She hardly understood herself! Why did she care at all if Cameron de Vere, a reckless probable-thief, ran away from her? She didn't want to be with him, either.

Did she?

Clio glanced towards the door, frowning. "Who ran out into the street?"

"Lord Westwood, of course."

"You mean you were speaking with Lord Westwood out here, and he became so angry he just ran off…" Clio's stare shifted to the krater above their heads, and her green eyes hardened, turning oddly intent. "Oh, no, Cal. You surely did not accuse Lord Westwood of being the Lily Thief!"

Calliope covered her hot cheeks with her gloved hands, trying to blot out the memory of his anger. Of her own impulsive ridiculousness. "I—may have."

"Cal…" Clio groaned "…whatever has come over you? I could see Thalia doing such a thing. She would challenge the devil himself to a duel! Not you. Are you ill? Do you have a fever?"

"I wish I did, then I would have some excuse."

Clio shook her head. "Poor Cal. I am sure he will not speak of it to anyone, since his father and ours were such friends."

"No, he won't speak of it. Except maybe to the governors of Bedlam."

Clio laughed. "There, you see! You made a joke. All is not lost. Perhaps next time you see him you can say you were simply overcome by the power of the music."

"Or drunk on the wine," Calliope muttered. She smoothed her hair and shook out her skirts, feeling herself slowly coming back to her usual calm presence. "I wish we never had to see him again at all."

"That's not likely, is it? Our world is so very small." Clio looked again to the krater. "But tell me, Cal, what made you suspect Lord Westwood of being the Lily Thief?"

Calliope shrugged. "It seems the sort of hot-headed thing he would do, does it not? He sent his own antiquities back to Greece; perhaps he thinks others should do the same, willy-nilly. I don't know. It was just a—a feeling."

"Now I *know* you have a fever! Calliope Chase, going by a mere feeling? Never."

Calliope laughed. "Tease all you like, Clio. I know that I usually have to carefully study a thing before I make my point…"

"Study it to death," Clio muttered.

Calliope ignored her. "I like to be certain of things. But don't the exploits of the Lily Thief just seem like something he would do? A person must be clever to get in and out of such fine houses undetected. They must be knowledgeable about art and antiquities, for only the finest and most historically important pieces are taken. They have to be sure of their cause, as Lord Westwood is. And they must be very misguided. As Lord Westwood also is."

"Why, Cal," Clio said softly. "It sounds as if you admire the Lily Thief."

Calliope considered this. Admire the Lily Thief? The most dangerous of criminals, for he stole not only objects but history itself? Absurd! "I admire his taste, perhaps, but certainly not his goals. I abhor the disappearance of such treasures. You know that."

Clio nodded. "I do know how passionate you are in your own cause, sister. But pray do not let it overcome you again when it comes to Lord Westwood! We have no proof he is the thief."

"No proof yet." Behind the closed drawing room door, the strains of music faded, replaced by the ring of applause. "It seems the concert is ending. Shall we fetch Thalia and go home? It grows late."

Chapter Four

"Good morning, Miss Calliope!" Mary sang as she drew back the bedchamber curtains, letting the greyish-yellow light of late morning flood across the room.

Calliope squeezed her eyes tighter shut, resisting the urge to draw the bedclothes over her head. How could it be time to wake up? She had only just fallen asleep. The long hours of the night she had spent tossing and turning, going over and over her hasty words to Lord Westwood. The anger she saw in his eyes.

Clio was surely right. She *was* fevered. It was the only explanation for showing her hand so early. She would never catch him now.

She needed to regroup. Strategise. It would surely all come back together at the Duke of Averton's Artemis ball. The Ladies Society would see to that.

"Did you enjoy the *musicale* last night, Miss Calliope?" Mary asked, arranging a tray of chocolate and buttered rolls on the bedside table.

"Yes, thank you, Mary," Calliope answered. She propped the pillows up against the carved headboard, pushing herself upright to face the day. No one ever won a battle lolling around! "Tell me, are my sisters up yet?"

"Miss Thalia has already departed for her music lesson," Mary said, rifling through the wardrobe. "And Miss Clio is at breakfast with your father and Miss Terpsichore. She left you a note on the tray."

As Mary organised the day's attire, Calliope munched on a roll and reached for Clio's message.

Cal, it read in Clio's bold, slashing hand. *I think we need an outing to clear our heads. Shall we take Cory to see the Elgin Marbles? She loves them so much, and we can talk there without Father overhearing.*

Calliope sighed. Perhaps Father would not overhear them at the British Museum, but the rest of London would. Still, Clio was right. They needed to clear their heads after last night, and where better than among the glorious beauties of the Parthenon sculptures? Terpsichore—Cory— was a delightful girl, just turned thirteen now and wanting so much to be a young lady, and she deserved a treat after being separated from their younger sisters, who stayed in the country with their various nurses and governesses.

And surely they wouldn't run into Lord Westwood there. The man probably didn't rise until two at the earliest, and the Elgin Marbles must represent all he abhorred: treasures taken from Greece and displayed for Londoners.

"Mary, I shall need a walking dress and warm pelisse," she said, swallowing the last of her chocolate. "And my lap desk. I need to send notes to the Ladies Society."

They had battle plans to draw up.

The Chases' *de facto* second home when in town was always the British Museum. They had been brought there since earliest childhood, escorted from artefact to artefact by their parents, instilled with a love for the past by the beauty of the pieces and by their father's vivid tales. Many of their favourites—Greek vases, Egyptian sculptures, Viking helmets—were immortalised for them in their mother's sketchbooks, kept by Clio since Lady Chase's death in birthing the youngest Muse, Polyhymnia, three years ago.

But their mother had never seen the sisters' favourite room of all, the Temporary Elgin Room—which was showing signs of becoming rather more permanent. This was where they went now, after climbing up the wide stone steps and passing through the massive pillars into the sacred hush of the museum.

"May we visit the mummies after we see the Marbles?" Cory asked eagerly.

Clio laughed. "Morbid child! You only want to scare your little sisters with gruesome tales of them in your next letter. But we can visit them, if there is time."

Cory wrinkled her nose. "There won't be. You two always spend *hours* with the Marbles."

"You enjoy them, too, silly monkey, and you know it," Calliope said. "Perhaps after the Marbles and the mummies we can have an ice at the shop across the way."

Smiling happily with the promise of dead Egyptians *and* a sweet, Cory went off to sketch her favourite sculpture yet again, the head of a horse from the chariot of the Moon, his mane and jaw drooping after an exhausting journey across the heavens. Calliope and Clio strolled over to the back wall, where the frieze depicting the procession of a Panathenaic festival was mounted. It was quiet there for the moment, despite the milling crowds, tucked behind the massive carved figures of Theseus and a draped, headless goddess.

Calliope stared up at the line of young women, all of

them gracefully poised and beautifully dressed in chitons and cloaks, bearing vessels and libation bowls as offerings to the gods. They were not as well displayed as they deserved; the room was cramped and ill lit, the walls dark. But Calliope always loved to see them, to revel in their classical beauty, in the procession that never ended. And today she was glad of the dim light, for it hid the purplish circles of her sleepless night.

"I have called for a meeting of the Ladies Society tomorrow afternoon," she told Clio.

Clio's gaze did not turn from the figure of the head girl in the procession, the one that held aloft an incense stand, but her lips curved down. "So soon? We usually only convene once a week."

"This is an emergency. The Duke of Averton's ball is coming up soon. We must be prepared for whatever might happen there."

"Do you still think you-know-who plans to snatch the Alabaster Goddess away that night?"

"I'm not sure. That is why I said we need to be prepared for anything. Even nothing. The ball might pass off quite peacefully—or as peacefully as anything could at Averton's house. The sculpture will stay in place…"

"But it will *not* stay in place!" Clio hissed. Her hand tightened on the head of her furled parasol, and for a moment Calliope feared she might stab it into the air, or at an unwary passerby. "Averton is sending it off to his infernal fortress in Yorkshire, where no one will ever see it again! He is a vile, selfish man with no care for his collections. Do you think that is a better fate for poor Artemis than to fall into the hands of the Lily Thief?"

Calliope bit her lip. "It's true that he is well named the Duke of 'Avarice'. I like him no better than you, Clio. He is a very—strange man. But at least we would know where the statue is, and one day a museum or legitimate antiquarian could acquire her. If the Lily Thief took her, she would vanish utterly! We would learn nothing from her then."

"Honestly, Cal! I do love you, but sometimes you don't seem to understand." Clio stalked away, her parasol swinging, and left Calliope standing alone.

Calliope stared up again at the carved procession, swallowing hard against her pricked feelings. She and Clio were as close as two sisters could be, drawn together by their love of history, by the need to be "mothers" to their younger sisters in the wake of their own mother's death. And she knew Clio had a temper that subsided as quickly as it flared. That did not make their little quarrels any easier, though.

What was it lately, Calliope wondered, that caused such arguments? First Lord Westwood, now her sister. Her eyes itched with unshed tears, and she rubbed at them hard. When she looked up again, she feared she was hallucinating. Lord Westwood stood right beside her, staring down at her solemnly, his glossy curls brushed carelessly from the sharp, shadowed planes of his face so that he seemed one of the sculptures himself.

She blinked—and found he was still there. She drew in a steadying breath, and offered him a tentative smile. "Lord Westwood."

"Miss Chase," he answered. "I trust you are enjoying your outing?"

"Yes, very much. My sisters and I visit the museum whenever we can." She gestured towards Cory, who was still sketching the horse's head with Clio leaning over her.

"I come here often, as well," he said.

"Do you? I—I imagine it reminds you of your mother's

homeland," she said carefully, wary of yet another quarrel. How could one speak of these controversial carvings without starting a fuss, though?

But he simply answered, "Yes. Her tales when I was a child were always of gods and goddesses, and even muses."

Calliope smiled. "Perhaps then you have an understanding of how changeable a muse can be?"

He smiled in return, a quick grin that seemed to light up their dim corner of the room. "I have heard tell of such things. One day the muse will smile on you, the next she has vanished. Perhaps that is simply part of her allure."

Allure? Did he then find her—alluring? She would have thought "prickly" or "annoying" more likely adjectives he would use. But then, did she not think the same of him? Annoying, and yet strangely alluring. She shrugged away these distracting thoughts and said, "Sometimes, too, a muse forgets her manners. Says things she should not. Then she must apologise."

"Is that what this is, Miss Chase? An apology?"

Calliope sighed. "I fear so."

He clutched at his heart, staggering back as if in profound shock. "Never!"

She laughed. "I would not have you think I was not properly brought up, Lord Westwood. I should not have said those things to you last night. My sister says I should blame it on the spell of the music or on the wine, but in truth I do not know why I said them. I was just rather out of sorts."

"I suppose I have been out of sorts with you in the past as well, Miss Chase. Perhaps we can start anew. Cry pax."

"Pax, then. For now."

"For now. Come, let me show you my favourite of these friezes." He offered her his arm, and though she only laid her fingertips very lightly on his fine wool sleeve, she could feel the warmth of his skin, the strength of his coiled muscle beneath the layers of cloth. His arm tensed under her touch, as if he felt it, too. That strange, gossamer tie. "There, that wasn't too hard, was it?"

"Not at all," Calliope answered.

He smiled, and led her to the end of the marble procession, where it curved around to the next wall. There was etched the very reason for the procession—Athena, seated in profile as she observed her offerings. She did not wear her usual helmet on her curled hair, but held her aegis on her lap and bore a spear in her right hand.

"She is your favourite?" Calliope asked.

"You sound surprised."

"Perhaps I imagined you preferred one of the Lapiths and centaurs from the metope, drunkenly breaking up the party. Or Dionysus over there with his leopard skin."

He laughed. "Oh, come now, Miss Chase! I do enjoy the pleasures of life, but I am hardly a centaur. Or a Dionysus. Were we not just speaking of orgies last night? His soirées tend to end so badly, with the participants tearing each other limb from limb and devouring the raw flesh. No, indeed, cannibalism is not for me."

Calliope felt herself blushing again, an embarrassing red heat flooding up her throat to her cheeks. "I never quite imagined *cannibalism* as one of your vices, Lord Westwood. But tell me why you like Athena here so very much? She seems too rational and measured for you."

"It is exactly those qualities—her rational calm, her dignity. My life has never held much of those qualities, pulled from pillar to post with my parents, and I crave them. I can find them right here, carved in this marble."

Calliope blinked in surprise. True, the two of them had

declared peace only moments before, but she could never have expected such an instance of confidence from Cameron de Vere, of all people. A wistful longing was etched on his handsome face, driving out the careless mockery.

"She is my favourite, too," she admitted.

"And so she should be, for you are very like her."

"I, like Athena?" she said, startled. "She would never have been rude to you at a *musicale*."

"No, she would have struck me down with her spear. I must feel fortunate you wield no such weapon. Your tongue is quite sharp enough."

Before Calliope could answer, there was a sudden commotion in the doorway, disturbing the church-like hush of the room. A ripple of comment, of tension. Calliope peered around the bulk of a headless goddess to see that the Duke of Averton had just made an entrance.

He was a handsome enough man, Calliope thought, she would give him that much. Tall, slim, with flowing red-gold hair that fairly shimmered in the dim light, and bright green eyes that took in everything around him in one penetrating glance. The only flaw on his handsome face was a slightly crooked nose, as if it had once been broken and not healed straight. His dramatic, almost Celtic looks were emphasised by his flamboyant way of dressing—a long cape where all the other men wore wool greatcoats, a yellow satin waistcoat, tasselled boots, and jewelled rings on his fingers. Rubies and emeralds.

The duke stood there for a moment until he was certain everyone watched him, then he swung his cloak from his shoulders in a great arc and deposited it with one of the many lackeys trailing behind him. The sweep of his arm seemed to encompass and embrace all the sculptures as if they belonged to him alone.

"Ah, the glories of Greece, the ancient spirits—we meet again," he said, softly but carryingly. Then he turned and made his way towards the metope section, his entourage hurrying behind him.

Calliope almost laughed aloud. The Duke of Averton so seldom went about in town; it was part of what made his upcoming ball the talk of the *ton*. But when he did it was more amusing than Drury Lane.

"Ridiculous toad," Lord Westwood muttered darkly. "What is the purpose of such a preening display?"

Calliope glanced up at him to find him glowering towards the duke, his long fingers curled into fists. Where was the lighthearted Apollo now? Westwood resembled no one so much as the ill-tempered Hades, lurking in his black underworld, wishing he could feed the duke limb by limb to his snarling Cerberus.

Calliope had to admit she rather liked that image herself. Of all the selfish collectors in London, all the people who hoarded their treasures while denying scholars all access, Averton was the worst. He never scrupled about where or from whom he bought his treasures, and the precious objects always disappeared into his Yorkshire fortress. But she had not known that *Westwood* had a quarrel with him. Indeed, Westwood seldom seemed to dislike anyone—except her, of course.

Yet it was more than mere dislike she saw on his face now. It was dark, unadulterated hatred, raw and primitive. And very frightening.

Calliope shivered despite the warmth of the close-packed room, and edged away from him until she felt the hard edge of a stone base against her hips. He seemed to notice her wide-eyed regard, and that glimpse of jagged emotion was quickly concealed behind his usual smile.

"I did not realise you knew the duke well," she murmured.

"Not well," Lord Westwood answered. "Certainly better than I would like. We were at Cambridge together, and the Duke of Avarice has certainly not changed much since those days. Except to grow even more vicious and brainless."

Vicious and brainless? The duke was a menace, certainly, and had a reputation for eccentricity and rapaciousness. But vicious? Calliope waited, full of anticipation, for Westwood to elaborate, but of course he did not. Their brief moment of confidence was gone, and Calliope was soon distracted by the sight of the duke drawing close to Clio.

Clio did not even seem to notice the man's theatrical entrance, or his stately parade around the room as everyone cleared a path for him. She was leaning close to a goddess sculpture, frowning as she examined it through her spectacles. The duke, much to the consternation of his followers, suddenly veered from his trail to stop at her side.

As Calliope watched, puzzled and concerned, he edged closer to Clio until his bejewelled hand brushed her arm. Clio spun around, startled, bumping into the goddess.

"Your sister should have a care around that man," Westwood muttered.

"I have no idea what he could be saying to her. We hardly know him."

"That won't stop him when it comes to ladies. Even respectable ones like your sister."

Calliope saw Clio's hand edging back and up, towards the sharp pin that skewered her silk bonnet. Clio's frozen expression and demeanour never altered, yet Calliope knew she would have no compunction about driving that pin into the duke's arm. Or more sensitive areas.

Calliope took a step forward, intending to intervene, but Lord Westwood was there before her. He strode across the room, reaching out to practically shove the duke away from Clio. As the duke smirked at him, Westwood leaned in to mutter low, harsh-sounding words that carried to Calliope's ears as only the rushing noise of a stormy sea. Clio eased away from the men, her hand dropping to her side, as everyone else in the room edged closer. A quarrel between a duke and an earl in the middle of the British Museum was not something to be seen every day! This was certain to be much talked of for days to come.

If only she and her sister were not in the midst of it, Calliope thought, perturbed. Yet even she could not help but stare at the two men, Westwood so full of barely leashed anger, Averton still smirking but growing in agitation, if the spasmodic opening and closing of his fists was any indication. It was a scene that hardly belonged in civilised London. More like those Lapiths and centaurs, wrestling in ancient stone.

Calliope shook off the strange spell that urged her just to stare at the growing fight, and hurried to Clio's side. She took her sister's arm and whispered, "We should take Cory out of here, don't you think?"

Clio shuddered, as if she too were bound by some strange, wicked enchantment and only Calliope's voice shook her out of it. "Of course," she said, and rushed over to where Cory still sat sketching. Clio overcame her protests with renewed promises of mummies, and ushered her out of the Elgin Room.

As soon as they departed, Westwood and Averton broke apart, Westwood striding from the room without a glance backward. The duke straightened his waistcoat and returned to his friends, laughing as if nothing had happened.

Puzzled, Calliope stared after Westwood. How very angry he seemed! And to think, for a moment there, when they smiled and talked together so easily, she had thought herself silly for imagining him the Lily Thief.

Now, after witnessing that strange scene with Averton, she was more convinced than ever that he had to be the thief. And she was determined to prove it. One way or another.

Chapter Five

What does it matter, de Vere? The girl is a tavern wench, free for the taking!

Cameron heard the echo of Averton's voice in his mind, the laughing, mocking words from many years ago. He saw the man's smile, that knowing smirk of smug entitlement, that only vanished when Cameron had planted his fist in Averton's face, bloodying that aristocratic nose. It had been small comfort indeed to the girl, no more than sixteen years old, who had run away sobbing, her dress torn. And it was hardly a balm to Cameron's white-hot fury, for he knew he would not be there to rescue the next girl. Or the next purloined vase or sculpture.

As Cameron's friends had dragged him away, he had been able to hear Averton mutter, "Let him go. What do you expect from the son of a Greek street mouse?"

It had taken ten men to pull Cameron out of there that day, and he had soon left the suffocating confines of Cambridge to begin his travels anew. To find himself among the "street mice" of Italy and his mother's beloved Greece. Those years of wandering had erased the memories of

Averton's words, of the feeling of his fist meeting bone and flesh. Until today.

The sight of Averton hovering so close to Clio Chase, of Calliope's helpless concern, had brought back that day in the dingy tavern, that girl in the torn dress. Brought it back with a vicious immediacy that frightened him.

Averton was known as an eccentric now, a semi-recluse who only came out to show off his ancient treasures. His Alabaster Goddess. Cameron had not even seen the man since he returned to town. Yet surely the duke's vices were only hidden now, tucked away behind his stolen antiquities. Who would dare challenge him? Who would even seek out the crimes of a rich and powerful duke?

Cameron stopped at the museum gates, roughly raking his fingers through his hair until he felt his anger ebb. Cold thought was needed now, not the impulsive fisticuffs of his youth. No Dionysus. Athena was the god he required.

He stood there for a long time, the wind catching at his hair and his coat, ignoring the flow of London life around him. He thought of his mother, of her tales of great warriors like Achilles, Ajax, Hector. Their downfalls always seemed to be their tempers, their rush to battle without planning, without forethought, driven by their passions.

"You are too much like them, my son, and it will get you into trouble one day," she would say. "There are better ways to win your fights."

As he stood there, leaning against the cold metal gates, the doors of the museum opened and Calliope and Clio Chase emerged, their younger sister between them, holding their hands. She chattered brightly, but the two older Muses seemed silent and serious, as if their thoughts were far away from the windswept courtyard. Calliope kept shooting Clio concerned little glances.

Cameron ducked behind a large stone planter as they passed by. He could not speak to Calliope now; she had been taken aback by his violent behaviour, and he could not explain it to her. He could not even explain it to himself. But he fell into step several feet behind them, watching carefully until they climbed safely into their carriage and set off for home, without being accosted by the duke or any of his minions.

If Averton thought he could get away with meddling with any of the Chases, he was very much mistaken.

"Lord Mallow. Mr Wright-Helmsley. Mr Lakesly."

Calliope stared down at her list, biting the end of her pencil as she examined each name by the light of her candle. They were certainly all men of means and some intelligence, as well as collectors of antiquities. Could they really be candidates for the Lily Thief?

She tapped her chin, running through all the men of her acquaintance who were not children or infirm. Or who showed not a speck of ingenuity, like poor Freddie Mountbank. "Lord Deering. Sir Miles Gibson. Mr Smithson."

Yet, in the end, she always came back to one name. Lord Westwood.

She had begun by being so very certain it was him! He had all the necessary qualities—intelligence, interest, plus a certain recklessness, probably born of his years in Italy and Greece. He had the courage of his convictions, as misguided as those convictions were. But now something bothered her, some irritating little voice at the back of her mind that whispered doubts. Could it be—was it—that she was growing to *like* him?

"Piffle!" Calliope cried, tossing down her pencil. Of course she did not like him. How could she? That very recklessness went against all she believed was important. That voice was surely just her inborn female weakness, lured by a smile and a pair of handsome eyes.

He was still the most likely candidate for the Lily Thief. His dark, sizzling anger towards the Duke of Averton only emphasised that fact. Westwood had an edge to him, like the fire-honed blade of a dagger that was usually hidden in its velvet sheath, but could flash out and wreak destruction in only an instant. Lady Tenbray's diadem had already fallen victim to its slice. Was the Alabaster Goddess next?

Calliope stared down at her list, and slowly reached for her pencil. *Lord Westwood*, she wrote.

Her bedchamber door creaked, warning that she was no longer alone. Calliope hastily shoved the list under a pile of books and drew her shawl tighter around her shoulders.

"Are you working, Cal?" Clio said quietly, slipping into a chair next to the desk.

"Just reading a bit before I retire. I couldn't sleep."

"Me, neither." Clio fiddled with the edge of one of Calliope's notebooks. She seemed rather pale tonight, her green eyes shadowed and large without the shield of her spectacles. Calliope had noticed she didn't eat much of her dinner, either.

Blast Averton, anyway! Why did the man have to go parading through the museum today, upsetting their outing, pestering her sister? Why did he choose Clio? And why couldn't he just stay hidden away at home with his ill-gotten Alabaster Goddess?

Yet if he did that, she wouldn't have the chance to catch the Lily Thief once and for all. The Alabaster Goddess was an alluring bait like no other. If only Clio didn't have to be caught in the middle of it all.

"What did he say to you this afternoon, Clio?" Calliope asked.

Clio stared down at the notebook. "Who?"

"Averton, of course. You have been so quiet tonight. You didn't even seem to be listening when Father read from the *Aeneid* after dinner."

Clio shrugged. "I am just tired, I think. As for Averton, he is of no importance."

"But his behaviour this afternoon—"

"Is of no consequence! He is like so many men of his exalted ilk, he thinks all women are his for the asking. No, not even asking, just taking. Like an ivory box, or an alabaster statue from a Delian temple. When he meets one who wants nothing to do with him, it only makes him more determined. But I have twice the determination he does."

That Calliope knew to be true. No one was more determined, more single-minded than Clio. Expect perhaps Lord Westwood. "I did not realise you even knew the duke."

"I don't. Or about as much as I *want* to know him. I have encountered him once or twice at galleries and shops. He seems to have taken a ridiculous fancy to me of some sort."

Calliope stared at her sister in astonishment. She always thought they were as close as two sisters could be, yet she had no idea of this "fancy". "Clio, why didn't you say something?"

"I told you, Cal, it is of no importance!" Clio cried, slapping her hand down on a pile of books. The volumes toppled, revealing the list beneath. Clio reached for it. "What is this?"

"Nothing, of course," Calliope said, trying to snatch it away.

Clio held it out of her reach. "Lord Deering, Mr Smithson, Mr Lakesly. Is this a list of your suitors?"

"Certainly not!" Calliope finally succeeded in retrieving the list. She folded it in half and stuck it inside one of the books. "I would never consider a suitor like Mr Lakesly. He gambles too much."

"I noticed Lord Westwood's name on there, too. Certainly you would not call *him* a suitor, though I did notice you two were having quite a coze at the museum."

"We were discussing Greek mythology, that is all. And this list is merely something for our Ladies Society meeting tomorrow."

"Ah, yes, the meeting. What is it really all about, Cal?"

"I told you. To make plans for Averton's ball. We must all be extra-vigilant that night, so there is no repeat of Lady Tenbray's rout. Unless…"

"Unless what?"

Calliope bit her lip. "Unless you don't want to go to the ball. It would be completely understandable, given the duke's deplorable behaviour! We don't even have to talk about this any more, if you don't care to."

Clio slumped back in her chair, arms crossed and face set in stony lines. Calliope had seen that mutinous pose since childhood. "Cal, really. It's not like the man tried to slit my throat in the middle of the Elgin Room. He merely said some—words to me. Nothing I cannot manage. Surely you know better than to treat me like a piece of fragile porcelain."

Calliope smiled reluctantly. Oh, yes, she did know that. When they were children, Thalia could always outrun them all in foot races, a veritable Atalanta. But Clio was the first to climb up trees—and leap down from them as if she had wings. The first to swim streams and scramble up peaks.

The duke didn't know what he was up against.

"Of course," Calliope agreed. "No more porcelain."

"So, tell me about this list. I would guess they are your candidates for the Lily Thief."

Calliope drew the list back out, smoothing it atop the desk. "Yes. Some of them are a bit far-fetched, I know."

"A bit? Mr Emerson couldn't tell an amphora from a horseshoe. And Lord Mallow is shockingly myopic."

"Hmph." Calliope pushed the list towards her sister. "Very well, Clio, since you're so clever, who would *you* put on the list?"

Clio pursed her lips as she examined the names. "Not Mr Hanson. He would be utterly paralysed at the thought of his mama's disapproval. And not Mr Smithson—he is far too honest. What about Lord Wilmont?"

"Oh, I hadn't thought of him! That's very good. Remember that krater he had that no one had ever seen before?" Calliope added the name to the others. Now Westwood was no longer at the bottom of the list.

"And Lord Early. Remember when he nearly fought a duel with Sir Nelson Bassington when that unfortunate man declared Early's Old Kingdom stela was clearly Amarna Period?"

"What bacon-brains the two of them are. I think they should both be on this list."

They sat there long into the night, debating the merits of each suspect. Names were added; others erased. The only one that stayed in place, black and solid, was Lord Westwood.

Chapter Six

"I call this meeting of the Ladies Artistic Society to order," Calliope announced. "Miss Clio Chase will take the minutes."

The chatter and rustling among the members slowly ceased, as they put their teacups back on tabletops and faced Calliope once again. Their pretty faces were alight with curiosity.

"What is our subject today, Calliope?" Lady Emmeline Saunders asked. "It must be something very important, since this is not our regularly scheduled day to meet."

"Oh, something truly dreadful must have happened!" moaned Lotty Price. "A murder. An illness. A poisoning!"

"Someone needs to take away that girl's novels," Clio muttered under her breath.

"Do let Calliope talk, Lotty," said Emmeline.

"Indeed there hasn't been a murder, by poisoning or any other method," Calliope said. "And I hope that we may prevent one from ever happening."

Emmeline gave her a sharp glance. "You suspect a murder is about to occur?"

"I knew it!" Lotty cried. "There is a dreadful plot afoot."

Calliope sighed. "I fear Lotty is not far wrong this time."

"Whatever do you mean?" asked Thalia. "Who is to be killed? Should we not arm ourselves?"

"No, no, I don't mean it in that way," Calliope said quickly, trying to stem the rising tide of panic she sensed among her friends. "I have no knowledge of any *human* murder being planned." *Yet.* "The plot I refer to concerns the Alabaster Goddess."

The ladies subsided back into their seats, yet there was still a distinctly unsettled feeling in the air. "So, you still think the Lily Thief intends to steal her?" Emmeline said.

"Yes, probably from the duke's masquerade ball, as we discussed at our last meeting," Calliope answered. "We must formulate a plan to prevent it."

"I am ready to defend her at any moment!" Thalia cried. She leaped up from her chair, eyes aglow as she no doubt imagined herself wielding a sword against any would-be thief. "Only give me the signal and I shall do battle."

"Thalia, dear, do sit down," Clio said, shaking her head. "We don't need Boadicea and the Iceni hordes to keep an eye on one little statue."

"You never know," Thalia said, plopping back into her seat. "What if the Lily Thief has a partner? An army?"

"Even if he had a battalion—which he does not, for how could a battalion sneak into Lady Tenbray's library?—he could not get by us," Calliope said.

"What is the plan?" asked Emmeline. "What are we to do?"

"I made up a list of anyone who might even remotely be suspected of being the Lily Thief," Calliope said, holding up her list from last night's sleepless hours. "Everyone in the *ton* received an invitation to the ball, so they are sure to be there. You will each be assigned one or two names. Your task will be to ascertain what each man's costume is, and then keep an eye on them, make certain they do not try to slip away."

"I hope you do not want me to trail Freddie Mountbank," Emmeline said. "He's already made himself a nuisance in my life!"

"Mr Mountbank is not even on the list," Calliope answered, remembering the quarrel Mountbank got into with Lord Westwood right in view of these very windows. "And we must not be at all obvious about our observations. We wouldn't want to give the wrong idea."

"Perhaps we should work in pairs," Lotty suggested. "That would make it easier for us to trail anyone who might try to slip away."

"Oh, very good idea, Lotty," Calliope said. She reached for Clio's pen and quickly made the amendments to the list. "All right, then, ladies, here are your assignments."

Thalia handed out the papers to the Society members. They bent over them eagerly, laughing and exclaiming.

"Mr Emerson!" Lotty said. "It would certainly be no hardship to watch *him*. He is so handsome."

"Nor Lord Mallow," said Emmeline. "But what of Mr Hanson? I wouldn't have thought he could plot a stroll to the end of the street, let alone a theft."

Calliope rapped her gavel against the table, bringing order back to the gathering. "Now that you have your assignments, this is how we shall proceed on the night of the ball…"

"Do you think it will work?" Emmeline asked quietly, coming up next to Calliope, who stood staring out the window.

Calliope glanced back at the others, gathered around the

pianoforte as Thalia played them a Beethoven nocturne. "I don't know," she answered honestly. "The ball is sure to be a dreadful crush. How can we watch just a few people? People in disguise, no less. Yet I can't just stand here and let that statue be stolen without at least trying to do something."

"I know. We all care so very much, we want to save them all. Make sure they are all properly looked after and studied," Emmeline said. "There are only five of us, though. But we will do our very best to save the Alabaster Goddess, Calliope, never fear. She never had more devoted acolytes, even in her temple in Greece."

They were quiet for a moment, listening to Thalia's beautiful music, watching the traffic on the street below. Emmeline leaned closer to murmur, "Did you assign yourself Lord Westwood to watch, Calliope?"

Calliope looked to her, startled. "I thought Clio could do that."

"Oh, no, I really think it should be you. The two of you are always circling each other like wary hawks anyway."

"We do not!" Calliope cried. The others glanced towards them, and she hastily lowered her voice. "I do not *circle* Lord Westwood, Emmeline. Whatever do you mean?"

"Oh, Calliope dear. Everyone sees it. Whenever you are in a room together smoke practically billows. My brother even tells me you are in the books at his club."

"The books! People are *wagering* on me?" Calliope felt a sick, sour pang deep in her stomach, an ache of sinking embarrassment. "How dare they! What—what are they saying?"

"Are you sure you want to know?" Emmeline said, her eyes full of concern. "I should never have brought it up."

"Of course you should. If people are talking about me, I want to know."

"Well, half of them wager you will be married by the end of the Season. The other half wagers one of you will be in Newgate for murdering the other."

Calliope pressed her hand against her stomach. "What does your brother wager?"

"Calliope! He would never do that to a friend."

"Come now, Emmeline. He is a man. Wagering seems to be in their very veins. They cannot help themselves."

"Well, if he does he doesn't tell me about it. I was much too angry with him for not putting a stop to it."

"People are always full of such tittle-tattle. They must be desperate for gossip indeed to make up Banbury tales about such a dullard as me! Where do they find that kind of nonsense?"

Emmeline eyed her closely. "It is not entirely made of whole cloth, you know. You and Lord Westwood snap and quarrel every time you meet, or if you don't speak you glower at each other from across the room. What are people to think?"

Calliope now felt ill in earnest. She sat down heavily in the nearest chair, wrapping her arms tightly around herself.

"Calliope, dear, you really didn't know?" Emmeline asked.

"I have been so engrossed in my own studies," Calliope murmured. "Worrying about the Lily Thief. I suppose I was just oblivious. My mother always did say that living in my own little world would get me into trouble one day."

"It is hardly trouble," Emmeline said. "It's not as if you were caught kissing him! You're right, it's just silly gossip from people who have nothing better to do. It will soon be gone, replaced by something else and forgotten. My brother says they also wager on whether or not Prinny is the Lily Thief, so you see how serious their betting books are!"

Calliope laughed reluctantly. The vision of the prince, fat, red-faced and encased in a creaking corset climbing in windows and picking locks was so absurd it nearly drove out those sick feelings.

"Just ignore them, Calliope," Emmeline said. "Their ignorance deserves no response. In the meantime, why don't we go for a stroll in the park? It is too fine a day to stay indoors, and we all need time to think over our plan for the ball."

"I would like some fresh air," Calliope admitted.

"Excellent! I will tell the others."

Calliope caught Emmeline's arm as she turned away, staying her for a moment. "Emmeline, what do *you* think of Lord Westwood and me?"

Emmeline gave her a gentle smile. "How can I say? I'm just an unmarried lady like you, with Freddie Mountbank my most serious suitor. I know little of romance. You say you dislike him. Very well. But are you *sure* that's all there is to the matter? Maybe you should ask Lotty what would happen in one of her novels."

Calliope watched Emmeline walk away, more confused than ever. Antiquities she knew about; they could be studied, classified. Men never could. Especially Westwood.

Maybe she really should take up reading horrid novels, and not so much Aristotle and Thucydides. It was obvious that her powers of observation, her knowledge of modern life, of what passed for romance, was sadly lacking. Would *The Prince's Tragic Secret* fill that gap? Surely everything could be learned, with the right tools. Herodotus was no help here. Perhaps *By An Anonymous Lady* could be.

Calliope pushed herself up from her chair and made her

way resolutely towards her friends, who were gathering up their shawls and bonnets in preparation for their walk.

"Lotty," she called. "Could I speak to you for a moment?"

As it was a fair day, cool and dry after the morning's rains ceased, Hyde Park was quite crowded. Riders cantered along Rotten Row, stopping by the barriers to chat with each other, or with friends who rolled past in their open carriages, showing off their newest fashions. Nannies in starched caps and cloaks watched their charges as they sailed tiny boats on the calm, murky waters of the Serpentine or rolled hoops along the gravel pathways.

Calliope smiled as she watched them, their laughing faces turned like smooth-petaled flowers to the sun. She remembered days when her own nannies, or sometimes even her mother, would bring her and her sisters here. They would pretend the Serpentine was the Mediterranean, the trees and rocks the grove of Apollo's Oracle at Delphi, and they were Muses in truth. The fount of all art and wisdom.

Suddenly, she felt a sharp pang, a yearning for that innocence that seemed so far away now. The days when she thought any dream was possible, that she could attain any goal she longed for. Even the wisdom of the Muses. Now—well, now she wondered if somehow their father had cursed them by giving them their names!

Yes, she did wish now for childhood's blissful oblivion. For as she walked the pathways now, she imagined every person, every polite greeting, concealed smirking laughter. *There is Calliope Chase! You know, the one who is pursuing Lord Westwood.*

Emmeline linked arms with her, smiling in her cheerfully determined way. "There now! Is the fresh air not bracing?"

"Yes, indeed," Calliope answered. She could be

cheerful, too. After all, Emmeline was quite right. Any rumours about herself and Westwood were merely the product of idle minds and sure to pass soon. Especially if she gave them no more heat for their scandal broth.

"Oh, look! There is Mr Smithson. Was he not on your list of suspects?" Emmeline said.

"Hmm," Calliope said, watching the gentleman in question as he strolled past, politely doffing his hat. "I will admit he is a bit of a long shot. He's so slender, one can hardly envision him pulling himself through a window."

"And not Lord Deering over there! They do say the dowager Lady Deering is such a dragon. She would incinerate her poor son if he disgraced the family name."

Calliope laughed. "Quite so. But I think we must examine every possibility, no matter how farfetched."

"Yes. Appearances can be so deceiving."

Calliope nodded. Surely no one knew that better than herself, after all her studies of the ancient world. The ancient Greeks had such an appearance now of rationality, of cool, pale beauty. Yet in truth their statues and temples, which were so slavishly recreated now in Adam foyers and white muslin gowns, had been brightly painted. Their ideas of order, their great philosophy and tragedy, concealed a love for madness, ecstasy, the paranormal that was distinctly *irrational*.

People were like that, too, in modern London or ancient Athens and Sparta. Layer upon layer, concealing whatever truly lurked at their core. A mystery.

And the greatest mystery of all was strolling into her view. Lord Westwood himself, of course. No wonder people gossiped about the two of them, Calliope mused, for he so often appeared just where she happened to be!

Unlike when he stormed out of the British Museum, all

Hadean fire and anger, he was back to sunny Apollonian charm. A small parcel was tucked under his arm, half-hidden by the folds of his greatcoat. He smiled at the people he passed, pausing to kiss giggling ladies' hands or chat with friends.

Layer upon layer. Where was the real man?

Calliope's steps froze as he moved nearer, bringing Emmeline up short.

"What is amiss?" Her eyes widened as she followed Calliope's gaze. "Oh. The man himself, I see. And so handsome today!"

"Perhaps we should turn back," Calliope said. "We've left the others so far behind…."

"Nonsense!" Emmeline said, continuing on their path so resolutely that Calliope had no choice but to follow. "It would only fuel the gossip if you were seen avoiding Lord Westwood, Calliope. We must be polite and say hello."

When Lord Westwood saw them, Calliope thought she saw a frown between his eyes, a whisper of solemnity. But whatever it was quickly vanished, replaced by a sunny smile, a flourishing bow.

"Miss Chase, Lady Emmeline," he greeted. "A lovely day for a walk, is it not?"

"Indeed it is. We were just discussing our costumes for the Duke of Averton's ball, weren't we, Calliope?" Emmeline arched her brow at Calliope so she had no choice but to nod, even though they had been discussing no such thing. "A Grecian theme, of course, so we were hoping some of the park's statuary would inspire us."

Westwood's lips tightened. "I am sure that whatever you two ladies wear you will be the loveliest in the room."

Emmeline laughed. "Miss Chase might. She looks like a Greek statue all the time!"

He glanced at Calliope, but she could read nothing in his eyes. They were as opaque as the waters of the Serpentine. "That she does."

"Oh!" Emmeline suddenly exclaimed, detaching her arm from Calliope's. "I see someone over there I absolutely must speak to. Excuse me for a moment, Calliope. Lord Westwood."

What on earth was her friend up to? Calliope tried to catch Emmeline's hand, but she was off, dashing away like the traitor she was. Leaving Calliope alone with Lord Westwood.

Well, not entirely *alone*, of course. Not with half of London around them, and Clio and the rest of the Ladies Society not far away. Yet it felt as if they were alone. Calliope felt dizzy, her vision blurring until she saw only him, not the crowds.

She clasped her hands together, reminding herself of her purpose. Cause no scenes; act perfectly calm and normal. No scandal broth.

"So, you plan to attend Averton's ball?" he said. His voice was as unreadable as his face.

"Of course. Isn't everybody? I do long to see the Artemis again. Unless…"

"Unless?"

Calliope remembered how murderous he looked at the museum, when the duke edged so close to Clio. "Unless there is a reason it might be unsafe."

"And you think I might know that reason?"

"Perhaps. Better than some. And I would hope, Lord Westwood, that you would tell me if you know of any reason why my sister or I should not go. I know that you and I are not exactly friends…"

At last there was a glimmer of emotion, a tiny smile like

the sun peeking through grey clouds. "Are we not, Miss Chase? Friends, that is."

"I—well," Calliope said, flustered. "Perhaps we *could* be."

"If we were not both such stubborn spirits?"

Calliope took a deep breath. Infernal man! Just when she thought she had him figured out, he fooled her. Revealed another layer. He lured her from her resolve to be cool and polite. "Lord Westwood, tell me! *Is* there a reason Clio and I should not go to the ball?" A reason such as that he was planning to snatch the Alabaster Goddess while everyone else danced in oblivion?

He shrugged. "As you say, everyone will be there. Averton won't try anything in front of the entire *ton*. You should be safe enough. As long as you don't do anything rash."

"Rash?" Calliope cried. "What do you think I would do? Rashness is much more your style than mine, Lord Westwood. I merely plan to examine the statue, have a glass of the duke's fine champagne, and depart. In peace."

"Of course. As befits a Muse," he said. His smile was now that maddening full-fledged grin.

Cool and polite! Calliope berated herself. "Will you be there?"

"Oh, I wouldn't miss it. I always enjoy fine—champagne."

"Are you sure that's wise?" Calliope asked doubtfully.

"I never overly imbibe, Miss Chase. Not in polite company."

She had to resist the urge to childishly stamp her half-boot on the walkway. "You know what I mean."

"Oh, yes. You are remembering our scene in the Elgin Room. I do so often seem to show myself at my worst to you, Miss Chase, and then I have to apologise. It's true that I have no liking for the duke, or he for me. But I do know better than to cause a scene at a ball, though I've given you little cause to trust my word on that."

"I don't believe you would cause a scene at a ball," Calliope admitted, bemused. "It doesn't seem your way to turn a grand ballroom into Gentleman Jackson's parlour."

"Just a museum, eh? Well, you and your sister may attend the ball in peace. We'll all be masked, won't we? Averton himself won't even know I'm there. Neither will you." He bowed to her again, the paper of the parcel under his arm rustling. "Good day, Miss Chase. Enjoy the rest of your walk."

Calliope turned to watch him leave, to watch him greet Clio and the others, then hurry on his way, obviously a man with an errand on this fine afternoon.

Oh, but you are wrong, Lord Westwood, she thought. *For I will certainly know if you're there.*

Cameron leaned back in his chair, surveying his library. At least nominally it was "his" library, but ever since he returned from his travels to take his place as Earl of Westwood it felt like his father's library. His father's house. Everywhere Cameron looked he saw his father's furniture and carpets, the niches where his collections once resided. Their country seat was one thing; the furnishings there were old family pieces and not personal. This townhouse had been his father's, the place where he indulged his love of Greece, his passion for collecting.

But that was about to change. For too long now Cameron had lived with someone else's life. It was time to begin his own. One piece at a time.

He stood up and reached for the parcel on the desk. It was small, flat, carefully wrapped in brown paper. Cameron carried it over to the carved fireplace mantel,

gazing up at the painting that hung there. It was one his
father had acquired on his own Grand Tour many decades
ago, an indifferently executed murky scene of Egyptian
pyramids. Cameron had never much liked it, even though
it hung there through his childhood. The perspective was
all wrong, the colours dim, conveying no sense of the desert
brightness, the mystery of the Egyptians.

He reached up and unhooked it from the picture rail, lifting
it down at last. It left a pale square on the topaz-coloured silk
wallpaper. Then he tore the wrapping from his new package
and lifted the pyramid's replacement into its place.

Cameron stepped back to survey the image. He had
seen it in that gallery window and knew it was meant to
be his. Meant to hang just here, where he could see it every
day as he worked at the desk.

It was an image of Athena, standing framed between
the shining white pillars of her temple. The sacred fire
burned behind her, outlining her slim figure in pleated
white silk. One arm was outstretched, holding her grey
owl, while the other hand rested on the shield propped
beside her. Her golden helmet rested at her feet, and her
hair, a river of glossy raven-black, flowed over her shoulders.

Her beautiful face, a pale oval set with wide-spaced
grey eyes, was solemn and knowing. She was beautiful, oh
so serious, set on her own course come what may.

She was, in short, Calliope Chase. Or very, very like her.

Cameron smiled up at her, not sure she would appreciate
such levity. The *real* Calliope Chase certainly wouldn't appreciate knowing he had her double hanging in his library.
Yet he could never have passed up this painting. It was so
lovely, just as her modern counterpart was.

Why was he always so drawn to her, when their

meetings so often ended in strife or farce? He should stay far away from her, from all her family. The Chases were trouble he did not need, now most of all. He had important work to do, and couldn't afford to be distracted by a beautiful Athena with fire in her eyes. Fire just waiting to scorch him if he got too close.

Yet he never could stay away. Every time he saw her he was pulled to her side, he couldn't help himself. Lately it seemed quarrelling with her was more fun than making love to another woman would be. The thought of quarrelling *and* making love with Calliope was enough to make his head explode! Her fiery nature would surely take hold even in bed, and her pale skin and black hair against his sheets…

"Blast," Cameron cursed, spinning away from Athena's knowing gaze. The chances of Calliope Chase ending up naked in his bed were slim to none. She wouldn't even come near his house once she found out what he had done with his father's antiquities. Not even Aphrodite could help him with that Muse, no matter how much he desired her.

But he *could* keep her safe from Averton. Safe from her own folly concerning the Lily Thief, perhaps. She said she would be at Averton's ball. Well, so would he. And he would not let his Athena out of his sight.

Chapter Seven

"Oh, Miss Calliope! You look lovely," Mary said, putting the last touches on the hem of Calliope's costume.

From her perch atop a stool, Calliope surveyed herself in the mirror. "You don't think it's too much?"

"Not at all. It'll be the finest costume there."

Calliope *did* rather like it. She had worked closely with the modiste to replicate an etching her father owned of the Athena statue that had once stood in the Parthenon. The soft, thin white muslin was pleated and fastened at the shoulders with gold brooches, bound at the waist with gold cord. The sandals were also gold, and she wore antique bracelets and earrings that had once belonged to her mother. Waiting for her by the bedchamber door was a helmet, shield and spear.

Calliope fiddled with the cord, unaccountably nervous. Ordinarily she would be excited about a Grecian masquerade. Yet this was no ordinary ball.

What if the Lily Thief *did* appear? It was one thing to talk about catching criminals in her own drawing room, quite another to face a real, living thief bent on taking the

Alabaster Goddess. What if she could not stop him? What if Artemis did indeed vanish, never to be seen again?

Don't be faint-hearted! she told herself sternly. *You can't fail. This is much too important.*

She glanced towards the spear and shield. The weapons, pasteboard and glitter, would never hold against steel. But they reminded her of her purpose. She had to be Athena, and protect those in her charge from harm.

No matter who the Lily Thief was. No matter what might happen.

"Shall we finish your hair now, Miss Calliope?" Mary asked, putting away her needle and thread.

"Yes, thank you," Calliope said. She stepped down from the stool and went to her dressing table, where gold ribbons and combs waited. "We don't have much time left, the carriage is ordered for nine."

Mary had just started brushing out Calliope's hair, twisting the strands into long ringlets, when there was a quick knock at the door and Clio appeared.

"Oh!" Calliope gasped. She hadn't yet seen her sister's costume, or even known its theme, and the effect was dazzling. Dazzling and strange.

Clio was not an Olympian goddess, all pale perfection, or even the Muse of their namesakes. She was instead Medusa. Her gown was of vivid green silk, the sleeves like long wings, split and folded back from her shoulders. The green robe revealed glimpses of a gold-tissue underdress, embroidered with tiny green glass beads that winked and sparkled. An emerald kirtle, a rare medieval piece that had also been their mother's, caught the rich fabric around her waist.

But it was her headdress that was truly extraordinary— a twisting, tangled nest of gold-tissue snakes, their scales overlaid with greenish, brassy embroidery. More of the beads formed their eyes, and they seemed to gleam malevolently, as if the snakes were alive. Only a few long tendrils of Clio's own auburn hair escaped, revealing that here was a real woman and not a vengeful Gorgon.

"What do you think?" Clio asked, twirling around in all her frightening splendour.

"I think there will be no one else like you at the party," Calliope answered, bedazzled by those snake eyes. "Wherever did you find such a creation?"

"Madame Sophie made the gown," Clio answered, adjusting her sleeves. "And I did the headdress myself. Cory helped me, you know she's quite the budding artist. They look quite fearsome, don't they?"

"Terribly," Calliope said with a shiver. A frown from Mary made her sit still again, facing the mirror so her hair could be finished. "I doubt the duke will attempt to harass you with *those* staring at him."

Clio laughed. "I'm not afraid of the duke!" She brandished her staff, a tall gold-and-green, ribbon-wrapped pole topped with yet another snake, a puffed-out cobra. "I shall just turn him to stone."

"If only it was always that easy to deal with men," Calliope muttered. "What are Thalia and Father dressed up as?"

"Thalia is Euridice, and Father is Socrates, of course."

"With his cup of hemlock?"

"Hmm, yes," Clio said. She stepped up to Calliope's mirror to make sure her snakes were straight. "Or rather a cup of lemonade with sprigs of mint floating in it. We shall have to make sure he doesn't bore everyone in sight at the ball, for he is already wandering around the drawing room, declaiming to the furniture."

"If there is no youth to corrupt, a hassock will do. Is that a direct quote from Socrates as he drank the hemlock? If not, it should be." Calliope watched as Mary finished the curls and ribbons and carefully lowered the helmet over her creation. "How do I look, Clio?"

"Perfect, as always. Surely there can be no finer Athena," Clio answered. "Too bad Cory's pet owl died last year, it would have made an excellent prop."

"A prop that would fly off and get lost in the chandeliers. I told Cory a barn owl didn't want to be a domestic pet. This one here will do very well." Calliope hoisted up her shield to display the enameled owl on its face. "Shall we go?"

Athena, after all, was never late to battle.

The Duke of Averton's grand townhouse, Acropolis House, was lit up like the Colossus of Rhodes set down in the middle of London. Even from their place far back in the long line of carriages, Calliope was dazzled by the amber glow.

Acropolis House was not the usual among aristocratic townhouses. No plain white stone, no mellow red brick set in tidy rows for the duke. No. Acropolis House was like a vestige of medieval London, a fortress of solid, dark rock, turreted and many-chimneyed, the shutters of all its mullion windows thrown open to let out all that candlelight. It was set back in its own small garden, surrounded by high walls. The iron-tipped gates were usually closed and chained tight, but tonight they were open to admit the flood of carriages, the gawking curiosity seekers. As their own conveyance entered the gates, Calliope peered out to find leering gargoyles staring back at her. They topped the gates and lined the walls, discouraging the curious.

Calliope shivered and drew back into her shawl.

"You'd think the duke was Charlemagne," Thalia

sniffed. "And look at that obelisk over in the corner of the garden! Twenty feet high at least."

"Terribly pretentious," their father agreed. But Calliope thought she saw a tiny glint of envy in his eyes as he peered at the towering obelisk. "I wonder where he obtained it? The hieroglyphs are quite fine."

"Somewhere he had no business being, I'm sure," Clio said tartly.

Calliope did not answer, for their carriage at last rolled to a halt before the massive, iron-bound front doors and it was their turn to alight at last. The duke's footmen, clad in chitons and sandals for the evening, hurried forward to assist them. Calliope held tight to her spear and shield as she followed Clio's glittering green train into the very lair of the Duke of "Avarice".

The foyer, where they surrendered their cloaks to more classically garbed servants, was a soaring, octagonal space with black-and-white marble floors and walls inlaid with dark wood panels. Tall, wrought-iron candelabras provided the only light, flickering on tightly closed doors, on Minoan frescoes of slim bull jumpers, on suits of armour, and bristling maces and swords, and on two massive Assyrian lions guarding one of the doors, as if ancient Persia rested just beyond that portal.

"My, what eclectic tastes our host has," Clio muttered, as they joined the line of revellers making their way up the twisting staircase towards the ballroom.

"To say the least," Calliope answered, eyeing the treasures tucked in niches. Sculptures, vases and amphorae, even Byzantine icons. They were all impressive pieces, beautifully restored, elegantly displayed. Yet Calliope noticed something odd about them all. Unlike her father's own antiquities, which depicted the gods and Muses, wise scholars, merry parties, the finest of human endeavours, these pieces all had some element of violence about them. Battles, fights, sacrifices. Even the icons depicted martyred saints: Catherine and her wheel, Sebastian and his arrows, and St George driving his sword into the dragon.

Calliope turned away from them, disquieted.

"Or perhaps not so eclectic as all that," Clio said quietly. "Murder and bloodletting are sadly a part of every civilisation. The duke seems bent on reminding us of that fact."

"Indeed he does," Calliope said.

The higher up they went, the more the noise of the party grew, a hum that expanded into a vast river of sound as they spilled into the ballroom. Calliope usually had little use for balls and routs that earned the coveted society accolade of "dreadful crush". There was little real conversation possible amid such clamour, just overheated air and far too much noise. Tonight, though, she welcomed the crowd. It seemed a bright haven of normalcy in this very bizarre house.

The ballroom was not as eerie as the foyer and staircase, but was merely a large, bright space with white walls and gleaming parquet floor. The domed ceiling was painted with an elaborate fresco of an Olympian banquet where, thankfully, no one was killing anyone else. Around the walls were more ancient frescoes, no doubt snatched from some Italian villa, scenes of cosy domestic life. Marble statues were interspersed with the paintings of scantily clad nymphs, satyrs, gods and goddesses that echoed the costumes of the revellers.

As Calliope expected, there was no one quite like Clio among the crowds who were forming a dance set or milling among the statues, sipping champagne and nibbling on lobster patties and mushroom tarts—rather *un*Grecian hors-d'oeuvres, Calliope thought. There was a Minotaur, hulking and hairy, flirting with Ariadne and her ball of twine; several Achilles and Hectors; some giggling Aphrodites with various versions of Ares and Cupid. Their father soon joined a cluster of other philosophers in the corner to argue about how man could examine his reasons to be in harmony with the cosmos, and Thalia was swept into the dance by an Orpheus, their respective lyres deposited with a footman.

Calliope tucked her spear under her arm and reached for a glass of champagne from a passing servant's tray. It was the finest quality, of course, a rich, tart golden liquid that blended well with the exotic setting, the swirl of music and laughter. For a moment, she felt transported from London, from everyday life, and lifted into some phantasmagoric fantasy world where reality was gone, vanished amid the sea of masks.

She held the glass up to the light, wondering if the enchanting little bubbles concealed some hallucinogenic elixir, some Shakespearean "love in idleness".

"Is something amiss with the champagne, Miss Chase?" an amused voice asked.

Calliope whirled around to find their host standing behind her, a smile on his lips. He was as unusual as his house, dressed as Dionysus with a leopard skin over his chiton, his long, red-gold hair loose over his shoulders. Dionysus, the god of wine and revels. Of maddened followers who tore their victims limb from limb in their bloodlust.

Or stole treasures that did not belong to them.

Calliope stiffened under his intense regard. "Not at all, your Grace. The champagne is excellent, as are your arrangements. Your house is most—extraordinary."

"That is high praise, indeed, coming from a Chase. For you are all experts in art and antiquities, are you not?"

"I would not say *expert*. We are all students, in our own ways."

"And is *your* interest strategic warfare?" he said, gesturing towards her Athena shield.

"Or perhaps olives," she said flippantly.

"Ah, yes. For it was Athena who ordered olive trees planted on the hills of her Acropolis. The very foundations of her followers' prosperity."

"Until rapacious thieves ordered them dug up, in search of buried treasure. Now glorious Athens is just a dusty little town. Or so I hear."

The duke laughed. "My dear Miss Chase, how kind of you to defend a people you do not even know! Yet if your so-called rapacious thieves did not dig on the Acropolis, think what would be lost to us. So much beauty and learning. Is it better that these things should moulder in the ground, disintegrating in the care of people who have no regard for them?"

Calliope grudgingly had to admit that he said nothing she herself had not argued. But his smug tone of voice, his patronising smile, made her want to quarrel with him. To slap that expression off his face. She shrugged, and drained her glass of champagne.

"Come, Miss Chase, let me show you one of the treasures that would have been lost for ever," he said, taking the empty glass from her hand.

"The Alabaster Goddess?" Calliope asked.

"Are you trying to gain an early glimpse of the masterpiece of my collection? No, she will be revealed later. At the right moment."

"One last chance for her to be admired before she is shut away?"

"She is hardly a cloistered nun. She is being taken to a

place where she can be properly protected, unlike other antiquities in our fair city of late," he said. He took her arm in a light clasp, steering her around the edges of the crowd, calling jovial greetings to the noisy guests.

Calliope had to grit her teeth to resist the urge to pull away, to run from him. When Lord Westwood took her arm just so at the British Museum, it was warm and easy. The duke's touch felt like a cold shackle. She pinched her lips together and walked faster as they moved past candelabra and frescoes.

He led her to the end of the room, where tall glass doors led on to a dark terrace. The crowd was lighter here, the air cooler. Calliope almost feared he meant to lead her out on to that terrace, away from the noise and light, and then—then what? Push her off to the stone walkway far below?

Calliope almost laughed aloud at her own foolishness. He did not know of her plans to keep his Alabaster Goddess safe, to prevent her from being stolen like all those other lost pieces. To keep her from disappearing into Yorkshire, too, if she could help it at all. He did not know of her great aversion to him, of how frightened she was by his behaviour towards Clio at the museum. He couldn't know any of that.

Nevertheless, when his clasp on her arm loosened, she wasted no time in moving away.

"What do you think of this, Miss Chase?" he asked, gesturing towards another statue displayed between the glass doors.

Calliope forced herself to turn her wary attention from him, to take in a deep breath as she examined the piece. Art, as it always did, slowly worked its magic on her senses. The duke and the crowd subsided to a whisper.

It was beautiful, of course, as everything in the duke's collection was. Beautiful in a strange, violent way. This depicted not a battle or brawl, but Daphne at the very moment she was transformed into a tree by her father Peneus, after Daphne called on him to stave off Apollo's unwanted advances. She was running, her body twisted as she looked frantically back over her shoulder. Her legs and upflung arms were turning to branches. Her long hair flowed back like a river.

"What do you think, Miss Chase?" the duke asked.

"It is lovely. The sense of movement, the way the flesh of her arms transforms just here into wood—extraordinary."

"Exactly so. It is a Roman copy, of course, but still its great beauty is evident. And her face looks rather like your sister, does it not?"

Startled, Calliope stared up at the duke, shaken from the reverie the Daphne invoked. He did not watch her; all his attention was on Daphne's cold, carved face. He reached out one fingertip to touch her cheek, sliding a slow caress along the angle of her cheekbone.

It *did* look like Clio, Calliope had to admit. With that hair, and the sharp, thin angles of the face and bare shoulders. And that made his rapt attention all the more chilling.

"She has the same independent spirit, you see," the duke murmured. "But in the end, one way or another, she will belong to the gods. Run though she will."

Calliope's throat was dry, and she knew she had leave, to find Clio. She slowly backed away from the duke, who still seemed lost in his own world. His own fantasies of poor Daphne.

"Excuse me," Calliope murmured. "I see someone I must speak to."

She hurried back into the midst of the crowd. There seemed to be even more people packed into the ballroom than before, knots and skeins of humanity laughing and drinking, oblivious to any nightmarish quality this house might hold. Yet there was no Clio anywhere, not even a glimpse of her shimmering green silk. Thalia was still dancing, as she probably would do all night. Their father was nowhere to be seen. Probably he had gone off to the card room with his philosopher friends, continuing their discussion over a hand of *vingt-et-un*. She did see Emmeline, dressed as the Delphic Oracle, talking with one of her assigned possible thieves. She gave Calliope a small nod and smile. All was going as planned in that corner.

If only Calliope could say the same! She so hated when her plans went awry. But then, what could she expect from someone like the Duke of Averton? He was a strange one, to say the least, and there could be no predicting what might happen in his house. She had to stay calm. Remember her goal—to protect the Alabaster Goddess.

And surely in such a vast crowd Clio was safe enough. The duke couldn't hurt her here, couldn't turn her into a tree. He probably couldn't even find her. Still, Calliope would feel better if she could talk to her sister, warn her to be on her guard.

Hoisting her shield higher, Calliope threaded her way through the ballroom. Several friends greeted her, but there was no Clio.

"Where *are* you?" she muttered, straining on tiptoe to see over the crowd.

"I am here, grey-eyed Athena," a voice said, slightly muffled, close to her shoulder.

Half-fearing the duke had crept up on her again,

Calliope turned. There was no Dionysus, though. It was Hermes, in his winged sandals and helmet, muscled arms bare in a white chiton. The visor of the helmet was down, but Calliope recognised the unruly dark curls that escaped its golden confines. She also recognized Hermes' scent, the clean smell of citrus soap with something darker, more complex and alluring, underneath, like cinnamon or sunshine, salty sea air.

A strange sense of relief flowed over her. She was not alone in this crowd any longer! "My eyes are brown, Lord Westwood," she said, resisting the urge to hug him, to cling to those strong arms. It was surely just another measure of how bizarre this evening had become that she was so very happy to see him.

"Always so logical," he said, pushing back the visor to reveal his smile. "How did you know it was me?"

"Your soap."

"My *soap?*"

Calliope shook her head. "It's not important. Have you by any chance seen my sister?"

"Miss Clio? I don't think so, but then anything is possible in this crowd. What is her costume?"

"Oh, you couldn't miss her. She is Medusa, in a green-and-gold gown, with snakes on her headdress."

"Snakes? Never say she brought reptiles in here! But then, I would not really be surprised. You Chases always do things in your own fashion."

Calliope had to smile in spite of herself. "I dare say Clio might have brought real snakes in, if she didn't know how I dislike them. But she only has cloth snakes. With green glass eyes."

"I fear I've seen no Medusas at all. Is something amiss?"

"No, I just need to tell her something. I'm sure I will see her later. Unfortunately, I can glimpse little in this crowd."

"Did I not predict it would be a 'dreadful crush'?"

"You did. Surely what every hostess most desires."

"Or host." His expression hardened. "I saw you were speaking to Mr Dionysus."

"For a moment," Calliope answered cautiously. "He was showing me a statue of Daphne." The memory of the duke's hand on that marble cheek made her feel cold all over again, and she trembled.

"Are you cold?" Lord Westwood asked solicitously.

"Just a bit. Though I'm not sure how I could be, it's so overheated in here!"

"Such a mausoleum as this place can never be truly warm. Come, Miss Chase, dance with me. I think the exercise will do us both good."

Calliope glanced towards the dance floor to find a new set forming. Emmeline was there with Mr Smithson, as was Thalia with the strange Minotaur. Still no Clio. Yet surely a dance *would* do her good. Take her whirling thoughts from the duke and his bizarre actions, the Alabaster Goddess and the Lily Thief, and warm her chilled bones. Westwood was right—this place was a mausoleum. Only music and dancing could bring it to life again.

Especially a dance with Lord Westwood, for surely no one could be more alive than he was. His cognac eyes, the golden glow of his smooth skin, fairly breathed youth and vitality and strength. After the duke's brief, cold touch, the breath of his corruption, she craved that heat. Yearned for it. Even if it *was* with Westwood.

But he was not Westwood tonight. He was Hermes. She

was Athena. And this was not an ordinary London ball, but an Olympian revel. For the length of one dance, anyway.

"Thank you, Lord Westwood," she said. "I would be happy to dance with you."

Chapter Eight

Clio glanced back over her shoulder as she tiptoed along the narrow corridor. Empty. No one followed her. Probably they did not even notice her absence from the ballroom, not in such a crush.

Perfect.

It was silent here, unlike the roar of music and shallow conversation. So quiet it was almost like a cave, lit only by a few lamps built to resemble flickering torches. The shifting light touched the dark, linenfold panelled walls, the low, carved ceiling and the gilt-framed paintings, making them glitter and waver as if alive.

Clio paused to slip off her heeled shoes, peering closer at one of those paintings. It was a modern creation, an oil of the Minotaur in his labyrinth. A great, hulking, hairy beast with red, fiery eyes, lurking in a dark space much like this corridor. All around him were smoking torches, stone walls painted with strange, glowing symbols.

The duke must feel some affinity for this particular myth, Clio thought as she studied the scene. She had seen several depictions of it tonight, in stone as well as paint, and in that one odd costume in the ballroom. Well, she knew that everyone had within them a dark heart—a Minotaur. And that sometimes a person had to venture into the labyrinth to confront that side of themselves. To confront the truth.

Was that not what she was doing now?

Clio turned her back on the Minotaur and hurried on stocking feet to the end of the corridor where there was a small, winding staircase, a miniature of the grand one soaring up from the foyer. The duke was being very cagey about the Alabaster Goddess's whereabouts tonight. But his servants were not all so secretive. Clio was able to persuade a footman to tell her where Artemis waited.

At the top of the stairs ran a long gallery, almost the entire length of the front of the house. Its bank of windows, uncovered, looked out at the front garden and the street beyond, the open gates that still admitted latecomers to the ball.

The gallery was dotted with tall, heavy iron branches of candles, half of them unlit. No doubt waiting for the "grand reveal" after supper, when they would spring to life as if by magic. Right now the light was dim, falling only in shimmering bars on some of the treasures displayed there, leaving others in darkness.

Clio found herself holding her breath as she crept along the gallery, peering right and left at all the wonders jumbled together. Her father's friends were all great collectors and loved to show off their prizes, so she had grown up surrounded by beautiful antiquities. But this—this was something else entirely. A cabinet of curiosities such as she had never seen before.

The gallery almost resembled a warehouse, it was so thick with objects. Ancient stone kouros, stiff and precise, their empty eyes staring back at her. An Egyptian sarcophagus, with traces of bright paint still clinging to its surface. Bronze warriors; marble gods finer than any she had ever seen; cases full of gold Etruscan jewellery, lapis scarabs, tiny cat mummies in gold coffins, jewelled perfume bottles. Steles propped against the walls. Shelves of vases, kraters, and amphorae. All jumbled together, just to serve one man's vanity.

Clio frowned as she remembered the duke at the British Museum, pressing so close to her she was overcome by his spicy cologne. That strange light in his green eyes…

She shook her head, her satin snakes trembling. She couldn't think about him now. She didn't want to think about him *ever*.

At the end of the gallery, alone in a pool of candlelight, was an object covered in a drape of black satin. Only a bit of the separate coral-coloured marble stand was visible. Clio approached it carefully, half-expecting some sort of trap, some alarm. All was silent, except for the whining hum of the wind past the windows. She reached out and carefully lifted an edge of the drape, peering beneath.

"Oh," she sighed. It was really *her*. The Alabaster Goddess. Artemis in her solitary glory.

The statue was not large. It was easily dwarfed by many of the more elaborate creations in the gallery. But she was so perfectly beautiful, so graceful and elegant, that Clio could understand why she had become such a sensation.

Carved of an alabaster so white it seemed to glisten, almost silver, like a first snowfall, she stood poised with her bow raised, an arrow set to fly. Her pleated tunic flowed over the curves of her slender body as if caught in a breeze, ending at mid-thigh to reveal strong legs, tensed to run. Her sandals, the little, ribbon-laced shoes every lady had copied this Season, still bore bits of gold leaf, as did the bandeau that held back her curled hair. A crescent moon was attached to the band, proclaiming her to truly be the Goddess of the Moon. Her gaze was focused intently on her prey, not heeding mortal adulation.

Clio stared up at her, enthralled, as she imagined the Delian temple where this goddess once resided, where she once received her worship from true acolytes of the moon. Not just *ton* ladies with their "Artemis" coiffures.

"How beautiful you are," she whispered. "And how sad."

Clio reached out to gently touch Artemis' foot in a gesture of silent sympathy. As she did, she noticed that the goddess stood on a modern wooden base, a thick block of mahogany. A thin crack ran along its centre. She leaned closer, trying to see if that crack was a fault or deliberate. It seemed such a strange perch for a beautiful goddess.

"Ah, Miss Chase. Clio. I see you have discovered the whereabouts of my treasure," a voice said, quiet, gloating.

Clio ducked away from Artemis, spinning around to find the duke standing halfway along the gallery, watching her intently.

Even in the dim light, his eyes gleamed like the snakes in her headdress. He smiled at her gently, shrugging his leopard pelt back from his shoulders. Clio thought of that scene from the *Bacchae*, where Agave, under the evil influence of Dionysus, tore her son Pentheus to death, thinking him a lion. Then she carried his severed head back home, still delusional.

He moved closer, light and silent, as if he was a leopard himself. "She is beautiful, is she not?" he said, still so quiet. So soft. "I knew you would be drawn to her, as I was. She is quite—irresistible, in her mystery."

Clio edged back against the goddess. She had indeed

found Artemis irresistible. So much so that she let her
guard down, and that was not like her. As the duke came
closer, she reached behind her, her fingers just touching
Artemis' cold sandal. She slid her touch down, finding that
strange crack in the wooden base…

Calliope took her place in the set with Lord Westwood
just as the music began, a quick, lively tune that made her
toes tap in her sandals. She was not Terpsichore, the Muse
of Dance, but she did love the movement, the rhythm of
the music, the swirl of other dancers around her as they
formed the patterns and picture of the dance. Usually, it
could lift her out of herself for a few moments, send her
into a world where there was only the music.

Tonight, though, the beat was not soothing, not transport-
ing. There was so much in her mind—Clio's disappearance,
the plan to protect the Alabaster Goddess. And, not least, the
fact that her partner for this dance was Cameron de Vere.

Never would she have imagined they would be dancing
together at a ball, quite as if they were—well, as if they
were friends! No one was shouting or scowling or throwing
things. He stood across from her in the line, smiling at her.
Calliope smiled back, and all at once she felt the old magic
of the dance come upon her once more. A new energy
surged through her veins, lifting her up on to her toes as
she stepped forward to meet him. Their hands touched, and
they turned to move down the line, swirling among the
other dancers in a quick, intricate rhythm.

He was a good dancer, light and graceful, but then she
did not expect anything less after seeing him drive his
phaeton. No jerky, ham-handed movements for him. He
moved his horses—and his dance partners—with gentle
persuasion, and made it all look easy. Calliope barely felt

she had to move, so easily did he twirl her from step to step, spinning her until she vowed her feet left the floor and she was flying!

As they were separated by the design of the dance, Emmeline leaned close and quickly whispered, "Is he the thief, then, Calliope?"

As Calliope turned in a circle, she glanced towards Lord Westwood. Surely he had the fleetness to climb in a window, the strength to carry off the Alabaster Goddess. But… "I don't know. What of Mr Smithson?"

Emmeline shrugged, and was spun away into another circle. Westwood caught Calliope's hand again, drawing her near as they turned in allemande. "You are a fine dancer, Miss Chase," he said, not even out of breath.

Calliope, though, felt suddenly winded as she stared up into his eyes. "I could say the same about you," she answered. "Where did you learn such grace on your travels?"

"Oh, I am a man of *many* talents, Miss Chase," he said, catching her against him for a moment, so very close she could feel the damp heat of his body, the tense strength of him. Their bare arms brushed together, and his skin was so smooth and warm. "You have no idea."

No. But Calliope thought maybe she was beginning to have an inkling.

They slid back into their own places in line as the music ended, and Calliope ducked into a curtsy. Her heart fairly pounded, as if she had run a mile rather than just danced an easy reel. It was as if the earth shifted under her feet, an earth she had always been so certain of, and it had not yet re-formed. Perhaps it never would.

Westwood held out his hand to help her rise. She slid her fingers into his clasp, still warm from the exercise, and let him lead her from the dance floor. The ballroom was even more crowded than before, newcomers swelling the throng until it reached the very walls, spilled out on to the terrace and the grand staircase. Yet Calliope could hardly hear them for the humming in her head, could not feel their press, their clamour. She only felt his hand on hers.

"Did I tell you that you look quite lovely tonight, Miss Chase?" he said, so close to her ear that his breath stirred the loose curls at her temple.

Calliope shivered. "I—thank you, Lord Westwood. You did say I made a plausible Athena."

"I would not be surprised if you started a battle right here, leading us to victory over the Spartans."

Calliope laughed nervously. "I don't think I could, Lord Westwood. Even Athena could not find her way through this crush. And I can't find my sister. A poor goddess I would make."

"Perhaps she went to peek at Artemis," he suggested.

"But the Alabaster Goddess is hidden! The duke said she would only be revealed later."

"Ah, yes, you did speak to our notorious host. Or should I say inadequate host, for I have not seen the man since I arrived."

"Yes, I did see him, but not in quite a while. It was over there, by that Daphne…" Calliope paused, remembering the duke's caress on Daphne's cold cheek. "I would feel better if I could find Clio."

"I'll help you search," he said. "This is a big house, to be sure, but she has to be in it somewhere."

"Oh, would you? I don't want to take you away from the dancing. Or the cards."

"A mystery is always more fun than a game of loo, Miss Chase. And 'find the missing muse' should be more interesting than a dance—unless it's with Athena, of course." His tone was light, but Calliope thought she sensed disquiet in his eyes, in the tight line of his jaw. It made her own uncertainties stronger. She was very glad of his help, not at all sure she wouldn't get lost in this vast mausoleum on her own.

Plus, if he was with her he couldn't steal the Alabaster Goddess!

"Thank you, Lord Westwood," she said. "I appreciate your assistance."

"What!" he cried in mock astonishment. "Calliope Chase *appreciates* something about me? Never say so."

"I won't let it become a habit," she said. "And I will appreciate it even more if you actually find Clio."

"Then let us waste no time. I'm sure two instances of gratitude in one evening would be quite more than I could bear."

He steered her adroitly through the crowd, deftly sidestepping human barriers and looming statues until they found their way out the ballroom doors. There were also people in the small foyer at the head of the grand staircase, and in the card room and antechambers, but none of them were Medusa. Clio was also not in the ladies' withdrawing room, which Calliope checked without Westwood's assistance. Nor had anyone seen her.

Even more unsettling was the fact that no one had seen the duke for quite a while, despite the persistent buzz of gossip about him.

Calliope rejoined Westwood in the foyer, removing her helmet from her aching head. The headache forming behind her eyes was pounding and persistent, insisting that something was amiss.

"Did you say you know where the Alabaster Goddess is?" she asked Westwood.

"I've heard a rumour."

"I think we should look there, then. Unless you think Averton has a secret dungeon somewhere?"

He gave a humorless laugh. "I wouldn't put it past him. But we'll ask Artemis first."

He turned on his heel and set off from the foyer, finding a deserted narrow corridor. Calliope followed closely as they left the light and noise of the party behind. The duke's house was even more of a crypt than she had first thought, or perhaps more of a catacomb. An odd, twisting series of corridors and chambers. Unlike the Roman version, though, these catacombs held not human bones and ashes, but the bones of civilisations. A jumble of marble and basalt and mosaic, all piled together with no concern for the various cultures and time periods.

Calliope thought of her father's own collections, so carefully labelled and placed neatly in glass cases. How much each piece meant to him, and his daughters, so much more than a mere beautiful object. More than something to possess and show off, they meant knowledge, a link to lives long turned to dust. A way to understand the past, or at least begin to understand it.

It was obvious from this opulent clutter, this clash of Minoan, Archaic, Classical, Egyptian, Assyrian, Roman, Celtic, that the duke did not see them in this way. Their true value was lost to him.

As was surely the true value of her sister. Wherever Clio was.

At that unsettling thought, Calliope stumbled, reaching out to catch herself on a stone Egyptian lioness.

"Ouch!" she gasped.

Westwood spun around, and her hand landed not on the

cold statue but on warm, shifting flesh. His arm went about her waist, holding her steady.

Only she felt even dizzier now, pressed so close to him, than she had falling towards the ground.

"Are you all right?" he asked, his voice rough.

"Yes," Calliope answered slowly. "I must have stumbled on something."

"Easy enough to do in this warehouse."

Calliope eased herself away from him, leaning back against the kore until she could catch her breath. "I was just thinking it was a catacomb."

"A most apt description, Miss Chase. A pile of dead things, hidden away from the daylight."

Calliope studied the reclining Egyptian lioness, her muscles coiled and massive paws flexed, as if she would rise at any moment. How fierce she looked! How unhappy at being caged. Would she try to run away like Daphne? "Do you think they are dead?"

"Let us say sleeping, rather," he said. He ran his hand over the lioness's head, and Calliope felt as if she, too, could experience that touch. Rough and chipped, battered by the centuries, but still holding the imprint of her creator. "They can't breathe in such a gloomy place."

"Exactly. With no one to see their true worth." She paused, turning her gaze from the lion's obsidian stare to meet Westwood's. In this shadowed light his eyes were just as dark, just as mysterious. "But we don't agree on what their worth is."

"Do we not?" His hand tightened on the rippled stone. "I think we agree on far more than is first apparent, Miss Chase."

If only that were true! Calliope remembered her long-ago daydreams, that he could be the one man who understood her, who shared her dreams. Those hopes were shattered when she had found the Hermes statue gone. "How so, Lord Westwood?"

Instead of answering her, of telling her what she found she yearned to hear—how they could find common ground and be friends at long last—he just smiled. "Do you not think that sometimes you could call me Cameron? I still look around for my father when I hear 'Lord Westwood'. Everyone I met in Italy and Greece called me Cameron. Or Cam."

"I'm not sure." *Cameron.* How informal it sounded. How—inviting.

"Come, now! No one can hear us but our friend the lioness. And she won't tell. She loves to keep secrets."

Indeed, there did seem to be a satisfied gleam in those obsidian eyes, as if she relished having one more secret to add to the vast store she had collected in her long lifetime. Like the Aphrodite statue in the conservatory, and her remembered orgies. "Do you not think she holds enough secrets as it is? I'm sure this house has more than its share."

"No doubt you are right. Nasty secrets. But, while she is the duke's captive, she is *our* friend. She wants us to be in accord."

"Very well. I suppose I could call you Cameron, when only inanimate objects can hear us."

"Shh!" He put his hands over the carved ears. "She's not inanimate, remember? Only sleeping."

"When will she awaken? When she's taken from this place at last?"

"When she sees the sunlight again?"

Calliope remembered Lady Tenbray's Etruscan diadem, far from the sun of its homeland. "And will you be the one to liberate her—Cameron?"

He gave the lioness a considering glance. "Do you think

I'm strong enough, Miss Chase? Calliope?" he said teasingly, flexing his—admittedly impressive—arm muscles.

"Are you a hidden Herakles, then?"

"Ah, fair doubter! But as I am not Herakles, merely Hermes, I fear your doubts are justified. She would be much too heavy for me, winged sandals or not. One day, though, someone will free her from this place. Free all these things."

"Send them back where they came from?"

He shrugged. "Some place where they can be safe. I don't think anything can be safe here."

"Oh!" Calliope cried, sharply reminded of their errand. "Clio."

"Yes, we should move on. If you're quite recovered?"

"Of course."

He held out his arm and she accepted his support, letting him lead her down yet another corridor towards a narrow, winding staircase. She couldn't help but glance back at the lioness, so silent and stolid. Except for that gleam in her eye. That secret glint.

Had she seen Clio tonight?

"The Alabaster Goddess is up here," Cameron said, clambering up the steps.

Calliope looked up. She saw only a stout wooden door, somewhat ajar, and yet more shadows. More darkness. "How do you know?"

"Still so suspicious! And after I asked you to call me by my given name and everything."

"The duke said her location was a secret."

"I have my ways. Come, do you want to see or not, Athena?"

She glanced again towards that doorway. It could conceal anything at all. She half-expected a many-headed Hydra to leap out at them, snarling and slavering. "I want to see."

"Follow me, then. I may not be Herakles, but I promise I'll keep you safe."

He held out his hand, beckoning, and Calliope reached out and clasped it. Held fast to it, like a lifeline in a stormy sea. They climbed up the last of the stairs together, and slowly pushed open the silent door.

That entrance led not to Hades or a vast black river, but to a long, narrow gallery. Tall windows let in moonlight, which mingled with the glow of sputtering candles and cast a soft illumination on more antiquities, more statues and stele and sarcophaguses. Calliope blinked at the light, at first unable to see anything beyond the rich clutter.

Next to her, Cameron stiffened, and a curse escaped his lips in a soft, ominous explosion.

"What…?" Calliope began. Then she saw it.

The Alabaster Goddess, the pride of the Duke of Averton's collection, lay on her back on the floor, her bow aimed upward at the inlaid ceiling. Her gleaming alabaster body seemed intact, tangled with a length of black satin, but her wooden base was split and splintered.

And, at her feet, lay the duke himself.

Cameron dashed forward, Calliope close on his winged heels. The duke's bright hair was darkened with a spreading stain, his eyes closed, his skin as pale as Artemis's. His leopard skin was torn beneath him, and the coppery tang of blood was thick in the cool, dusty air.

"Is he dead?" Calliope whispered.

Cameron knelt down beside the prone duke, reaching out to touch the base of his bare neck. "Not yet. I can feel a pulse, but it's thin. See here," he said, gesturing to a gash along the duke's forehead. "It matches Artemis's elbow."

Calliope glanced at the goddess and saw that her arm was indeed stained, a dried smear of rust-coloured blood.

"He must have been here for quite a while, for it to dry like that. Do you think the statue fell on him?"

"Maybe her base broke as he was gloating over her. It would seem to be poetic justice of a sort."

"Or maybe..." Calliope leaned closer, pushing down her nausea. "No. It can't be."

"What?"

Shivering, Calliope gestured towards the duke's hand.

Clutched in his fist was a ripped swathe of green-and-gold silk. Half-hidden underneath his arm was a scattering of sparkling green beads.

"What is this?" Cameron asked tightly.

"Clio," Calliope groaned. "These are from her costume."

Cameron straightened, peering intently into the shadows. But Calliope could not be so cautious. She shot to her feet, dashing behind the marble plinth Artemis fell from. "Clio!" she cried. "Where are you? Clio!"

"Shh!" Cameron caught her hand, pulling her up short. "What if whoever did this is still lurking about? What if your sister...?"

"No! Clio couldn't do this, or if she did I'm certain she had a good reason. You were at the British Museum, you saw. We have to find her."

"And we will. But there are no other bloodstains on the floor, are there? She isn't hurt. We need to get help for the duke first. He's still alive."

Calliope looked at the man sprawled on the floor. He was still pale, yet she could see that he stirred. "You would help him? Even though you loathe him?"

He laughed wryly. "I may be tempted to leave him to die, done in by his famous Alabaster Goddess. But I would loathe *myself* even more than him if I did that. I will run back to the ballroom and fetch help, if you think you can stand guard for a few moments. I promise I won't be gone long."

Calliope sucked in a deep breath. "Yes. I can stay."

He studied her closely, as if to gauge her words. Finally, he nodded. "Of course you can, you're Athena. When you hear people approaching, hide behind that sarcophagus. It would never do for anyone to know that we were alone here!"

Calliope thought of the rumours Emmeline told her about, the gossip about Westwood and her, the bets. How upset she had been by that! Now it hardly seemed to matter. "Not at all," she said tartly. "Then you would be forced to offer for me."

"A dreadful fate." He caught her close in a swift, hard embrace, pressing a kiss to her brow. "I won't be gone long."

Calliope watched as he dashed back down the gallery and out the door, as fleet as any true Hermes. When he was gone, the silence gathered around her, thick and muffling, like a true London fog. The shadows also seemed to gather closer, creeping around as if they sensed doom, fed off it.

Calliope wrapped her arms tightly around herself to ward off the cold, to hold Cameron's embrace close. Some of her stout, Athena-ish courage was ebbing away without him to hold it up, but she knew she had to hold strong. Hold on to her composure. So much depended on it.

Steeling her nerves, she knelt by the duke and reached for his hand. Swallowing a sudden bitter rush of bile, she loosened his fingers to pull free the strip of telltale silk. His grip tightened, as if reluctant to relinquish his prize, but she tugged it loose. Then she set to gathering the green beads, the scattered snake eyes.

As she picked up the last one, she noticed the broken wooden base of the statue. Even though it was splintered, it appeared to not be broken so much as split along an opening. Calliope peered closer, and saw that a tiny, torn bit of paper protruded.

"How odd," she whispered. A secret compartment? To conceal—what?

Before she could investigate further, she heard the echo of voices and footsteps coming up the staircase. Gripping the silk and beads, she ducked back behind the sarcophagus, lying on her side. It was even darker, colder back there, the floor hard on her hip. She pressed herself tight against the carved, painted hieroglyphs, holding her breath as she listened to the shouts and exclamations.

She had never felt more alone in her life.

Chapter Nine

Calliope crept up the stairs of her own home, her steps weary and slow. The house was quiet; no one expected them back for hours yet, and the servants were tucked away in their own quarters. Her father and Thalia were still at the duke's, her father to observe all the excitement, and Thalia to look for Clio. Calliope had come home to see if Clio had returned, but she had also come for herself. For the comfort only her own surroundings, her own well-ordered space, could provide.

After such a long, bizarre night, there was something in her that craved the sight of *home*.

"Perhaps I will write my own horrid novel," she muttered, catching up a warm shawl draped over a chair and wrapping it tightly around her bare shoulders. Wouldn't Lotty enjoy *that*?

She would call it *The Duke's Revenge*. Or perhaps *Vengeance against the Duke*. Yes, that would be more fitting.

Calliope shuddered. It would be a very long time before she forgot the way Averton looked, so pale except for that crimson gash. The confused clamour when the crowd burst into the gallery and carried him away, while she huddled behind that sarcophagus.

"Oh, Clio," she whispered. "What has happened to you?"

And what had happened between Calliope and Westwood—or Cameron? For those brief moments it seemed they were allies, united in one cause. *That* was something she never thought to see happen. Never thought to be so affected by. But his humour, his kindness, the quick, cool way he dealt with the duke…

No. She couldn't think about that right now. It was too baffling, too dizzying. And she had to find her sister. Find out what had happened in that gallery.

There was a thin line of light beneath Clio's bedchamber door, flickering and shifting like flames. Calliope didn't even knock, just gently eased that door open, holding her breath as she paused on the threshold.

And Clio *was* there. After all the searching through the labyrinth of the duke's house, she was in her own chamber. The room was in darkness except for the blazing fire in the grate. Clio knelt beside the flames, wrapped in a white dressing gown, her auburn hair loose down her back. The red-orange glow reflected on her spectacles as she fed scraps of green silk into the fire. Her face was utterly expressionless.

"Clio," Calliope called softly.

Clio jumped, spinning around on her heels, crouched for battle. "Calliope!" she cried. "Don't creep up on me like that. I nearly had apoplexy."

"I'm sorry. I wasn't even sure you were here or just a mirage." Calliope slowly moved to Clio's side, hands held out as if in surrender. She knelt beside her sister, studying the torn remains of the Medusa costume.

"What happened tonight, Clio?" she said. She reached

out to touch the ragged edge of a gold sleeve. It was stiff with smeared blood.

Clio stared straight ahead into the flames. "What do you mean?"

"Lord Westwood and I found him. The duke. He held a scrap of this very silk in his hand."

"Was he—dead?"

"No, not yet."

"And what did he say?"

"He was unconscious. Lord Westwood went for help, and when they carried the duke away I came home. To find you." Calliope couldn't hold herself back any longer. She seized Clio, drawing her into a fierce hug. "Oh, Clio, I was so frightened!"

Clio held herself stiff for a second, then she gave a great shudder and fell against Calliope's shoulder, clutching at her. "Cal! It was—was horrible."

"My dear, you're safe now. We're all safe, I promise," Calliope said, struggling to convince herself as much as Clio. "Why were you alone with him?"

"I was a fool." Clio drew away, wiping her cheeks with her dressing gown sleeve. "I wanted to see the Alabaster Goddess without all the gawking crowds. I got one of the footmen to tell me where she was, and I slipped away for a peek. But he must have been watching me. He followed me to that gallery, and just as I saw the goddess, he…"

"He what?"

Clio shook her head fiercely. "I don't want to say. I swear he did not get very far, though, Cal. He just kissed me. Artemis saved me."

Calliope gave her a gentle smile. "You mean she leaped off her pedestal and coshed him on the head?"

Clio laughed. It was a strained, choked sound, but very welcome none the less. "Well, she did need a bit of mortal help. I grabbed her by that wooden base and swung it towards him. I just wanted to scare him, make him back away. I thought for a moment he was dead, and I didn't mean to kill him! I wouldn't *mind* if he was dead, but I don't want his blood on my hands." She held out one trembling hand, palm up. "Of course, it's there anyway."

"No!" Calliope took that hand, holding it tightly. "He is alive, and will probably recover, more is the pity. Hopefully his wits will be scrambled enough, though, that he won't hurt anyone else."

"And so he won't talk of this to anyone?"

"Why would he? Being known as an attacker of women—and being so weak a woman could attack *him* and bring him low—could hardly be what he wants."

"For a normal man, perhaps. I don't have any idea what a man like the duke could want."

They sat there for a long moment, clinging together, the only sound the snap of the fire. Outside the window the sky was beginning to lighten, a lark twittering in the trees. London coming to life again for one more day.

"There is something I want to show you, Cal," Clio said. She rose unsteadily to her feet and crossed the room to her bed. From under the mattress she drew a folded, rumpled sheet of paper, covered with a spidery black hand. One corner was ripped away.

"What is it?" Calliope asked, as Clio came back to the fireside.

"I'm not sure. When I—well, when Artemis made contact with the duke's head, the wooden base split and this paper came out."

"Oh, yes!" Calliope exclaimed, remembering that

broken base, the tiny scrap of parchment. "I saw that it was broken. But what is the paper?"

"A list of some sort." Clio smoothed it out on the hearth rug. "I can't quite figure it out, though."

Calliope leaned closer, peering at the tiny words. "Cicero. The Grey Dove. The Sicilian. The Purple Hyacinth. Nicknames?"

"Perhaps. There are ten of them in all, and they're each so strange. I wouldn't have thought the duke was one for secret societies, he seems so solitary, but after seeing his Gothic horror of a house I know anything is possible. What could they be nicknames for?"

Calliope ran her finger down the baffling list. "Charlemagne. The Golden Falcon. I have no idea. It must be very important, though, to hide it in the Alabaster Goddess like that."

"Important—and illegal, no doubt. Immoral goes without saying."

Illegal contacts? "Oh, Clio," Calliope breathed. "Do you suppose the duke is the Lily Thief?"

Cameron splashed cold water over his face, hoping the icy drops would finally wake him from the bizarre dream this whole evening had been. It didn't work, though. When he opened his eyes, slicking back the wet strands of his hair, his rumpled Hermes costume was still tossed over a chair. And he faced himself—eyes bloodshot, face strained—in the mirror.

In his travels to Greece, he and his companions were chased by bandits and rebels on occasion, running through the rocky hills with bullets zinging at their heels. That was surely dangerous, but also exhilarating. Life-affirming. After a narrow escape, they would drink and sing around campfires until dawn, when they would run again.

Why, then, did he feel so weary *now?* So—old, almost. Was it because bandits and bullets had a strange honesty to them? Unlike whatever it was that had happened at Averton's house tonight. *That* had a murky, corrupt air, a mystery he didn't care for.

Would he have left Averton to die, if Calliope Chase's solemn dark eyes weren't watching every move he made? He was surely tempted to, and the world would be better off. In the end he couldn't. He couldn't even let a man he detested die. Because of some weakness in himself? Because he didn't want to seem less than good, seem the flawed man he was, in front of Calliope?

Cameron shook his head, droplets flying, and reached for his dressing gown. He drew the warm brocade over his chilled nakedness, watching as the first light of day, grey-pink and fuzzy, peeked through the window. Now wasn't the time for agonised self-examination. He had never been good at that, anyway; he was no poet. Now was the time for action, for solving whatever it was that had happened last night. Someone had tried to kill the duke. Perhaps they had tried to steal the Alabaster Goddess.

The duke himself was always up to something. What did he want with Clio Chase? What did she have to do with last night's events? What was going on with the Chase sisters?

Cameron went to the window, staring down at the street coming to life for the day. Milkmaids and greengrocers hurried along on their errands; a maid scrubbed at the white steps next door. She yawned as she worked, but Cameron, despite his long night, was suddenly wide awake, his earlier weariness quite forgotten.

Something had happened between him and Calliope

Chase, as they made their way through those dark, moul-
dering rooms. He had always thought her beautiful, of
course. And sharply intelligent, sure of herself as only a
truly clever person could be. But also stubborn and maddening!

Last night there was a new connection, a new spark that
intrigued him, drew him in, even as his suspicions grew.
He *would* find out what was going on with her, with his
deep Athena who hid so much. It wouldn't be easy to gain
her trust, her confidence. In fact, he had the feeling it
would be the most difficult thing he would ever do. But
something was afoot in the small world of antiquities collecting, in the world of the Chases, and he was determined
to find out what that was.

Even if he had to spend time—lots of time—with
Calliope Chase. Not that that would be a terrible hardship,
he thought, remembering the way her Athena costume
clung to her bare, white shoulders. But someone had to
solve this riddle, before more artefacts like the Alabaster
Goddess fell victim to its spell.

And he was just the person to do it.

Chapter Ten

Calliope tied the ribbons of her bonnet into a jaunty bow just under her left ear and examined herself in the mirror. Did it really look well on her? It was her favourite hat, chip straw trimmed with blue satin ribbons. But was it too—plain?

And why was she so very worried about hats, when there were so many other more important things to be concerned about? Clio and the duke, the Lily Thief, the Ladies Society.

She knew why the sudden preoccupation with fashion, though, and she didn't like it. She was worried because she was to wear the bonnet to go driving in the park with Lord Westwood.

Cameron.

With a frustrated sigh, Calliope pulled off the bonnet, completely disarranging Mary's careful construction of curls, and reached for the note that had arrived over breakfast.

"Miss Chase, would you do me the honour of driving with me in the park this afternoon? I think that there, surrounded by hundreds of people, would be the only place where we could really talk. If you are agreeable, I will call for you at half past three."

If she was agreeable. The gossips would certainly have a splendid time to see them together in Cameron's yellow phaeton. Calliope idly wondered what the betting books would say. She didn't *want* to be talked about, especially now, when she needed to move as unobtrusively as possible in society to discover the Lily Thief. Was it the duke? Westwood? The mysterious Minotaur from the ball? Or someone she had not yet even thought of? She could never find out if everyone was watching her, laughing behind their fans.

But she did need to talk to Westwood. He was the only one, besides Clio and the duke, who knew what really had happened in that dark gallery. Perhaps he could help her now, but she had to be careful. It was possible he was also her biggest obstacle.

Calliope pushed the bonnet aside and reached for the newspapers from that morning. The more disreputable ones were full of news from the masquerade ball, nearly all erroneous. One had the duke's head split completely open, blood and brains spilling forth on to the floor. It didn't mention how the man still lived after such carnage. One had jewels stolen from the house, ladies fainting, masked thieves brandishing pistols. Or swords. Or daggers.

None of the accounts were as bad as her own memories, though. Of the smell of coppery blood mingling with dust. Of that scrap of silk in the duke's hand.

Calliope shuddered and shoved the papers away. Under all those black headlines, under her own confused memories, there lurked the truth. And she intended to find it. Surely it was the only way to stop the Lily Thief, and keep Clio safe.

Yet she couldn't do it alone. She was no Athena. She

needed as many allies as she could find. Her sisters, the Ladies Society. Cameron de Vere?

Could she trust him? Last night he had been like a rock amid chaos and confusion. But that did not erase his old attitudes towards antiquities, their old quarrels.

There was only one way to find out. Talk to the man. Try to see beneath his light, charming façade to the truth beneath.

Calliope reached again for her bonnet and popped it on her head. She wished it had some flirtatious feathers or bright fruit and flowers, or that she herself possessed Thalia's blue eyes or Emmeline's fine figure. Brown eyes and skinny limbs, clad in classical white plainness, weren't likely to coax secrets out of any man, let alone one as admired by the ladies as Westwood.

It was no use worrying about it, though. She was who she was, and there was nothing to be done about it. And she was going to be late if she didn't hurry.

Calliope retied the bow under her ear and reached for her blue spencer. Maybe she didn't have flirtatious azure eyes, but she did have one thing she shared with Cameron—a knowledge of history and antiquities. They could speak the same language, if they just tried.

As she pinned a tiny brooch, a golden owl of Athena, to her collar, a knock sounded at her chamber door.

"The Earl of Westwood is waiting for you in the morning room, Miss Chase," the footman announced.

"Thank you," Calliope called. "I will be down directly." She touched the owl and whispered, "Courage."

The fashionable hour was just beginning as Calliope and Cameron turned into the gates of Hyde Park, his dashing yellow-and-black phaeton rolling smoothly along the lane, joining in the bright parade. Calliope opened her parasol, turning it over her shoulder to block the afternoon sunlight—and some of the stares of the curious.

"Are you quite well today, Miss Chase?" Cameron asked, steering his horses down a slightly quieter pathway. She had been right about his driving skills. His gloved hands were featherlight on the reins, his horses perfectly responsive to his slightest touch. Just as she had been responsive when they danced.

"A good night's sleep and a strong pot of tea can do wonders," Calliope answered, nodding at Emmeline as they passed her and her mother in their carriage.

"Did you sleep well, then?"

Calliope laughed ruefully, and shook her head. "Hardly at all. I had such dreams!"

"Dreams of falling statues?"

"Of being chased by hairy Minotaurs down endless corridors."

He gave her a sympathetic smile. "That house would be quite enough to disturb anyone's dreams, even without other—events."

"Quite. I hope never to see Acropolis House again."

"Or its owner?"

"Him, too. Will he live, do you think?"

"The doctor who was summoned last night says his prognosis is quite good. Once his brain is set right. Whatever *right* might be for such a man."

Calliope swallowed hard, her throat suddenly dry. "And have you heard what the events of the night are supposed to be?"

"That the duke was examining his treasure, and she fell from her unsteady base. A tragic accident."

"At least until the duke awakens and tells the truth."

"Until then. How is your sister today?"

"Quiet, but well enough. Clio does not stay discomposed for long. But her account of events is much what you would think, I fear. The duke surprised her as she examined the Alabaster Goddess, and when he tried to do—something, she hit him with the statue."

"Well done for her."

Calliope laughed. "I think she is mostly disappointed she didn't finish the job."

"Well, I'm sure one day someone will—finish the job. The duke has many enemies."

"Like you, Lord Westwood?"

He glanced at her from the corner of his eye. "Perhaps. One can never predict what might happen in the future. And I thought I asked you to call me Cameron."

"When we are alone."

"Aren't we alone now?"

Calliope looked around at the crowd of carriages and equestrians. "Hardly."

"No one can hear us."

"All right, then—Cameron. I hope that, if something *does* one day happen to the duke, it won't be by your hand."

"You wouldn't like to see me in Newgate, then?"

Calliope had a vision of him locked behind stout bars, dishevelled, waiting for the noose or the ship to Botany Bay. Once it might have made her laugh; now it made her shiver. "Not for the likes of the Duke of Averton. I don't want to see you or my sister hurt because of him."

"I don't want to see such a thing, either, believe me."

"Then how can we prevent it?"

"We?"

Calliope examined the passing scenery, the neat rows of trees, feigning a carelessness she was far from feeling. "I think we worked together well last night, did we not?"

"Yes," he agreed slowly. "Certainly we prevented anyone knowing what really happened in that gallery, though I'm sure there is no power on earth that could stop speculation."

Calliope thought again of those rumours Emmeline told her about. The wagers on how soon she and Westwood would be betrothed—or would kill each other. "No, indeed. People do like their gossip."

"But not us," he said teasingly. "We are above all that. We care only for the benefit of *art*."

Calliope laughed. "I am not so high in the instep as all that, I hope! I confess I do indulge in a spot of, shall we say, speculative conversation now and then."

"Never! Not Miss Calliope Chase."

"Sad, I know, but I must be honest." Calliope sighed.

"And what do you speculate about?"

You, she almost said. She bit her lip, turning away again to peer at the passing pedestrians on the walkways. They were in a more sparsely populated part of the park now, most of the stylish gawkers behind them. Here were mostly serious strollers, nurses with their charges, footmen with dogs on leads. The phaeton rolled past them slowly, at a snail's pace. "Oh, this and that. Bonnets, of course. Parisian fashion papers. Fans and plumes. Don't ladies always interest themselves in the latest styles?"

Cameron shook his head. "Some ladies perhaps, Miss Chase. Not you, nor, I dare say, your sisters, or your friends in that Ladies Society of yours all the females of the *ton* are so anxious to join. You can't fool me."

She hoped she *could* fool him, at least some of the time. He couldn't know how much they really did talk about him at Ladies Society meetings, how most of her acquaintances were half in love with him, called him their "Greek god". He couldn't know why she needed his help so much now. Why she had to keep an eye on him.

And he *really* couldn't know that she was beginning to like him.

There. She said it, at least to herself. She was beginning to like him, to look forward to his conversation, his smiles. It surely wouldn't last, though. Such silliness rarely did. She knew this from watching ladies like Lotty, who were infatuated with a different gentleman every week.

It was like one of Lotty's beloved novels, turned farce rather than Gothic tragedy. *The Folly of Calliope*. At least it was folly with a purpose.

"Very well," she admitted. "Sometimes we *do* talk about hats, and sometimes suitors. Mostly we talk about art and history. And books." No need to mention that once in a while the books were things like *Lady Rosamund's Tragedy*.

"I knew it. Did I not say you cared only for the benefit of art?"

"You did. And that, Lord Westwood—Cameron—is why I need your help."

He glanced at her, his brow arched. "My help? Dear me, Miss Chase, I fear I shall swoon!"

Calliope lightly slapped his arm. "Don't tease! I'm serious."

"As am I. Who would have thought this day would come? I'm quite dizzy with surprise."

"Hmph." She snapped her parasol closed, just in case she was required to rap him over the head with it. "Do you want to hear what I have to say or not?"

"Always."

"Very well, then. I think we both agree the duke is an odious man, yes?"

His smile melted, the corners of his beautiful, Greek god-ish lips turning down. "Of course."

"You know that better than I, I'm sure. You went to university with him. I only have his behaviour towards my sister to judge by. And his rapacious collecting habits. Those are quite vile enough."

"Believe me, my dear Miss Chase, you don't want to see what the man is like outside of polite society," he said darkly.

My dear? Calliope peered closer at him, trying to read his face under the shadowed brim of his hat. It was as smooth as a statue, as Hermes. Only an obsidian glint in his eyes betrayed the depths of emotion roiling inside.

"No, I don't," she said softly. "But I will, if that's what it takes."

"If that is what *what* takes?"

"To protect my sister. And the Alabaster Goddess."

"The Alabaster Goddess?"

"Of course. It is too much to think I could protect all those objects in that dreadful house. The lioness, the sarcophagus, Daphne. But I think Artemis is in the most immediate danger. Both from the duke and from whoever might think to take her from him."

"The Lily Thief again?"

"Perhaps. He is not the only petty criminal about, you know. She could be in danger from any number of people."

"You think some pickpocket from Whitechapel is likely to break into Acropolis House and steal a Greek statue? Maybe some of those cat mummies while he's at it?"

Calliope sighed. "Put like that, it does sound silly. No, I don't think some cutpurse is going to haul the goddess away. There are plenty of criminals with more sophistication who could carry off such a crime, though. She is a prime target. Not too large, in beautiful condition…"

"Too famous to sell on the open market."

"That wouldn't stop a collector who wants only to gloat over her in private."

"As the duke has done?"

"Yes, just so."

He turned the phaeton on to yet another lane, this one more crowded. Their progress slowed even further, caught in a knot of vehicles. "Say the Lily Thief—or someone else—does steal the Alabaster Goddess. How is she worse off than she was in Averton's possession?"

"At least with him we know where she is. There is a chance she could pass to a museum or a respectable scholar one day. If she is stolen, she would likely never see the light again. Never be studied properly."

Cameron shook his head. "Calliope, she *has* been studied, as much as can be. Taken from her original context, most of her lessons are lost for ever anyway. The duke does not deserve her."

"I won't argue with you about that. He doesn't deserve any of those antiquities in his house! But he *does* own them, for good or ill, at least for now."

"And so you think that gives him the right…"

Calliope reached out and pressed her fingers to his tense arm, stilling his angry growl. This was that old quarrel of theirs, and there was just no time for it now. She needed him. "Please, Cameron. I need your help. Let's not argue."

He stared down at her intently, perfectly still under her touch. "My help with what exactly?"

"I told you—to keep Artemis safe. No matter what our disagreements are, we both want that, yes?"

"Yes, of course."

"Then can we declare a truce? A new alliance, to save the Alabaster Goddess?"

He was silent for a long moment, until Calliope half-feared he meant to reject her truce, to set her down here in the park and drive away, laughing at her folly. Finally, though, he pressed his hand atop hers. "Very well. A truce. Now, how do your propose we protect our divine charge? Put surveillance on the duke's house? Follow him around town—once he is conscious, of course."

Calliope laughed in sheer relief. "I'm afraid I haven't thought that far ahead. That is one reason why I need your help."

"I thought strategy was Athena's strong point."

"I fear I had to put my helmet and shield away and don this bonnet instead. But I am sure we will soon think of something. Come to my house tomorrow evening. My father is having a small card party, and we can talk more there."

"Strategise over a game of astralasi, eh?"

"Perhaps if the Trojans had done so rather than make war, things might have ended better for them." Calliope sat back in her seat, opening her parasol again. She felt a new, warm glow of satisfaction. The truce was begun; a new game was afoot. "Thank you, Cameron. You won't be sorry, I promise."

You won't be sorry.

Cameron laughed aloud as he bounded up the steps of his house. That was where Calliope Chase was wrong, for he was already beginning to be sorry. If he joined forces with her, allied with her to protect the Alabaster Goddess, he would have to spend time with her. And then how would he ever stop himself from kissing her?

When he looked at her today, the sun dusting her fair skin with glistening gold, her cheeks flushed with the excitement of her mission, her lips parted on a breath, it took everything in his power, every ounce of self-control, not to grab her. Not to pull her close and kiss those pink lips, feel their softness, their warm yielding. He was so hot to kiss her, embrace her—*her*, Calliope Chase of all women! A woman who always seemed to regard him with suspicion and disapproval. A woman who was beautiful, but oh so stubborn.

Until that blasted masquerade ball, anyway. The drama and danger, the strange nightmare quality of that evening, had changed something between them. The old distrust cracked and broke, but hadn't yet reformed into something he could identify.

Except lust. And he'd always had *that* for her.

Now they were to be allies in some scheme she had to "save" the Alabaster Goddess from the Lily Thief, the duke, and who knew what else.

Cameron opened the door to the library and found Athena's painted image, her solemn grey-eyed stare. Aside from the fact that Calliope's eyes were brown—a deep, melting chocolate brown that a person could drown in, happily unable to extricate himself—they were the mirror image of each other. He wondered if Athena had been a member of a Ladies Society, too.

They were certainly up to something, Calliope and her Ladies Society friends. He knew that even before they found the duke in his gallery, when they were dancing and she and Emmeline Saunders kept exchanging glances and whispers. Everyone thought they were some sort of harmless study group, a way for ladies to occupy themselves before they married, yet Cameron had always suspected otherwise. Any society with the Chase sisters as members could hardly be called "harmless". And now he was somehow a part of it all, God help him.

If he was truly wise, he would stay far away from Calliope and her plans, would pack his bags and retreat to the countryside. Retreat, though, was never his way. Nor was running away from an intriguing puzzle. His curiosity had always got the better of him, especially since life was so dull since he had returned from his travels.

Cameron remembered the way his father would look at him, puzzled, taken aback, as if this son wasn't what he bargained for. He would shake his head, and say, "You *are* Greek, aren't you?" And he was. That insatiable curiosity, that temper that so often got the better of him—that weakness for a pair of dark eyes.

He laughed ruefully, as the painted Athena gave him a scolding stare. He was her acolyte now, a soldier in her adventure. Perhaps it *was* foolish of him. The last thing he wanted was to be involved in the Duke of Averton's sphere again, in any way. Perhaps he *would* be sorry. It was obvious Calliope and her sisters trailed trouble in their beautiful wake.

But he very much looked forward to it. He had been rather bored lately, floundering in his new English life. Unsure of his place, even though he was brought up to it. He was far from bored now.

Yes. He would *not* be sorry.

Chapter Eleven

Calliope surveyed the tables set up in the drawing room for the card games. All seemed to be in tidy readiness: the neat white cloths, the new decks of cards, the tea table for refreshments. Through the half-closed doors of the dining room she could hear the servants setting the table for a late supper. The clink of silver and china, the soft murmur of voices.

Drawing her shawl over her shoulders, she stopped to straighten some of the teacups, twitch a crooked cloth into place. There was nothing left to do in here. She should go up and dress, get ready for the guests' arrival. She was too restless, though. She wanted to keep moving, keep adjusting cloths and fidgeting with cards, not sit down to have her hair dressed!

Calliope stopped at the window, peering down at the darkened street. It was quiet now, a calm lull between the bustle of the day and the flow of evening partygoers. She should feel calm, too. There was surely no need for nervousness. She had played hostess for her father since her mother died, and while they certainly did not entertain as much as they once did, she could manage a small card party.

Perhaps it was not the party itself, but the guest list. Or one guest in particular.

Cameron de Vere was coming to the party tonight. And, what was more, he was going to help her in her schemes to save the Alabaster Goddess. Of course, she didn't yet know what the scheme would be, but surely with his help things would soon be figured out. He disliked the duke as much as she did. He wanted to see Artemis safe.

A lone carriage rattled down the street, a phaeton hurrying homeward. It was not bright yellow, yet for a moment she remembered staring down from here to see Cameron's equipage in that very spot, his laughing face turned towards the sun, hair tossed in the breeze. Free. He was always so very free, so careless of what others thought of him. So secure in who he was.

How she envied that.

Calliope sighed, and drew the curtains closed. Free or not, she had a job to do and not much time to do it. She was wasting precious minutes, reflecting on Cameron's handsome face, his self-confident ways. She just couldn't seem to help it, though! Thoughts of him crept up on her at the oddest moments. Perhaps she was infected by Lotty's novel-reading habits, after all.

But then, maybe in a situation like this—stolen antiquities, wicked dukes, mysterious thieves—horrid novels could be more help than Plato or Aristotle. Too bad those novel heroines always seemed to be such fainting cabbage-heads.

"Calliope? Are you not dressed yet?" she heard her father say. She turned to find him in the doorway, leaning on the walking stick he seemed to employ more and more these days. He glanced around with a puzzled air, as if surprised to find himself in his own quiet drawing room, and not the bustling Athenian agora of his studies.

Calliope gazed at him with concern. How frail he looked since her mother died! How distracted and distant. As if he was not of this world, but living more and more in the ancient past. Who could blame him, really, with so many daughters to worry over? So many wild Muses. At least his distraction gave them lots of free time. Time to track down thieves.

"I just wanted to be sure everything is in readiness," she said. She hurried to his side, taking his arm to lead him to his favourite armchair. "We want our guests to be comfortable, do we not?"

"Ah, Calliope. So much like your mother," he said with a sigh, patting her cheek.

"Am I, Father?"

"Certainly. Oh, Clio looks the most like her, with that red hair, but you have her spirit. Always thinking of other people, always wanting things to be right for them." He chuckled. "Whatever *you* think right is. You and your mother—always so certain of everything. How I always relied on her sureness…"

Calliope gently took his hand in hers. "You miss her very much. Just as I do."

"Indeed. She was an excellent companion, your mother, so intelligent and steady. Practical, as you are. And beautiful, of course. I can't seem to find my way without her." He covered her hand with his, holding her close. "But she left me you and your sisters. I'll always have a part of her. I tell you, Calliope, my dearest wish for you, for all my Muses, is that you find such a partner in life."

"Oh, Father," Calliope said carefully, fearful she might start to cry, "you and Mother were so fortunate to find each other. I fear I've never met anyone I could be so compatible with. Could love that way."

"No one? What of young Westwood?"

Calliope stared at her father, startled. Had he, too, heard those rumours? She thought he noticed nothing that hadn't happened thousands of years ago! "Lord Westwood? Of course not him, Father. We argue too much."

"So did your mother and I, when we first met. It's a sign of passion, y'know."

"Father!" Calliope cried, feeling hot embarrassment flood her cheeks. She turned away to fuss with an arrangement of chairs.

Her father chuckled. "You don't want some milquetoast who would just agree with everything you say, would you? Not my Calliope. You would be bored within an hour. And Westwood appreciates the same things you do. Art, history."

"His father appreciated those things, too, and you two were great rivals."

"So we were. And enjoyed every moment of our rivalry. One wants to be opposed at times. Life is so dull otherwise."

"I don't think I would want a rival as a spouse, though," Calliope protested. "And Lord Westwood's views are so different from mine."

"I'm sure he would come round to a more correct way of thinking, with my Calliope's help. One more for our cause, eh? You always did enjoy a challenge, my dear."

Calliope had to laugh. "I do indeed. He might prove too great a challenge, though."

"For a Chase Muse? Never!" He gave her a sly wink. "Lady Rushworth tells me Lord Westwood is considered quite handsome among the ladies. An Apollo to adorn your side?"

"Father!" Calliope said, kissing his cheek amid helpless laughter. "You should not try to matchmake, you do it ill. I will find the right gentleman, never fear."

He patted her hand. "I just want to see you happy."

"I *am* happy. But I will be even happier once I dress, so I don't have to greet our guests in my round gown and shawl."

"You run along, then, Calliope. I will sit here and savour the anticipation of trouncing Mr Berryman at cards. He won ten shillings off me last time."

"Such shocking extravagance, Father," Calliope teased. "While you sit here, make sure the servants properly arrange the cakes for the tea table."

"I shall, my dear. You can always trust me with cakes."

Calliope left the drawing room and went up the stairs, past servants bustling with final preparations. She should be thinking about refreshments and the guest list, too, but instead she thought only about her father's words.

For a man with such a crowd of daughters, he seldom showed any concern for their matrimonial prospects. He lived in his own classical world, where dowries and betrothals had little place. Had he really been looking to Lord Westwood with an eye for an engagement? Scheming a match, along with his friend Lady Rushworth? Was *everyone* around her expecting her to marry Cameron, simply because they were prone to quarrels?

Calliope stepped into her bedchamber, watching as Mary prepared yet another white evening gown. Had she grown so predictable, then? She feared she had—white gowns, arguments with Lord Westwood, the evening was set. Too bad life couldn't follow such easy patterns. It always insisted on throwing obstacles in one's path. Things like thieves, and dukes obsessed with one's sister.

And handsome young earls.

Calliope pushed all that away, and discarded her shawl to begin her evening *toilette*. A card party was not the place to suddenly become *un*predictable. But if society thought they really knew Calliope Chase—well, soon, they would just have to think again.

The scene in the Chase drawing room was a distinct contrast to the one that happened in the duke's grand ballroom. There were no fantastical costumes, no gods and monsters and nymphs, just ordinary mortals in stylish, if subdued, evening dress. No wild dancing, no crowds packed to the walls, and much less artwork. But at least *their* statues, Calliope thought with satisfaction, were legally obtained and properly looked after.

But one thing was the same. Lord Westwood was there. He sat across from Calliope at the card table, no Hermes with bare arms and loose curls, yet still as mysteriously alluring in a fashionable blue coat and impeccably tied cravat. Calliope peeked at him over the edge of her cards. He was obviously better at this sleuthing-subterfuge business than she was. He was his usual self, smiling and joking, calmly examining his cards, while she had to restrain herself from staring boldly into people's faces, searching for any minute, hidden signs of villainy.

Thus far her surreptitious glances revealed nothing. No avaricious expressions when looking at her father's antiquities. No careless words or frowns. No flush of guilt when the duke was mentioned. No ancient bibelots dropped to the floor to give irrefutable proof.

Calliope sighed as she studied her cards. What a dreadful Bow Street Runner she would make! She had no idea how to look beyond the obvious, how to see into people's hearts. How to find the motives of the Lily Thief.

Cameron was her ally now, an ally of convenience. Could he also be the thief? And what of the duke and his strange list? Who were Charlemagne and the Grey Dove?

The Purple Hyacinth and Cicero? It was all very vexing, turning her well-ordered world topsy-turvy. What would set it right again? Could anything?

"Well, now," said Mr Smithson, who, with Emmeline, played against Calliope and Cameron. "Shall we play?"

"Have you discovered anything yet?" Calliope asked, as she and Emmeline lingered by the tea table during a lull in the play. They had a quiet moment, since Calliope's father was holding forth on the Punic Wars, and a debate threatened to ensue as Lady Rushworth heartily disagreed with his point. There was really nothing these people loved more than a good argument over ancient wars. Unless it was speaking of imaginary "courtship" between Calliope and Westwood.

Emmeline shook her head. "I have been spending a great deal of time with Mr Smithson. He is most amiable, but I doubt he is our thief."

Calliope glanced at Mr Smithson, his open, freckled face avid as he listened to her father. Obviously he did appreciate history. It would be so convenient if he *was* the thief, for she did not know him very well. "Why not?"

"Well, for one thing I doubt he would know a lock pick from a candlestick. He is not very mechanically inclined. He can scarce drive his own carriage. For another, he was at his estate in Devon when Lady Tenbray's diadem was stolen. He spends a great deal of time there, cataloguing his collection of Hellenistic silver."

"Oh…" Calliope sighed "…I'm sorry you wasted your time, Emmeline."

"Not at all! I quite like him." A delicate pink stain flooded Emmeline's cheeks. "In fact…"

"Emmeline! Never say he has become a real suitor."

"Perhaps. We'll see."

"But don't your parents want you to marry poor Freddie Mountbank, who is so loudly in love with you?"

"They do, but surely they will change their minds when Mr Smithson comes up to scratch. His income is twice Mr Mountbank's. Mr Smithson hasn't said anything yet, though, so don't breathe a word to the rest of the Ladies Society!"

"My lips are sealed," Calliope vowed. Well, well—perhaps something good could come of this wild goose chase after all. If only everyone didn't start thinking the Ladies Society was just a matchmaking operation!

"What of you, Calliope? Any progress?"

"Not yet. At least nothing I can decipher." Calliope thought of that list hidden in the Alabaster Goddess's base, of Clio, pale-faced, burning her blood-stained costume. Clio sat beside their father now, sipping her tea, her gaze very far away.

Calliope's stare moved to Cameron, who played a lively game of Pope Joan with Thalia. He slumped back in his seat, ostentatiously defeated, as Thalia merrily clapped her hands. Calliope wondered what he would make of that list, if she showed it to him.

"It is all very puzzling," Emmeline agreed. "The stolen items are all so very distinctive. If the thief sold them to a collector we know—and we all do seem to know each other—he could never display it. We would recognise it in an instant."

"True. And I can't imagine any of this lot keeping such a secret." Calliope gestured towards the noisy debaters.

"Then where are they going?"

Calliope shook her head. "I have no idea."

"Do you think it is Lord Westwood?"

"I don't know that, either." Calliope laughed bitterly. "I don't know very much, do I? But it does seem that Lord Westwood is a bit too open to be the thief."

"Wouldn't one of the characteristics of the thief be good acting skills?"

"Very true."

"Are there any new suspects on the horizon?"

Calliope remembered the duke's jumbled house, Daphne, the lioness, the great piles of precious objects. Anything could be hidden in there. "The Duke of Averton seems quite greedy," she whispered.

Emmeline's eyes widened. "Greedy, to say the very least. And whatever could have happened to him at the ball? It's all quite sinister."

"Quite. I can't help feeling that the Alabaster Goddess is somehow the key. Oh, Em! If only he wasn't going to take her away..."

Emmeline smiled. "I think I may have a solution to that."

"What? Are you going to kidnap Artemis yourself?"

"If only we could! I don't think even the whole Ladies Society could manage that. We are simply not quiet enough. No, I have a slightly more legitimate plan."

"Do tell me! We need all the help we can get right now."

"You know my father has an estate in Yorkshire, near the duke's mouldy old fortress? We seldom go there; too rustic for Mama."

"So, you're going to Yorkshire to watch the duke's house? In the middle of the Season?"

Emmeline laughed. "Better! We will all go. We'll take the Season with us, the part that matters, anyway. My father has a great scholar coming to visit from the university at Cologne, his name is Herr Mueller and he is an expert on all things Greek. Papa is going to invite us all to a house party in Yorkshire, to meet this scholar and wander about the moors discussing history and such."

"All of us?"

"The Ladies Society and their families, of course. And Mr Smithson, Lady Rushworth, Lord Westwood, everyone. And most of the other suspects, if I ask him to. So, we can watch them *and* the duke. Or the outside of his castle, anyway."

Calliope grinned. "We could pretend to be bird watching. Oh, Emmeline, it's a brilliant idea! It will be so much easier to observe everyone in the country than here in town."

Emmeline laughed. "Easier to get Mr Smithson to pop the question, too! The invitations go out tomorrow."

"Calliope!" Thalia called. "What are you and Emmeline talking of so secretly? Come here for a moment, see how much I won from Lord Westwood."

Calliope gave Emmeline a nod, and hurried over to Thalia's side. "You did indeed triumph, Thalia. What a poor gamester Lord Westwood must be."

"Ha!" Cameron said, all mock-contempt. "Did we not win at whist, Miss Chase? Thanks to my clever strategy."

"We did win," Calliope agreed. "But I think it was mostly due to the fact that Mr Smithson kept losing track of his cards."

"Staring all moon-eyed at Emmeline, no doubt," Thalia said. "But Lord Westwood here tells me that there is to be a most interesting lecture at the Antiquities Society tomorrow, Calliope. A discussion of the Panathenic Games with Herr Mueller, all the way from the university at Cologne."

"You enjoy hearing about Athena, do you not, Miss Chase?" Cameron asked quietly. "Is she not your patroness?"

Calliope stared at him, their gazes meeting, clinging. For a moment, it was as if all the rest of the room vanished, became a mere muted blur, and they were all alone. Just as they had been in the darkness of the duke's house, bound in some ancient spell. She couldn't breathe, couldn't turn away.

"I fear Athena's wisdom is not often mine," she murmured. "But I enjoy learning whatever I can from her."

"It is settled, then!" Thalia said, her voice the last, strongest tether to drag Calliope back down to earth. "We will ask Father to take us to the lecture. Perhaps it will lift Clio from whatever doldrums she has fallen into."

"I hope to see you there, then," Cameron said. He was shuffling the cards, the pasteboard squares flashing through his long fingers. Calliope shivered, certain she could feel that touch on her own skin.

"Oh, yes," she murmured. "I hope so, Lord Westwood. There is something I would like to ask your opinion about…"

Chapter Twelve

"We might just as well have stayed at home," Clio muttered.

"Hmm?" Calliope said, distracted. They stood in the foyer of the Antiquities Society, waiting to go into the lecture hall, and she occupied her time by observing the people around her. The chattering, laughing groups, all so polite and civilised. How could ideas of theft possibly lurk behind one of those smiling faces? "What do you mean, Clio?"

"I mean we always seem to encounter the same people, just like at Father's card party. The same people having the same conversations," Clio said, her tone so quiet, so impatient. "We should just have one continuous party, instead of always changing our clothes and moving about. If nothing different is ever to happen…"

Calliope peered closer at her sister, puzzled. Ever since the—occurrence in the duke's gallery, she had been so quiet. So serious. Calliope could not blame her, of course, but Clio always seemed so resilient. So strong. The strongest of all the Muses.

She was certainly as pretty as ever tonight, in her turquoise-coloured gown, her auburn hair pinned up in a loose, classical knot bound with gold ribbons. Yet her eyes behind the spectacles were dull, her skin pale.

"Are you ill?" Calliope asked, concerned. "Do you want to go home?"

Clio made an impatient noise, fiddling with her fan. "No, I'm not ill. I'm just—oh, I don't know!" With that most uninformative outburst she stomped off, moving across the room to examine one of the plaster statues of gods and dying Gauls that lined the red-papered walls.

The statues had been there for ever, ever since their parents started bringing them here when they were girls. One of the "unchanging" things Clio complained of tonight. Calliope could look around this room, this building, and remember her first visits here, listening to tales of ancient wars, politics, heroic deeds, doomed romances. Most of the people she remembered from then, too, though perhaps they were a bit greyer now.

When she was an old lady, would she be here, too, surrounded by her children and grandchildren? By Emmeline and Lotty and their children? She had never thought of such a thing before. This was just how the world was.

Calliope frowned, feeling a prickle of some strange unease. Was Clio right? Did nothing ever change?

She thought of Cameron de Vere, of how he seemed to trail the intriguing allure of exotic lands behind him wherever he went. Even in stuffy drawing rooms, dull assemblies, he emanated adventure, intrigue. Danger.

Intrigue and danger were the last things she needed. She *liked* her well-ordered world, her old friends and familiar patterns. Or at least she thought she did.

"You seem very thoughtful tonight, Miss Chase," she heard a voice say. A deep, rough-edged voice that made her shiver. She knew who it was even before she turned. She always knew.

Cameron. How was it she had only to think of him and he appeared?

She pasted a bright smile to her lips before she faced him. He looked so handsome tonight, of course. Yet also rather sombre, in a dark burgundy coat, his hair smoothed back.

"One *should* be thoughtful before a lecture," she answered.

"Thoughtful of questions you can pepper the speaker with, eh?" he said, with a glimmer of his old smile. "I would wager you know far more than this—what's his name?"

"Herr Mueller, from the university at Cologne. Lady Emmeline Saunders and her parents have invited him to their house party, you know," Calliope said. "And I hope he knows a great deal, since we will have to listen to him for several days."

"Ah, yes. The house party. Strange, isn't it, how their estate just happens to be so near that of Averton?"

Calliope shrugged. "It is a lovely, rural spot for some academic contemplation."

"And a bit of spying, maybe?"

Calliope laughed, smothering the sound behind her gloved hand. The Antiquities Society was always such a hushed, serious place, not one for loud laughter. "I understand there is some interesting bird watching in the area, too. That would require the use of opera glasses, I think."

He laughed, too, but not behind his hand. The joyful sound caused several heads to swivel in their direction. *Oh, dear*, Calliope thought. *Yet more gossip.* Somehow, though, his warm chuckles made her feel too giddy to even particularly care. At the moment.

"So, you are planning your rustic intrigues already?" he said.

"Not really. I am finding I don't truly have a gift for sleuthing. We must hope that events provide us with an opportunity once we are there." Calliope glanced at Clio, who stood across the foyer with their father, his friend Lady Rushworth, and the head of the Antiquities Society, Lord Knowleton. She was still so quiet and watchful. "My sister tells me our lives are dull and full of sameness, anyway. That nothing unusual can ever happen to us. So perhaps I should not hope for much in Yorkshire."

"What do *you* think? Do you find life to be dull, Miss Chase?"

Not when you are near, Calliope thought. Ever since he had come into her life she wasn't sure of anything. "How can it be, with a thief among us, and dukes being coshed on the head in their own homes? I fear perhaps the excitement may prove to be too much."

"Perhaps a spot of bird watching might be just what you need, then."

Before Calliope could answer, the doors to the lecture hall opened and everyone began to file inside, discreetly vying for the best seats. Her father, Clio and Lady Rushworth vanished in the crowd. "I should find my father," she said.

"Let us look for him together," Cameron suggested, offering his arm. "I would be honoured to sit with the Chases and benefit from their wisdom in historical matters."

"As long as you don't whisper satirical comments, trying to make us laugh," she said, accepting his arm. It had become almost a natural gesture.

"Would I do such a thing?" he said, all wounded innocence.

"I am just warning you…"

* * *

"…as you see here, the young ladies of the procession carry the vessels for pouring offerings to the gods, in this case Athena. The *oinochoai* and the *phialai*, and here is the incense burner, the *thymiaterion*. The purpose of the maidens on this side, however, is less clear. Perhaps they carried the peplos, newly woven for the goddess, or perhaps they were even the famed *Arrephoroi*…"

Calliope tried to listen to the learned Herr Mueller, to study the large sketches of the Parthenon friezes set up behind the podium. She watched as the small, bespectacled scholar pointed out each figure in the carved procession she knew so well from days at the British Museum. But she could not seem to focus her thoughts where they should be, on the worship of the gods. Couldn't seem to sit still. And it was all due to Cameron, sitting beside her.

He, too, stared straight ahead, yet every time Calliope glanced at him from the corner of her eye his lips quirked with a barely suppressed smile. Finally, he caught her looking at him and raised his brows.

Calliope snapped forward again. *Ridiculous man!* Herr Mueller's speech was not so comical as all that, merely a bit—dry. Nothing to laugh about. Why, then, did she want to burst into giggles all over again?

Clio, seated on her other side, whispered, "Must I play Miss Rogers now, Calliope?"

Miss Rogers had been a particularly stern governess of their childhood, prone to furious frowns and threats of the rod. She hadn't lasted long with the young Muses. Thalia quickly dispatched her with the aid of a bag of frogs. "Of course not."

"Then tell me what you are laughing at, before I perish of boredom!"

"I don't know what I'm laughing at," Calliope admitted.

"…and here we see the nine Archons of Athens, or so they are assumed to be," Herr Mueller went on.

"I sense you are getting restless, *fräulein*," Cameron whispered. "You are not paying attention to the lessons. However will you pass the examinations?"

"Be quiet, or I'll have to pinch you," Calliope hissed. Were they really to be trapped in Yorkshire with endless lectures? For the first time, the intrigues of the Lily Thief, the mystery surrounding his exploits, seemed truly exciting to her. A most welcome distraction.

If she could survive the days in Cameron's company without completely losing her senses.

Calliope folded her hands in her lap, facing sternly forward again. But her calm attention was not to last. As Herr Mueller turned to the figures of the gods watching the procession, the doors to the lecture hall swung open. Everyone swivelled around to see who dared intrude on the sacred hush of the Antiquities Society, and slowly, gathering speed like an approaching thunderstorm, a chorus of whispers swept over the crowd. Even Herr Mueller sputtered away into nothingness.

"Oh! It's an avenging spirit!" Lotty, who sat behind Calliope, moaned.

If only it was something so mundane, Calliope thought, but they were not so fortunate. It was the Duke of Averton. He stood there for a moment, perfectly still, framed by the open doors.

His brow was bound by a stark white bandage, the skin of his face nearly as pale, yet he stood there unaided, unwavering, wrapped in a black, fur-trimmed cloak. His burning gaze swept over the assembly, as if it was his own private domain. His little kingdom. The demon emperor.

Oh, dear, Calliope thought. She *was* turning into Lotty.

Beside her, Clio stiffened. Calliope laid a gentle hand on her arm, but it was as if her sister took no notice. She just stared straight ahead, listening to a lecture gone silent.

"So, he didn't die," Cameron muttered.

"Are you sure?" Calliope answered. "Lotty says he's a spirit, and I half imagine she might be right."

As they all watched, as mesmerised as if they observed Hamlet's ghost at Drury Lane, the duke made his slow, stately way down the aisle to an empty seat near the front. Like Clio, he looked neither right nor left. Once it became apparent he was not going to do anything fascinating, the whispers abated and Herr Mueller began again.

"Though the gods are shown seated, the proportions are quite unusual, as their heads are parallel to those of the approaching humans…"

"I need some fresh air," Clio muttered tightly. Before Calliope could question or stop her, she leaped up from her seat and hurried out of the room, a turquoise silk blur. As some of the other ladies also took that opportunity to escape to the withdrawing room, her exit was unremarked.

Calliope stared after her, worried. She remembered how still and brittle Clio looked after the masquerade ball, bent over her ruined costume, as if she would shatter at a touch. Calliope sat there for a moment, unsure of what to do, scared of breaking into Clio's careful reserve. Finally, though, she could bear it no longer.

"Excuse me," she murmured, and followed her sister up the aisle.

There were a few groups milling about in the foyer, whispering together, speculating on the duke's sudden appearance. Or perhaps they were just congratulating themselves on their happy escape from the boring lecture. Clio was not among them, nor was she in the ladies' withdrawing room or the library. The study rooms and storage attics abovestairs were mostly locked tonight, so Clio would not be there.

Her concern mounting, Calliope rushed out the doors that led to the street, peering frantically both ways. The night was quite dark and chilly, broken only by the clattering rush of passing carriages.

"Clio!" she called out, even as she knew there would be no answer.

"Miss Chase?" she heard Cameron say, and turned to find he had followed her outside. The chilly breeze ruffled his hair, tugged at the folds of his beautifully tied cravat, but he did not seem to notice. He watched her solemnly.

Calliope had never felt more helpless in her life. Her family, the thief, the duke—she understood none of it. Every bit of her control was slipping away, and all she could do was grab at it frantically. Watch in horror as it slipped ever further away.

She held out her trembling hands. "I can't find her," she said, hoarse with unshed tears.

"I know," he answered. He came down the steps to her side, taking her hand in his. How very warm he was, how strong. He tucked her fingers into the crook of his arm and led her back into the building. "Your sister is a sensible woman. I'm sure she wouldn't just go dashing off into the night."

"Then where could she be?"

"Well, at least we know the duke isn't with her, as he is still sitting in the lecture hall being subjected to Herr Mueller. Perhaps she went to one of the study rooms?"

Calliope shook her head. "They are locked in the evenings."

"All of them?"

"I don't know." She glanced up the darkened staircase. The twisting corridors up there seemed silent and deserted, but one never knew. The Chase Muses were nothing if not resourceful, even in the face of locked doors. "Will you look with me?"

Cameron arched his brow at her, in that satirical expression she was coming to hate—and to find much too attractive. "Why, Miss Chase. How shocking of you."

"Don't go missish on me!" Calliope snapped. "No one will see us. And I—well, it's dark up there. What if the duke does decide to leave the lecture?"

"Ah, so you need protection from your friend's 'avenging spirits'?" he said, looking about at the thinning crowd. No one paid them any attention; they were all still too busy clucking about the main story of the night, the Duke of Averton. "Well, I'm always happy to play protective knight. Lead on, Miss Chase."

Before she could lose her nerve, Calliope dashed up the stairs, her slippered footsteps muffled by the thick red carpet. She didn't know what had come over her. Usually she was not such a ninny as all that! Not as wildly fearless as Thalia, to be sure, but surely able to search deserted study rooms by herself.

Ever since the masquerade ball, though, it was as if something had shifted in her world. The safe, cosy environs of her life had taken on new shadows, new uncertainties. Dangers she didn't understand and had never expected. Even this dull lecture seemed ringed round with them. She was glad of Cameron's solid presence at her back.

As they crept down the corridor, she was reminded of their journey through the Duke of Averton's mad house. Not that the dark, stolid Antiquities Society was much like the jumble of Acropolis House, yet there were all the statues and paintings. Shifting bars of dark and light on the red-papered walls, a hushed murmur from below them. And she was alone with Cameron, acutely conscious of the sound of his breath, the scent of his soap and starch and skin that floated over the miasma of lemon polish, dust and old books.

The first few doors they came across were indeed locked, and when she pressed her ear to their stout wood panels she heard nothing. Not even a soft footfall or sigh.

"How could she just vanish like that?" Calliope murmured, twisting yet another unyielding doorknob.

"We can hardly blame her," Cameron answered. "For not wanting to stay in there with Averton."

"She could have told me where she was going."

"Perhaps she didn't know. Come, let's try this room down here."

The next door was unlocked. It swung open to reveal one of the small studies used during the day by members of the Antiquities Society, since their books could not be taken out of the building. There were two desks and a few armchairs, a bookshelf, large pieces hulking in the shadows. The one window let in the meagre moonlight.

Calliope peered through its thick glass at the street below. Still no Clio. She wrapped her arms tightly around herself, around her waist in its thin white muslin, watching the parade of passing carriages.

"You knew the duke at university," she said.

"Yes, sadly enough." He did not come to her side, staying just inside the door, yet still she was aware of him. His heat and presence. It assured her, even as it made her nervous.

"And he—mistreated women then?" she said. "Behaved dishonourably?"

He sighed. "Oh, Calliope. I'm sure in many people's eyes he did nothing 'dishonourable'. Nothing most other young men of his rank do every day."

"But you don't agree."

"Most of the women he, as you say, mistreated were tavern wenches or shopkeeper's daughters, milliners or housemaids. Not fine ladies to be protected. But he took them whether they agreed or not, sometimes hurt them. One girl drowned herself."

Calliope gasped, closing her eyes tightly against a sudden vision of Clio sinking beneath cold waves.

Cameron came to her side then, his hand gentle on her arm. "I'm sorry. I shouldn't have said that."

"No, you were right to tell me. I'm glad to know the truth. He's a terrible man. Those poor girls…"

"Yes, poor they were. Unprotected, alone. Yet they were human beings, the same as us, and he had no right to treat them that way."

Calliope could feel the anger simmering inside of him, the fury of his memories. Yet his touch was still soft on her arm.

"No, indeed," she said. 'What could he want with my sister? She is hardly poor and unprotected!"

"Perhaps he wants to marry her, sire an heir."

Calliope snorted in disbelief. "He had best look elsewhere, then. Clio would never marry a villain like him, and he must surely know that after she knocked him unconscious."

"It's probably the challenge he enjoys. You Chase Muses are full of prickles and nettles. It takes a brave man to try to get close to you."

Calliope turned towards him, studying his face in the

moonlight. How beautiful he truly was, she mused, a creature of the Greek sun and sea, so full of youth and freedom. She lightly traced the chiselled line of his jaw, feeling a muscle twitch beneath her fingers. "*You* are close to me."

"I must be brave, then. Or very foolish." His hands circled her waist, tugging her closer. She went unresisting, overcome by curiosity and some heady, overpowering emotion she didn't understand. It was intoxicating, dizzying, and she clutched at his shoulders to hold herself upright.

She had never been so close to a man. How giddy it was, like too much bubbling champagne! Or like lolling in the grass on a hot summer's day. All her senses tipped and whirled, and she knew only him. The feel of him under his hands, hard and alive, hot, the strength of him bearing her up.

"Which do you think it is?" she whispered.

"Foolish, definitely," he answered, his voice so rough it was almost unrecognisable.

As if in a hazy dream, far away, yet more immediate than anything she had ever known before, his head tipped towards her and he kissed her.

The touch of his lips was soft at first, velvety, warm, pressing teasingly once, twice. When she did not, *could* not, move away, when she instead edged closer to him, tightening her clasp, his kiss deepened. Became hotter, damper, more urgent.

Something inside her heart responded to that urgency, a rough excitement that expanded and expanded until she feared she would burst with it! She moaned, parting her lips until she felt the tip of his tongue seeking entrance. The world utterly vanished, and there was only *him*. Only this one moment, this one perfect instant.

A moment that was shattered all too soon. A shout from

the street below broke into Calliope's dream, dragging her back down to earth, leaden and heavy. She tore her mouth from Cameron's, tilting her head back to suck in a deep breath of chilly air.

He stepped away, breathing hard. "Calliope," he said hoarsely. "Calliope, I—"

"No," she managed to say, though her chest was tight, her throat aching. She longed to cry, to burst into silly tears, and she didn't know why! Because she had kissed him? Or because they had stopped? "Please don't say you're sorry."

"I'm not. How could I be? But—"

"No 'but', either. I can't—that is, I…" For once in her life, Calliope Chase had no words at all. She spun around and ran out of the room and along the corridor, dashing down the staircase and into the empty ladies' withdrawing room as if a demon was at her heels. And surely a demon was—the spectre of her own wretched emotions. Her weakness.

She stared into the mirror that greeted her as she slammed and locked the door behind her, hardly believing she saw herself in the glass. Her cheeks were a hectic red against white skin, her hair mussed, and her eyes fever-bright. She looked…

She looked like Clio, as her sister fled from the Duke of Averton.

Chapter Thirteen

Calliope leaned forward to peer out the carriage window, scarcely daring to breathe as she waited for some new wonder to appear. It had been such a long journey to Yorkshire, days in the carriage with Clio and Thalia, reading aloud or playing cards. Not talking about what was truly on their minds. But it all must be worth it now, she thought, to see such a strange and glorious landscape.

Calliope had never really been much for the current craze for "nature" and wild emotion, fed by the fashionable poets. Classical order was what she craved, and in town, hemmed in by houses and shops, the neatness of squares and gates and parks, it was easy to believe that such order was possible. Here she could imagine no such thing. Here, she could begin to think the poets had a point. Could remember that the Greeks were not just about order, either, but about insanity and blood and monsters.

This country was beautiful, to be sure, but it was not the white beauty of a marble statue. There was such a wildness to it, a feeling of remoteness and profound solitude, a sense of being alone at the end of the world. Even Thalia had fallen silent, staring over Calliope's shoulder as the land rolled past. Crooked stone walls climbed bare hillsides, dark grey on greenish-purple, rugged squares and rectangles that disappeared over the summits.

Those old walls, clotted with moss, were one of the few signs of human life since they had changed horses at the last village. Only the occasional farmhouse, a wandering band of woolly sheep, spoke of present life. *Past* life there was in abundance—Romans, Vikings, Saxons, Normans had all passed this way, leaving their mark on the land. Even pirates, not too far away in Robin Hood's Bay. And perhaps something earlier, something even from beyond time, hidden in the hilltop tumuli and barrows.

Calliope lowered the window, letting in the cool breeze, the heavy, peaty scent of the earth. In the distance, she saw a narrow trail, a pale scar on the grey earth, leading to a ruined church. Its empty windows stared back, beckoning. Yes, the past was certainly alive here in this country, not just cold, dead stone. She could just envision Cameron here, galloping his horse over the windswept landscape…

Calliope slumped back in her seat. Why was it that he kept springing into her mind at every moment, no matter what she was doing? Reading, walking in the park, planning menus with the cook, playing cards with her sisters—it didn't matter. There he was. Yet she had not seen him since that night at the Antiquities Society. She had heard he had fled town, gone to see to business at his country estate.

It was so hard to think of anything else but that kiss they had shared, to concentrate on the things that usually made up her days. She would begin to forget him as she read a book on, say, the Trojan War, but then a mention of Hermes brought him right back. The glow of his eyes in the moonlight, the soft, hot press of his lips on hers, the smell of his skin. She had listened to her married friends whisper of their physical passion for their husbands, of course, had even read some of Lotty's silly novels, but had always thought such things must be exaggerated. How could a man's mere touch make one forget everything else?

Now she knew it was not exaggerated, for she had surely become as silly as any of them. Sighing over a man's kiss; longing for him to kiss her again, yet fearing it at the same time. What if it swept her away entirely, and she was lost, drowned, in him? All over Cameron de Vere, of all people! It was ridiculous.

He didn't seem to feel the same way, though, leaving town like that. She didn't even know if he would be at this house party, and she dared not ask Emmeline. She couldn't let anyone else know of her absurdity. Not even her sisters.

Would Clio even hear her if she *did* tell? Clio had also been so distant since the lecture, as if she was always thinking of something else. Something no one else could even fathom.

And Calliope and the Ladies Society were no closer to finding the Lily Thief. There had been no more thefts, no clues. This party, so near the duke's lair and the Alabaster Goddess, seemed to be their best chance.

"We should be almost there," Thalia said. "Oh, I can't wait to go walking over these fields! Do you think we could even go swimming in the river we drove past earlier today?"

"If you want to freeze your blood in its veins, Thalia," Clio answered, peering out the window as they lumbered up a steep hill.

"Pooh! It's not as if this is January. I'm sure the water is fine. Invigorating."

"As long as no one sees you," Calliope said. The Chase sisters had surely courted enough scandal of late. They were just fortunate they hadn't yet been caught.

"I am the picture of discretion. Oh, look!" Thalia said, pointing indiscreetly. "I think we're here."

They turned through a pair of open gates and rolled along a gravel lane, lined with wind-bent trees. At the end of the long, straight sweep was Kenleigh Abbey, the home of Emmeline's parents, the Earl and Countess of Kenleigh.

It was just as Emmeline had described at the last meeting of the Ladies Society, a medieval abbey half-converted for domestic life and gifted to one of her ancestors by Henry VIII, along with the title. Built of the local grey stone, it was weathered and harsh, overlaid by ropes of greenish moss. The upper floors boasted modern glass windows, while the lower still consisted of antique arches and walkways. In the watery sun of the afternoon, the light of the pale blue sky, it was odd and charming. At night, though, would the ghosts of old monks peer out from those empty arches?

That is it, Calliope, she told herself sternly. *No more novels!* First Byronic heroes galloping over the moors, now ghostly monks. Whatever would she conjure up next?

Around the front of the house circled a modern drive with a covered entrance, sheltered from the wind. The coach rolled to a stop just as the doors opened and Emmeline appeared, wreathed in welcoming smiles.

"You're here at last!" she cried as Calliope alighted, closely followed by Clio and Thalia. "It has been so dull waiting for everyone these last few days."

"Dull? With Herr Mueller to listen to?" Calliope teased.

Emmeline laughed. "He is very knowledgeable, to be sure, but I will be glad when he has a larger audience on which to impart his wisdom. Where is your father, by the way? Papa is most anxious to show him a new funeral stele he just purchased."

"He stopped in the last village we passed to examine their little museum," Clio said. "Something about Saxon arrowheads."

"Ah, well, no matter—you are all here now! Come inside and have some tea, you must be exhausted by your journey," Emmeline said, leading them through the open doors. They had barely a glimpse of drafty stone corridors and arches before she led them up a narrow flight of steps to a modern, firelit sitting room. Lotty was already there with her family, watching as the maids laid out a tea service.

"I have to tell you of everything I have planned," Emmeline said, pouring out the tea, slicing cake. "So many ruins to see! We can even go to the seaside, if you like. Robin Hood's Bay is a bit of a journey, but not too far, and terribly exciting."

"Where the smugglers are?" Thalia cried. "Oh, yes, we must. I have never seen smugglers' caves before."

"You probably wouldn't this time, either," Clio said. "Aren't smugglers notoriously choosy about who they let into their tunnels?"

"Clio, you are simply determined to ruin all my fun," Thalia answered. "When have you become such a fussy old lady?"

As she spoke, there was the sound of footsteps on the stairs, a woman's voice and the click of dog's claws on the stone floor. "It's just Mama," Emmeline said. "Shh! Don't let her hear you talk of smugglers, or she'll never let us go to the bay."

As Lady Kenleigh, a warm, welcoming older version

of Emmeline, came into the room, the conversation turned to town doings and the more genteel outings planned for their party.

As they chatted and sipped their tea, Calliope realised she had not thought of Cameron in fully twenty minutes. And she had not even asked if he was to be among the guests. Quite a feat, and surely it indicated that he was at last fading from her mind.

It simply had to.

Cameron paused at the top of the summit, gazing out over the grey-green landscape stretched out below. It was as if he could see for miles, over the great sweep of moorlands beyond, the dark lumps of farms and cottages. The roadway into the village wound below, a pinkish ribbon, but the only living being he could see was his own tethered horse, grazing at the bottom of the steep slope.

No wonder the Romans had built a fort nearby, now just a tracery of walls, the cracked remnants of a mosaic floor. They could see for ever from here, all the wild acres spreading out, full of freedom and magic.

Cameron took off his hat, letting the wind catch at his hair, buffet his skin. He had been stuck in town for too long, trapped by streets and crowds and stale smells. Here the wind carried only the scent of earth, of peat and heather, the hint of woodsmoke. He was alone at last, alone with the wind and the light, the old spirits of the fort.

Alone, except for the thought of Calliope Chase. She followed him even up here, the memory of her solemn dark eyes. The way her slender body felt under his touch, so warm and pliant. The taste of her lips, the innocent, passionate wonder of her. The way his body hardened, quickened, at the merest breath of her scent.

The way she ran from him, never looking back.

How he had longed to chase after her, to hold her, kiss her again! He even ran to the doorway of that dark room, frantic as her racing footsteps faded to nothing. Frantic to hold on to her again, to hold on to whatever that rare feeling was that grew between them when they kissed.

Yet something held him back. The look in those eyes, maybe, so very confused. The memory of Averton, so brutal with women—so unlike the way Cameron wanted to be. Muses were not as other women. They dwelled in their own world above mortal men. They were rare and precious, not to be coerced. Pressured. Not to be pursued like prey, lest they turn their backs on the man entirely, withdrawing their grace and shining good fortune from him for ever.

So, he did not run after her, even as every fibre of his being screamed at him that he must. Once his heartbeat slowed, and his body was fit to be seen without causing a scandal, he made sure that she was safe in the ladies' withdrawing room. Then he went home. For one fleeting second, he considered visiting Mrs Parker's discreet, expensive little establishment on Half Moon Street, where he was sure to find an enthusiastic welcome from one of her very pretty girls. But even as the thought occurred to him, he dismissed it. None of them would be Calliope, and it was Calliope alone he wanted.

How had such a thing happened? How had he gone from being exasperated by their quarrels, to longing to make love to her on the Antiquities Society floor?

The desire hadn't vanished, either, even though he stayed away. Even left town for his own estate. There he tried to bury his turmoil in long gallops, even labouring in his own fields, much to his tenants' astonishment. He

thought about not coming to this house party. Calliope
was certain to be there.

But he couldn't stay away. Not any longer. He didn't
want to frighten her, but his Greek blood burned too hot
now to be denied. He had to admit it to himself—he
wanted Calliope Chase.

And he intended to have her.

Chapter Fourteen

"Emmeline certainly has so much planned for this party," Lady Kenleigh said, pouring out more amber-coloured tea and passing around the porcelain cups. "Picnics by the river, nature walks, charades. There is even an assembly in a few days, in the village rooms. Not Almack's, to be sure, but amusing enough. You young people do need your music and dancing!"

"It sounds delightful," Calliope said, peering at Emmeline over the rim of her cup. Emmeline blushed. So, it was as Calliope suspected—her friend was using picnics and the like as a scheme for more time with Mr Smithson. "But will we have time, with Herr Mueller's lectures?"

Lady Kenleigh smiled knowingly. "You needn't worry, Miss Chase. There will be more than enough time for Herr Mueller. My husband thinks everyone should be able to live on Attic vase painting and the Punic Wars alone, but Emmeline and I know that is not always true. We want you to enjoy yourselves here. After all, you are away from the busy Season. We must make it worth your while, if we can."

Calliope smiled at her, but she was afraid she knew what Lady Kenleigh meant. After all, Emmeline's mother was one of the most notorious matchmakers in all England. Since she had seen her daughter almost settled—though not with poor Freddie Mountbank, her first choice!—she needed other objects for her attention. And who better than the motherless Chase sisters?

Calliope looked across the room to Clio, who was examining a book with Lotty. Clio was smiling as she listened to Lotty's chatter, yet there was still that shadow, that wisp of greyness that seemed to follow her about ever since that blasted masquerade ball. Calliope doubted Lady Kenleigh would have much success matching *her*. But maybe a distraction—like fending off "suitable" introductions—was just what Clio needed.

As for Thalia…

Calliope turned her gaze to her other sister, who was banging out a stormy Beethoven concerto at the pianoforte. The light from the windows touched her silver-gilt curls, the very picture of an English rose. But Calliope knew it would take a special, and strong, man indeed to match her inner Amazon.

And as for herself—she had no thoughts of marriage. She was too busy, with her father and sisters, the thief, the Alabaster Goddess. There was no man who could understand. None she had ever encountered, anyway.

Except…

Calliope had a sudden vision of the dark room at the Antiquities Society. The hot, rough feel of Cameron's touch on her skin, the press of his kiss. The undeniable rush of need, bubbling in her veins, curling her toes. *He* was not like any other man she had ever met.

But he was not for her. They were not for each other.

Calliope frowned. She felt suddenly sad, as if Clio's dark cloud spread its misty tentacles over her own head. She put her teacup down on the nearest table and drifted over to a window, the murmur of conversation and laughter trailing after her.

She found herself gazing down at a side garden, neat, narrow pathways leading out towards the dip of a ha-ha and beyond. On the edge of the manicured lawn, just before the careful landscape vanished into a stand of trees, she could see a pile of dark grey stones. At first it seemed haphazard, an odd structure rising up out of nowhere, yet she could see how closely the slabs fit together. Like the walls they drove past, bisecting the hillsides.

A barrow of some sort? They had seen such things on their journey, old structures on summits, built so sturdily by long-dead hands that they still stood, reminders of a vanished world. Lotty would surely be eager to explore this one, to build elaborate tales of ancient romance around the cold stone.

Emmeline came to her side, offering a fresh cup of tea. "I was thinking perhaps a walk to the falls would be interesting for tomorrow morning," she said. "It's quite picturesque. They even say there's a grotto hidden behind the water, though I don't expect any of us would care to look for it! Much too damp."

"Don't tell Thalia. I'm sure *she* would attempt it, given half a chance."

Emmeline laughed. "I won't, but I'm certain she'll hear of it from one of the tenants. They love to tell of local folktales."

"Is there one associated with that?" Calliope gestured towards the pile of stones.

"Those? I have no idea. They've just always been there.

Shall we go take a look?" Emmeline glanced back at her mother, who was talking quite intently with Lotty's mother. "She is determined to match Freddie Mountbank with *someone*, you see. Poor Lotty."

"A walk would be lovely," Calliope agreed hastily. Heaven forbid Lady Kenleigh turn Freddie Mountbank on to *her*.

With Emmeline's efficiency, it took only a few moments for everyone to gather hats and shawls and set off across the gardens towards the mysterious stones. Thalia dashed ahead, her hem quickly muddied, and leaned down to peer over the low wall.

"Emmeline!" she called, her voice echoing hollowly off the rocks. "How could you never have looked closely at this? It's quite fascinating."

"We just don't come here very often," Emmeline answered. "It's too remote and quiet for Mama. Why? What do you see?"

"It's very dark down there, but it appears to be stairs of some sort. Cut into the earth." Thalia would surely have leaped right down off the wall, if Calliope hadn't caught the sleeve of her spencer. "An ancient basement of some sort?"

"A Viking root cellar?" Calliope said doubtfully. She peered past Thalia's shoulder, but all she could see was dirt and blackness. Maybe those *were* stairs, but she couldn't tell.

"It must be a passage!" Lotty cried. "A secret tomb, where forbidden lovers lie cruelly murdered. I read about something just like it—"

"I'm sure," Calliope said hastily, before they were treated to a lengthy and detailed plot synopsis. "But if those *are* stairs, they appear to go nowhere. They must belong to a structure that's vanished. An old gardener's shed, maybe."

Lotty pouted. "It could be a tomb."

"Calliope is surely right," Clio said briskly. "These stairs just end, see? Blocked up. Thalia, come away from that, you'll get all muddy."

"I have to wash before dinner, anyway," Thalia protested. "A little dirt never killed anyone."

"But Mary would not appreciate having to clean your gloves yet again," Calliope said, suddenly impatient. Really, living with her sisters was like herding a particularly recalcitrant band of sheep! Or something more slippery, wilder. Foxes, maybe. A herd of arguing foxes.

Thalia muttered, but she did back away from the mysterious steps that led to nothing. She and the others wandered off towards the trees, and Calliope turned in the opposite direction, seeking just a moment of quiet.

She walked around to the front of the house, strolling down the tree-lined lane. In the far distance she could see the front gates, partly open, as if inviting her to dash for their promised freedom.

Her thin half-boots weren't up to dashing, though. Instead she walked along the gravel drive, wondering at her strange mood. Her sisters often squabbled; it usually didn't bother her at all. Probably it was just lack of sleep, worry over the Lily Thief and where he might strike next. It was making her impatient and snappish. This holiday was just what she needed. A few days to rest and regroup, to breathe fresh air, enjoy the picnics and waterfalls…

The gates at the end of the lane swung open, admitting a single galloping horse. The creature dashed towards her, and she saw her peaceful hopes vanish like chimney smoke into the sky.

Even from here she recognised the horse's rider. It was Cameron. He wore no hat, and his curls were even longer and more wild than usual, his greatcoat billowing behind him like wings. An English Perseus on his Pegasus. She glanced around her, and could see nowhere to hide. No place for concealment. She just stood there, frozen, watching as he drew ever nearer.

He reined in a few feet from where she stood, tossing up a plume of gravel dust. A faint sheen of sweat glistened on his brow, matching that of his horse's glossy coat. He had been riding hard, then. Trying to outrun this thoughts, perhaps, just as she was?

He stared down at her in silence, the only sound his rushed breath, the wind in the scrubby trees. Calliope half imagined he was a mirage, a dream figure, but then he swung down from the saddle and walked towards her, all too real.

Calliope took a step back, until she felt the rough bark of a tree trunk against her hips. He stopped several feet from her, just watching her as he stripped off his gloves.

Calliope swallowed hard. She didn't know what to do, what to say! Her mother's careful etiquette lessons had never addressed how to treat a man after one kisses him.

"Good afternoon, Miss Chase," he said.

"G-good afternoon, Lord Westwood," she answered. *This* she could do. Polite conversation. "How was your journey?"

"Most uneventful. I trust you are well? And your father and sisters? Especially Miss Clio."

"Quite well, thank you. Clio seems quite recovered. They are looking forward to hearing Herr Mueller."

The corner of his lips quirked. "Indeed? They did not benefit from his, er, great wisdom sufficiently in town?"

Calliope wanted to laugh, but she kept her face perfectly serious. She could not give in to hysterics now! "The country air will also be beneficial, I believe. We did hear that you have been taking advantage of the healthy qualities of the country of late. We missed seeing you at the Burke-Smythes' Venetian breakfast last week."

"I had business with my steward, so I went to my own estate on the way here."

"Indeed?" Calliope cast about for something safe to say. So, polite conversation was not so easy as all that after all. Not when she couldn't say what she longed to— why had he kissed her? And why had he left town so soon after?

Had she been so truly dreadful?

"I have heard that your estate is quite pleasant," she finally said.

"It is very pretty," he agreed. "But lonely since my mother died. The arrangements are sadly out of date and require a lady's touch."

A lady's touch? Calliope was suddenly back to not knowing what to say. She turned towards the house, walking quickly away. "You must be tired after your journey," she said. "Lady Kenleigh has tea in the drawing room. And Emmeline is planning many excursions. A walk to the waterfalls tomorrow."

Cameron caught up his horse's reins and followed behind her, catching up with her near the empty porte-cochère. The abbey's blank lower windows stared out at them, unblinking.

"Calliope," he said quietly. He stopped her flight with a gentle touch on her elbow. "I've been wanting to talk with you about that night at the Antiquities Society."

"Oh. Yes." Calliope couldn't quite meet his gaze. Instead, she stared past his shoulder at the quiet horse. He watched her with a large, liquid, completely indifferent gaze. Just like the house and all those ghost monks. "You must not feel you have to apologise. It was entirely my fault. I was so worried about my sister, about the Lily Thief, and I—well, I was not myself. I'm sorry. Think no more of it."

She hurried up the steps. "Tea in the drawing room, Lord Westwood," she called, not looking back.

His voice followed her, though. It was a quiet, rough mutter, but she could vow he said, "You can't run from me for ever, Calliope Chase."

Not for ever, perhaps. But she could surely run for now.

Chapter Fifteen

The excursion Emmeline organised for their first day was a nature walk, a trek to explore one of the area's many famous waterfalls. "You will love it," Emmeline said, as they strolled away from the house, bundled in cloaks against the morning mist. "It's so very mysterious. Like a place out of time."

A place out of time. Calliope could well believe it as she gazed around at the landscape, so different from anything she saw in her everyday life. The mist hung low to the ground, a net of silvery tulle over the dark green earth, clinging to the old stone walls. The silence was thick, broken only by the occasional bleat of a sheep or the hushed laughter of their group.

Cameron fell into step beside her, and she gave him a tentative smile. He, too, seemed different here, his fashionable town clothes and dashing yellow phaeton left behind in favour of plain scuffed boots and his blue greatcoat. His hair was carelessly brushed back, sparkling with a few bits of mist that clung to the dark strands like diamonds. Strangely, he seemed to belong here, just as he belonged at a society ball or on a Greek seashore. Wherever he went he was surely at ease.

Calliope did envy him that.

"We look like some ancient band of Norsemen, don't we?" she said. "Marching out with the dawn for some watery battle."

Cameron laughed, and as always the warm, champagne sound made her want to laugh along with him. "Do you know of the Vikings, then? I thought the Chases cared only for ancient Greece. Democracy, philosophy, the Olympic gods."

"Much like the de Veres, you mean?"

"Touché."

"It's true that Greece came first in our educations. But we read of the Vikings and Gauls, too. And once we had this governess who would tell us tales of longships and bloody raids. We did enjoy those stories."

"What happened to her? Your Viking nurse."

"She left, of course, and my mother found a new governess. One who taught us more *appropriately* bloodthirsty history of Greece and Rome."

Cameron held out a hand to help her over a low wall, and their gloved fingers clung together for a moment longer than was proper. Calliope felt quite unlike herself, for she longed for nothing more than to hold his hand tightly, to race recklessly with him across the fields.

"I hadn't thought of her tales in a long time," she said as they walked on, trailing behind the others. "This place just brings them back so vividly."

"It *is* different here," he agreed. "Mysterious."

"Do you think there were Vikings here?" she said. "Perhaps they lived among those stones up there, on the hilltop! Worshipping Thor and Odin and Freya."

Cameron laughed. "That was a Roman fort, but I fear that is the extent of my knowledge. The de Veres, much like the Chases, believe history ended some time around 300 BC."

Emmeline, strolling at the head of the group with Mr Smithson, turned back and called, "Catch up, you two! We're nearly there."

Calliope and Cameron hurried their steps, joining the others as they entered a small, gorge-like formation of rocks. The sun was beginning to peek between the clouds, burning off the mist, but not in here. Here shadows reigned, along with that ancient magic Calliope could not explain.

He took her hand as he had at the wall, holding her steady as they descended a steep, sandy path into the enchanted land. The soles of her half-boots slipped a bit, but she trusted he would not let her fall. The river, a quiet, silvery-blue stream, suddenly seemed to bubble and writhe, stirred to a wild froth by some invisible hand. It rushed down into the gorge and dropped, dozens of feet, into a pool, tumbling and arcing over rock slabs.

The smell of the earth was strong, dark green in Calliope's nostrils, wild garlic and moss, wildflowers that miraculously peeked out of the rocky bed.

Her steps paused, and she just stared and stared, captured by the otherworldly scene. She clung to Cameron's hand, and it was as if everything—her friends, her place in the world, even the Alabaster Goddess—disappeared. Everything she thought was important slipped away, and she had only this one moment.

"Calliope?" Cameron asked quietly, peering back at her. "Are you all right?"

"It's so beautiful," she whispered. "Have you ever seen anything more lovely?"

"Only once," he said, and one of his gloved fingertips

reached up to touch, ever so delicately, a curl that sprang free from her hood.

Flustered, her face hot, Calliope tugged away from him. Her moment of magic was gone, vanished in her old awkwardness, and she walked towards the group, as quickly as she could on the slick sand. How could he do that to her, every time she saw him? Make her forget herself, her task, her place in their oh-so-careful world.

He swept her up in his golden glow, all his freedom and beauty, and she forgot everything for that happy moment. She was as drawn to his spell as every other woman in London—"the Greek god", she remembered her friends sighing.

A god, one of light and merriment. And she was the most didactic of the Muses, full of practicality and lectures, the need for careful study and preservation. Not romance. Not wild paeans to nature and culture.

That was what she could not forget. She and Cameron were allies now, true, drawn together to save the Alabaster Goddess. But when Artemis was safe, they would still be themselves. Two very different people.

Once she reached Clio's side, she paused to gaze at the sky above them, a pale blue sliver that barely lit the dim grotto below. It was like her own mind—she almost grasped some truth, some hidden purpose, and it was like that bit of light. Far away and elusive, it slid away before she could grasp it.

She peered at Clio, who solemnly watched the tumbling falls. Somehow, her sister had become like this grotto, too. Dark and elusive, full of mysterious crevices where ghosts could hide. It frightened Calliope, because she would do anything to save Clio from whatever haunted her. Yet she couldn't save her, not if she didn't know what that was.

"I love it here," Clio said. "It's surely an ancient place. Older than human memory, than anything we can fathom."

"They say there's a cave back there, behind the falls," Emmeline said.

"I should swim over, then, to see!" Thalia said. She spoke teasingly, as if to recall their earlier quarrel. But Calliope closed her eyes in despair, for it was just the sort of thing Thalia really would do.

"You would catch your death," Clio said absently. "Do tell us more about these falls, Emmeline, for I'm sure there must be so many legends."

For the next hour, they all sat perched on the stone slabs by the water, listening to Emmeline's tales of ancient water spirits. Calliope was all too aware of Cameron's gaze on her, across the cold chasm of the magical river.

By the time they started for home, the sun appeared in earnest, breaking through the clouds to dispel the last of the morning mist. The land was no less beautiful, but it *was* less mystical, laid out for view in squares and rectangles divided by those ubiquitous walls. There were farmers in their fields, carts and hulking horses, white lumps of sheep meandering in search of fodder. Just daily life, free of magic.

Still, Calliope could not quite shake off the spell of the falls. That sense of being lost, even in her own mind. She didn't like these feelings, didn't like being confused.

There was only one way to break free. She had to concentrate on the Alabaster Goddess. She remembered the paper tucked secretly into her baggage, the list of names she had copied from the one Clio had found inside the Alabaster Goddess. Surely they meant something important? Perhaps they were that elusive clue that shimmered just out of her reach, and they would unlock all else.

She glanced back at Cameron, who strolled with Lotty, listening to her talk of her latest novel. He listened to her most seriously, nodding at all the appropriate moments, making polite comments. He betrayed not one jot of impatience. Maybe he was a reader of horrid novels himself.

There was really nothing else to do but show him the list soon. She couldn't decipher it herself, and perhaps he, knowing something of the duke and his world, would have some ideas. Or perhaps he would just indulge her whims, as he was doing with Lotty.

"Let's go this way," Emmeline said, breaking into Calliope's thoughts. "It's a quicker route back than the main road, and Papa said Herr Mueller wants to talk to us before luncheon. Something about Socrates, I think. Or Sophocles?"

"One can hardly wait," Clio muttered. "We'll be sitting there until after dinnertime, getting hungrier and hungrier. *Ja, fräulein…*"

Calliope laughed. "Shh! Herr Mueller is very distinguished. We're fortunate to benefit from his knowledge."

"If you say so," Clio said doubtfully. "Indeed, knowledge is never wasted. But I prefer the waterfall."

They followed Emmeline down a narrower path, between an arch of wind-bent branches that cast shifting shadows over the ground. It was quiet here, almost eerily silent, broken only by their own murmurs, the crackle of their footsteps on the underbrush.

"I believe Lotty would call this *The Lair of the Forest Witch*," Clio whispered. "Beware, o ye who enter here!"

Calliope laughed, but she had to suppress a shiver.

At last they left the wood, turning on to a wider, sunnier walkway, only to be faced with yet another enchanted scene. A castle, set high on a distant hilltop, framed by the vast sky.

It was not as old as the Vikings, but surely old enough. Fourteenth century, Calliope guessed, gazing at the rough stone walls, the crenellated battlements that needed only fluttering pennants to make them complete. Arrow slits stared out at them darkly, and no doubt a drawbridge and moat could be seen on closer inspection. It was silent, a solid hulk guarding the landscape. Beautiful, in its own way. Complete in a way other local castles, famous ruins like Bolton and Richmond, were not.

Permanent, and cold.

"That's Averton Castle," Emmeline said.

Somehow, Calliope was not surprised. The structure was so like the duke. Mysterious, beautiful, but in an off-putting way, strangely archaic.

The Alabaster Goddess was in that chilly fortress somewhere, locked away. Hidden.

Calliope reached for Clio's hand. Clio didn't turn her gaze from the castle, but neither did she pull away. Her fingers curled tightly around Calliope's. "Typical," was all she said. Then she drew away, and walked on.

Chapter Sixteen

"...In Oedipus, Sophocles shows us a man both cursed and blessed, vindicated through his many sufferings. He has lived out the themes of both freedom and destiny, as you see from this passage here..."

Calliope shifted slightly in her chair, watching Herr Mueller politely as he talked on about the Oedipus plays. Really, tonight she had no time for men killing their fathers, marrying their mothers, and ending up blind and wandering the countryside! She had concerns of her own.

Concerns that hopefully would end a bit better than tangling with "freedom and destiny".

She folded her hands over her beaded reticule, feeling the edges of the paper folded within. Across the room sat Cameron, also watching the professor. But his eyes seemed curiously blank, as if his true self had slipped off somewhere.

What was he thinking about? she mused. The Greek lands Oedipus wandered? She could almost see it—sun beating down on broken marble statues. Lizards skittering through dried thistle. A different place of old spells, of heat that never ended.

Maybe that was really what they were trying to recapture here, with their lectures, their endless discussions of old politics, old gods. Not freedom really, *or* destiny. Just that Greek sun, and the old creatures who reigned there. Gods and nymphs and naiads.

She glanced again at Cameron, who always seemed to embody those very dreams. Summer laziness that concealed a quicksilver changeability.

He shifted in his seat, catching her gaze. He smiled at her, and she nodded, tucking the reticule more securely in her clasp. After the lecture, she would have to find some way to speak to him alone, without incurring her friends' speculation—or Clio's questions. Somehow she wasn't yet ready to tell her sister she had enlisted Cameron's help.

Calliope turned her gaze to her sister, who sat on a chaise with Thalia and Lotty. She appeared to be listening to Herr Mueller, but her fingers kept plucking at her skirt, pleating the Turkey red muslin. Like Cameron, she seemed far away.

Soon enough, they would surely have all the answers. The thief would be caught, the goddess safe, and life would go back to normal.

Only Calliope feared that "normal", whatever that was, would be quite impossible after all this. After Cameron. He had turned "normal" topsy-turvy, and she wasn't sure she could ever right it again.

Or if she even wanted to.

Lady Kenleigh at last managed to bring Herr Mueller's lecture to a long-winded close, long after the light of sunset had vanished beyond the windows and night's chill set in. Calliope's father and a few of the others clustered around the professor with their questions, while Emmeline led the younger set into the dinning room, where a buffet supper was laid out.

"Hearing about Oedipus's travails certainly does work up an appetite!" Thalia said, reaching eagerly for her plate.

"I certainly feel that way after hearing about a good eye-gouging," Clio muttered. "Just tea for me, thank you."

Calliope strolled casually to Cameron's side, keeping an eye on her sisters to make sure they stayed together, too far away to overhear.

"And what do *you* think of poor Oedipus, Miss Chase?" he said, handing her a cup of tea from one of the footmen.

"Herr Mueller's views are most interesting," she answered.

"His views are most commonplace. They're what every scholar says these days. When will someone come out and say something shocking, such as that Oedipus's downfall was a Spartan plot? Or a Persian ploy?"

Calliope laughed. "Is that what you really believe?"

Cameron shrugged, but grinned at her laughter. "I have no strong feelings about Oedipus at all, I fear."

"Neither do I, I confess. I'm too fanciful. I prefer tales of gods and goddesses."

"'Fanciful', my dear Miss Chase, would be the last word I would think of to describe you."

Then what word *would* he use? Calliope ached to ask, yet truly she feared to know the answer. Would it be "dull"? "Annoying"? But all she said was, "I fear you may change your mind once I show you what is in my reticule."

A light glinted in his eyes. "I burn with curiosity, Miss Chase."

"I can't show it to you here. Emmeline is going to organise a game of charades later. I'll excuse myself to repair my hem or something, see if you can meet me in the small sitting room off the library. It won't take long."

She gave him a nod, and moved away to chat with Emmeline and Mr Smithson. Would this work?

Of course it would. It simply had to.

Calliope stood by the window of the little sitting room. The view was not of the terraced gardens as her own windows were, but of the sweep of the front drive, the long avenue of trees leading out the gates where she had watched Cameron come galloping in. The moon was bright tonight, the sky clear, and she fancied she could see the battlements of the duke's castle.

That was silly, of course, for that fortress was too far away. The duke's presence seemed to make itself felt all over the countryside, though. He lurked over all, like a great bird of prey.

Calliope took the list out of her reticule, smoothing it over the windowsill. What did those names mean? How did they fit together?

Behind her, the door clicked open softly. She looked back to see Cameron, outlined for an instant by the light from the corridor before he shut the door behind him. He stayed across the room, leaning back against the wall, but the space was small and she could feel his presence most acutely. Smell him, feel his warmth. She remembered the last time they were alone in the dark, in that study at the Antiquities Society. He kissed her then, and she had not been able to forget the way it felt.

Calliope tugged her shawl closer about her shoulders. "Did anyone see you leave?" she asked.

He shook his head, the movement distinct in the chalky moonlight. "Most of the gentlemen excused themselves for a quick brandy before being forced to play charades. I just slipped away at the same time—the ladies will think I went with the men, the men will think I stayed with the ladies. For a few minutes, anyway."

"Very clever."

"Of course. Is my cleverness not why you summoned me here? Or was it my handsome—eyes?"

"Both, as a matter of fact."

"Indeed? I'm intrigued." He came closer, standing with her by the window.

"I need your eyes to look at this, and your cleverness to tell me what it means," she said, firmly setting away memories of that kiss. Or trying to, anyway. She handed him the paper.

Cameron tilted it to the light, a frown touching his brow. "The Golden Falcon? The Purple Hyacinth? I fear my cleverness is not equal to this task. It seems like gibberish. Where did you get this?"

"Clio found it on the night of the duke's ball. Hidden in the base of the Alabaster Goddess."

He glanced at her in surprise. "This?"

"Well, this particular list is a copy. Clio has the original. I can't figure it out at all. Is it a code, do you think?"

"I have no idea." He read it over again. "At university, I remember Averton and his equally noxious friends had some ridiculous nicknames for each other. I don't think these are they, but it may be something similar."

"A list of his friends? Some kind of secret society?"

"Like your Ladies Society?" he said, smiling.

"Our Ladies Society is hardly secret," she huffed. "And we don't give each other silly monikers."

"Of course not. It's others who call you the Chase Muses."

"I didn't ask to be named Calliope, you know. I would have much preferred Elizabeth. Or Jane."

"Really? You don't strike me as a Jane."

"I'm much more a Jane than a Calliope. And we are off the subject! What do you think this list is? A criminal ring?"

His smile faded as he examined the list again. "I wouldn't put it past Averton. The man is capable of anything when he's bored, or determined. But I can't decide why. The days of smuggling French wines and silks are past, yet from here he does have access to the old tunnels at Robin Hood's Bay for whatever he has going on." Cameron stared out the window, as if he, too, imagined he could see those forbidding battlements. "I need to think about this, and you should get back to the drawing room. May I keep the list?"

Calliope nodded. Those odd names were surely burned into her brain by now. "Of course. But won't you come back, too?"

"Not yet." He smiled at her, reaching out to briefly, softly touch her hand. "Whatever would people say, if they saw us come into the room together?"

Calliope laughed. The gossip would increase, of course, and they would have to become engaged. And that would be terrible.

Wouldn't it?

Calliope opened her eyes to find herself lying not in the comfortable, curtained bed in her guest chamber, but on a cold stone floor. She blinked into the darkness around her, her mind as heavy and hazy as if it was wrapped in cotton wool. She slowly pushed herself upright, confused. She didn't remember leaving her bed! And certainly didn't remember seeing anything like this.

It was a grotto of some sort, a room all of rough stone, treacherous as daggers. The only light came from a mys-

*terious source high overhead, a pale, wavery yellow-green.
As if from far away, she heard a dull, rushing noise.*

Oh, *she thought.* I'm behind the waterfall.

And, in the same moment, I must be dreaming.

*Of course. A dream. But what could it mean? Why
would her dreams be of a spot she had never actually
seen? A cold, stony place full of chilly draughts and dank
smells.*

*Calliope pushed herself to her feet. She wore her
dressing gown and bedroom slippers, but was not cold at
all. Now that she knew it was only a dream, she had only
curiosity. What in her sleeping mind had brought her here?
She followed the source of the light.*

*It led out of the grotto room down a long, narrow
corridor. The ceiling was very low, the stone floor under
her thin shoes slippery. Strangest of all, the walls were
lined with objects she remembered from Acropolis House.
Daphne, the Egyptian lioness, Pan with his flute. Their
marble eyes followed her as she rushed past, their mute
stares accusing.* Why didn't you save us? *she could almost
hear them whisper.* Why did you leave us?

*Calliope's steps quickened until she was running,
dashing down the corridor as if she could leave them
behind. Their cold stares, their eerie voices. She ran until
she tripped, falling forward into rushing wind, into nothingness. Too terrified even to scream, she covered her eyes,
waiting for the crushing death she was sure awaited her.*

*It never came. Instead she landed on what felt like a
feather bed, soft and enveloping. Warm. Cautiously, slowly,
she lowered her hands, peering around her.*

*It was not a bed, but the sarcophagus she was laying
on. And in front of her was the Alabaster Goddess, bathed
in that murky green light, her bow held aloft. Like the*

statues in the narrow corridor, her eyes seemed alive, yet not accusing. She looked—compassionate. Concerned. That was odd, for Artemis was surely one of the least caring of the rather callous Pantheon! She had no compunction about turning men into deer and shooting them full of arrows if they displeased her.

Don't be foolish, *Calliope chided herself, sitting up on the sarcophagus.* This is only a dream. A friendly Artemis made as much sense as a grotto full of antiquities.

"What am I doing here?" *she asked.*

"I summoned you, of course," *Artemis answered. Her marble lips didn't move, yet her voice echoed all around. She sounded just as Calliope would have imagined— young but full of authority. Confidence. She seemed, in fact, much like Clio.*

"Why?" *Calliope dangled her feet off the sarcophagus's gilded edge, but dared not jump down. She could see only darkness below.*

"You and your friends have loved and served me well," *Artemis said.* "I must warn you, though. Your mission here holds many dangers."

"Dangers?" *Calliope thought of the duke lying on the floor bleeding. Of Clio's ruined costume. Cameron kissing her in the dark.* "Surely we have already faced dangers."

She fancied Artemis looked pitying. "Not like what is to come, my Muse. I have many hidden enemies, you know. Enemies that are yours now. You must stay strong. Stay your course—my course—and all will be well in the end. Remember that when you have doubts. Remember this when the enemies at last reveal themselves, and you find all is not as you thought."

"But…" *Calliope began, even as Artemis faded away into the shadows. She fell again, toppling from the sar-*

*cophagus into that waiting blackness below. When she
landed, it was not on a hard floor or jagged rocks. It was
a grassy summer meadow. She felt herself rolling, rolling,
down a slope scented with sunshine and wildflowers.*

*Her headlong trajectory was only halted when she
collided with a pair of polished boots. Stunned, breathless,
Calliope stared up to find Cameron peering down at her.
He was outlined in brilliant sunlight, dazzling after the dim
grotto, his curls tangled in the breeze.*

*"Calliope," he said, his tone coaxing. Alluring. He leaned
down, smiling at her. That merry, careless grin she loved so
much. What did it hide? "Please. Let me help you…"*

*He held out his hand, and she wanted to take it more than
she had ever wanted anything. To feel his skin on hers. But
she remembered Artemis's words.* Hidden enemies.

*She scrambled to her feet, backing away from him—
from what she felt. It was no use, though, for she found
herself all alone in that meadow. And a cloud was passing
over the sun…*

Calliope awoke with a gasp. She glanced around frantically, half-expecting to find herself back in the damp
grotto. She was in her bedchamber, though, the fire burnt
down to glowing embers and the bedclothes twisted and
kicked away. The canopy and half-drawn curtains, so dark
and heavy, red brocade so unlike her own blue-and-white
chintz at home, seemed suffocating. Engulfing. She
climbed out of bed, wrapping herself tightly in her dressing
gown as she went to the window.

The moon was still bright as it glimmered down on the
deserted gardens. Silvery-green, it turned the fountain and
statues below into shimmering, magical objects so different from their solid, daytime presence.

Calliope took a deep breath, still caught in that dream. How very vivid it was! Usually she didn't remember her dreams at all, or if she did they were terribly prosaic and dry. No hidden enemies or water-fall rooms. No Cameron.

She remembered those antiquities in her dream, their empty gazes that seemed so alive. Their eerie whispers. Such objects had never really seemed *alive* to her before. Important, of course. Beautiful, to be sure. Symbols of something that had once been alive, of lessons to be learned. But not living, vital objects in themselves, with their own desires. Their own wills.

Their own proper place in the world.

Calliope crossed her arms tightly against the late night chill. The disturbing shift of something inside herself. Was this, then, what Cameron meant when he spoke about art? When he sent his father's collections back to Greece? She had not understood then. Truth to tell, she did not under-stand now. Modern Greece was *not* the Greece that produced such objects. But still…

Her roiling thoughts were interrupted by a ripple in the shadows below her window. Calliope leaned closer to the cold glass, peering down. Was she still dreaming? Seeing things that weren't there? The next thing she glimpsed could be the Alabaster Goddess herself, marching down the walkway!

But the figures that appeared, detaching themselves from the shadows to step into the moonlight, were all too real. A tall, lean person in a greatcoat and wide-brimmed hat, and a smaller figure swathed in a cloak. They lingered next to the fountain, heads bent close together as they talked.

Slowly, Calliope opened her window, careful of squeaks and creaks as the old latch gave way. Surely it was just a couple out for a rendezvous. But it wouldn't hurt to eavesdrop, just a bit. Artemis had warned about hidden enemies.

There was little breeze to carry voices to her ears, unfortunately. All she could make out were soft, indistinct murmurs, unidentifiable. Just a few words carried—
"…soon", "…tide", "…here."

Calliope frowned. Even she could make nothing of such meagre scraps! She still watched, listening closely to see if anything else would be revealed. After a few moments, the cloaked figure handed the other a letter, a pale square in the darkness. "Wait," Calliope heard. Then the hatted one hurried away, and the cloaked one turned back towards the house. For just an instant, the hood fell away and a silvery beam glinted on the glass of spectacles. A long braid of auburn hair.

Calliope gasped, drawing back to the concealment of the draperies. *Clio!* As she stared, disbelieving, her sister drew the hood back into place, rushing towards the house. She disappeared, and the night was silent once more.

Calliope pressed her hand to her mouth. What was Clio doing? Who was that person in the hat? Some sort of illicit romance? Yet the scene had not had a romantic quality. No furtive embraces, no passionate kisses. Clio surely had been behaving strangely of late. So solemn and short-tempered. Yet who could blame her, after what happened with the duke? Did this, then, have something to do with Averton?

Hidden enemies, Artemis had whispered. Calliope foolishly clapped her hands over her ears, but the words were still there. She feared they would never leave again.

Chapter Seventeen

The next day dawned bright and clear, as if in mockery of Calliope's late night. She opened the window of her bed-chamber, leaning out to breathe deeply of the clear, misty air, the cold, clean tinge of earth. The cold breeze lashed at her cheeks, reviving her after the strange dreams of the night. The image, equally dreamlike now, of Clio in the garden.

She scowled as she watched the gardens come to life, workers hurrying out on their morning tasks, the distant bleats of sheep. Had she made a mistake last night, showing Cameron that list? Especially since Clio was now somehow involved. She remembered his unreadable eyes, his non-committal response. And yet he had asked to keep the list, so the names must mean something to him.

She rubbed hard at her itchy eyes, trying to stop her thoughts from spinning so endlessly, trying to erase the vestiges of her dreams. She almost wished she had never seen that list at all, never heard of the Lily Thief or his deeds!

Oh, but then she would never have gotten to know Cameron, a treacherous little voice whispered in her mind. Would never have seen what he was truly like. She would still be caught in her old notions of him. Her old impressions of carelessness and empty drama.

But what was it she thought of him now? What had she seen behind the charming façade that convinced her to ask for his help, to show him that list?

He was a puzzle, and one she didn't have time to decipher this morning. She had to get ready for today's picnic, for more of Herr Mueller's lectures—even when the ancient world was so far from her mind. For once, the here and now seemed far more important. More urgent.

She reached out to close the window, to block the morning wind, but paused as she heard a door below open. Clio again? She leaned back out, watching in surprise as Cameron came into view. After her dreams last night, she could almost believe her thoughts had summoned him.

He seemed so much a part of this wild place, with his dark greatcoat, his hair tumbling free, no hat or cravat to restrain him. She remembered hearing gossip, vague drawing-room whispers that he had run with bandits in the Greek hills. She could believe that now, as he strode across the lawn, his boots scattering the morning dew on the grass. There was something not of this world, the everyday English world, about him. Maybe that was why she trusted him with the list, trusted him to see what it all meant. A Greek bandit would never react as any other man of her acquaintance, men of convention, would.

He *was* different, and that was what had both scared her and drawn her in from the first moment she saw him. Yet what would a man like him see in a woman like her?

"Cameron," she called softly.

He spun around, and saw her there in the window. His expression, one of serious thought, did not alter, but he lifted his hand to wave to her. She gestured at him to stay where he was and shut the window. Catching up her cloak from where she left it after their walk to the falls, she swirled it over her shoulders as she hurried downstairs. No one else was about so early, except for the maids with their firewood and buckets of water, and no one questioned her as she slipped outside into the fresh morning air.

Cameron waited for her on the gravel walkway near the fountain, the same place where Clio had met her mystery man. "You're up early," he said. She could still read nothing in his countenance, in his cognac-coloured eyes, not surprise or pleasure—or irritation that she had interrupted whatever errand he was on.

"So are you," she answered. "I couldn't sleep for thinking about everything." She couldn't tell him about the dream. About his place in it.

"The list," he said. "Yes. It puzzled me, too."

"Have you been able to decipher it yet?"

He shook his head. "It does seem to be a code of some sort. Without the key…"

"A list of some criminal circle?"

"Led by the duke?"

"Well, it *was* found in his statue. Would it surprise you to learn he led some sort of illegal antiquities scheme? That he was up to criminal deeds?"

Cameron laughed ruefully. "Not at all. But, really, why would he? He can gain any piece of art he wants by more straightforward means."

Calliope remembered the glow in the duke's eyes as he gazed at his Daphne. As he stroked her cold marble cheek, comparing her to Clio. "The thrill of the chase, perhaps. The *frisson* from doing something forbidden, when so little is denied a duke."

Cameron smiled at her, that serious, flat look vanishing

like the mist. "Forbidden—like talking to me alone in the garden, before the rest of the house is even awake?"

Calliope laughed. He did have her there, and it was yet another sign of how things had changed between them. The old Calliope would never have done this! "It is hardly on a level with stealing art. But I do suppose I understand a bit better now the attraction of the—unconventional."

"I knew you would be converted eventually," he said, and reached out to touch one long curl of her loose hair. His touch was light, teasing, yet there was something in his gaze that made her breath catch. Her stomach lurched nervously. *Silly*, she told herself. *It's because you haven't had breakfast.* She batted away his fingers and stepped back. "I haven't been 'converted' to the unconventional that thoroughly, sir," she said lightly.

Cameron shrugged, tucking his hands into his pockets as if to prevent them from touching her hair again. "It's only a matter of time, you know, Calliope. Freedom once tasted is addictive."

"Is that what you have found, Cameron?" she asked quietly. "Do you miss freedom?"

He smiled, yet she could see it was not his merry grin. It was a mere shadow. Like her dream. "Am I not free?"

"They say that in Greece you lived with bandits."

"So I did. For a time. They needed money for their causes, you see, and I paid them to take me to ancient sites most people never see. Temples and tombs, far from civilisation."

Calliope could almost see it—broken pillars, hidden gods in faraway caves, dusty, sun-drenched valleys, scrubby olive trees. "That is what I mean. It must be hard to go from that to—this."

"Being an English lord, you mean? We all do what we must. What we're born for. Is that not so, Calliope?"

Do what we must. Yes. For was that not what she always did? What was expected. What was her duty. "Do you never miss Greece? Want to go back?"

"Perhaps one day I will."

There was a noise behind them, a shutter opening, the splash of water pouring down the old abbey wall. The house beginning to stir in earnest.

"I should go in," she said reluctantly. She didn't want to go inside, she wanted to stay here and hear more about Greece. About sunshine and bandits.

"Yes," he said.

"But we do have to talk more about the list," she insisted. "At the picnic."

He nodded, and she spun around and dashed into the house. More servants were on the stairs now, carrying clothes to be pressed for the day, water for washing, breakfast trays. She hurried past them to her own chamber, chased by visions of those dashing bandits.

Cameron watched Calliope run away, watched even after she disappeared into the house, leaving only a whisper of rose perfume in the air.

He had never seen her hair down before. It was beautiful; long black curls spreading over her shoulders, down her back in untamed spirals and whorls. She didn't resemble Athena with that hair, but a wood nymph, running free, laughing with abandon among the primeval trees.

Primeval trees? Blast it all, he *was* in trouble now if he had resorted to such whimsy! Such cheap poetics. Calliope Chase was just a woman, a lady, and yet he was finding she was a woman like no other. A woman who wouldn't leave his thoughts, his fantasies.

New fantasies of walking with her, hand in hand, on a

Greek shore, the turquoise waves lapping at their bare feet. Of kissing her under the hot Mediterranean sun, tasting the salt and light on her lips.

Cameron turned away from the house, striding off down the pathway as if he could walk away just as easily from *her*. From the memory of that night at the Antiquities Society, and the soft press of her body against his in the darkness. She wouldn't be so easily abandoned, though, her pale ghost trailing beside him. *What about the list?* she whispered.

Ah, yes—that list. Those odd names, exactly like silly young men in a secret society would devise. Charlemagne, the Grey Dove, the Purple Hyacinth. It did seem rather like a gambit that would appeal to Averton, with his flair for the dramatic, the archaic. Yet to what purpose? Why write such a thing and then hide it in the Alabaster Goddess?

Cameron considered himself to be rather a straightforward person. Subterfuge was so very time-consuming. The duke surely had money and artwork aplenty. Why indulge in some kind of game of theft, unless it was just for the thrill of it? And what role did Clio Chase play in all of this?

He had to confess he couldn't understand it—yet. But he soon would. He was determined on it.

As the long afternoon advanced, the feast of their picnic put away, Calliope felt the lassitude of the day wash over her. The sun was warm on her head, her stomach happily full, and the sleepless night suddenly too much. She leaned back against the rough bark of a tree trunk in perfect laziness, closing her eyes as she listened to the murmur of the stream, the voices of the others as they strolled by the water. Their laughter rose and fell, an indistinct hum, soothing, familiar. How lovely this was, she thought, how easy, with dreams and worries far away for now. Just to *be* for a few minutes.

"'By the blue and shining lake, where the grasses trail, I hang my purple robes in golden rays of sunlight,'" she heard Cameron say.

She opened her eyes and smiled at him. He lounged at the edge of their picnic blanket, his face turned up to the light, hair falling back from his brow, his beautiful cheekbones. One finger reached out to touch the hem of her skirt, and she kicked at him playfully, not quite hard enough to dislodge him. He merely tightened his clasp, feigning to tug her down next to him.

Laughing, Calliope said, "I thought you were going walking with the others."

He shook his head, eyes still closed. "Not at all. I'm far too full of that excellent lemon tart to even think of moving. Besides, we should enjoy the sun while we have it. The sky will be grey again soon enough."

"Very true." Calliope tipped her head back against the tree, watching, mesmerised, as he stroked the fabric of her hem, smoothing it, caressing. "It's a splendid day. All blue and yellow."

"The ancient Greeks measured colours not as we do, in shades, but in light."

"'Violet-crowned Athens.'"

"Exactly. I never knew how true that was until I saw it. Such a strange luminosity."

Calliope lazily gazed at the others, who sat now by the side of the stream, singing, their shining hair and pastel muslins like flowers. She could believe that about colours and light today. The grey-green of the earth, the silver of the water. It glimmered in the sun, something so alive and vibrant. "Tell me more about Greece," she said, remembering the living statues. "I have studied it my whole life, yet I don't know it at all. Not as you do, not as a living thing. Full of bandits and such."

Cameron laughed. "Greece is *hot*. Dry, dusty. Yet there are bays of rugged coastline, which make the country seem half-land and half-sea. The sky and the sea are so brilliant a blue, sometimes turquoise, sometimes deep and mysterious, like a sapphire. The Greeks are attuned to nature, you know, in a way we aren't. Or at least haven't been since the days of that barrow up there. They people the mountains and woods and streams, the sky, even the salty breezes from the sea."

"Like the Muses in their groves, or Zeus from the peak of Olympus?"

"Just so. The land is truly alive to them."

"And did it come alive for you?"

He didn't answer right away. Instead he sat up, swinging around to stare at the stream, his knees drawn up to his chest. Calliope sensed he didn't see that satiny water, the cluster of their friends. Surely he was far from her, ensnared in hot, dusty Greece.

"One of my mother's favourite places was the island of Delos," he said. "Her father, who was a great scholar, used to take her then when she was a girl, and she would tell me tales of it when I was a child. Great sagas of how Apollo and his twin Artemis were born there, of how, long before the golden age of Athens, the rise of Delphi, Delos held all the great riches of the land in its marble sanctuary. Gold, silver, gems. The necklace of Eriphyle, the tiller of Agamemnon."

Calliope leaned forward, fascinated by this sudden glimpse of Cameron's soul, a solemn essence so often hidden behind his dazzling smile. "Did you go there?"

"Of course. It was not the place of my mother's tales, though. Like you, I grew up on stories of Greece as it was thousands of years ago. Marble pillars, great temples, the birth of freedom. It is not like that now, especially on Delos."

"Perhaps it is best I stay here, then! Preserve my illusions."

Cameron tossed her a grin. "I wondered that, too, when I first saw the dusty reality of modern Greece. And yet on Delos I found something I did not expect. Something—magical."

Calliope crept closer until she sat beside him, slowly, lest she break the spell the sunny day bestowed on them. "Tell me about it."

"You know the *Homeric Ode to Delian Apollo*?"

"A bit. 'How shall I receive the god, the proud one, the arrogant one who stands in the highest place, above all the gods and people of the teeming earth.'"

"Yes. From Delos Apollo became the protector of human reason. He may have ruled from Delphi, but he was born and raised on Delos. Yet it seems such an unpromising place for such youthful gods. Tiny, barely three miles long and one mile wide, barren, with marshes and crags. I first went there in the early morning; it was so grey and misty as the boat drew near. The place had the look of an abandoned quarry, littered with broken stone among the wild barley grass.

"Yet by noon the mist had cleared, the sun was out in full force. And I saw what my mother saw. The stones there are not the honey colour of the Parthenon, Calliope, but such a pure white it is almost silver. They glitter in the light, flashing off the water and marble. Never still. Alive in the hot silence where only lizards live."

Calliope could almost see it all. "Wasn't Apollo a scourge of lizards, among his many other talents?"

Cameron laughed. "So he was. He seems to have made peace with them, though. They dart among his sacred swans, as those stone birds peacefully circle their lost lake."

"The swans don't sound very careful of the island's treasures."

"They have no need to be. Artemis and her army of lionesses take care of that."

"Like our friend at the duke's house? Greek cousins, perhaps?"

"Indeed, I believe she must have been the ancestor of those Delian creatures. They are young, you see, hot for battle. Crouched and ready to spring. Once there were fourteen of them, they say; now there are only five, and one guards the Arsenal in Venice. But though they are fewer they are no less vicious. The swans happily circle their lake, while the lionesses guard."

"Yet they allowed *you* entrance."

"Perhaps they remembered my mother. Artemis was her favourite goddess."

Calliope remembered the Alabaster Goddess, poised with her bow, whispering of enemies. For an instant, she pictured her at the entrance to Delos, fierce and elegant, keeping intruders away from the circling swans sparkling silver-white in the intense sun. "How I would love to go there."

"One day you will, Calliope."

She shook her head. "I'm not fearless like you are. Not full of adventure."

He shot her an unfathomable glance. "No? I would think anyone who was determined to chase down a thief would have to possess a heart full of adventure."

"No. I just want to see justice done." If she even knew any longer what *justice* was.

Cameron just shrugged and reached for the picnic basket, rummaging about until he found the last of the lemon tarts. "I think you might surprise yourself, Calliope Chase."

He held out the tart, the bright yellow cream poised temptingly just beyond her lips. She bit into it, feeling the sharp burst of tart citrus on her tongue, echoing the sun overhead.

How she liked this day, Calliope thought as she swallowed the lemony morsel and smiled at Cameron. She liked the sun and sky, the whisper of the water, the nearness of her dearest friends. She liked the strange, ancient magic of this land. She felt free here, far from the prying eyes of town, the shackles of her own practicality. It seemed a time out of time, a short span where she didn't have to be herself. She could be whoever she wanted.

She could even be someone adventurous. And it was Cameron who made her feel that. Believe it. Because *he* was so free, she could be, too, as long as she was with him.

"What are you thinking?" he asked, reaching up with his thumb to wipe away a trace of lemon on her chin.

Calliope trembled at the brush of his skin, so rough on hers. "I was thinking what a very beautiful day it is."

He grinned at her, and leaned just a tiny bit closer. The dark glow of his eyes said he wanted to kiss her, and, despite the proximity of the others, she wanted him to. More than she had ever wanted anything in her life.

But before their lips could touch, a shadow descended over his face as his glance flashed over her shoulder. Suddenly cold with disappointment, Calliope looked back—and froze.

At the top of the slope that led down to their little sheltered valley was the Duke of Averton, mounted on a large black horse that snorted and pranced in place. With his long cloak and loose, bright hair, his expression intent as he stared down at their party, he reminded Calliope of an unhappy god. Hades, perhaps, breaking up a summer flower-picking party to snatch poor, unsuspecting Persephone.

Calliope turned frantically towards Clio, surely the prospective Persephone. She hadn't seen him, was examining a cluster of water plants with Thalia, laughing. It was surely the first time Calliope had heard her laugh for days, especially after her mysterious late night. Why did the duke have to come ruin things, as always?

Beside her, Cameron rose to his feet, all of his warm lassitude vanished. Calliope closed the basket where the cheese knives were—just in case.

In the end, though, there was no need to lock up weapons. The duke wheeled his horse around and galloped away, leaving only a ray of chalky sunlight in his place. Clio never even saw him.

Calliope sat back on the blanket, suddenly limp with relief. Cameron, though, still stood next to her, stiff and alert. Combative as any creature of Artemis.

"This can't go on," he muttered. "Not like this."

Clio *had* seen the duke. How could she avoid it, when the man insisted on appearing like some black wraith alighting on the hill? She didn't betray her notice, though, just went on talking as if a cloud hadn't just shadowed their lovely day.

Why did he have to plague her so? Why did he always have to appear wherever she happened to be, watching, reminding.

But she knew why. And she intended to be the victor in this particular game. There was simply no other way.

After a few moments, that icy sensation at the back of her neck vanished, leaving only the kiss of the sun, and she knew he was gone. She stood up, stretching her back as she gazed at the now-empty ridge. He wouldn't always be gone so easily, she knew that. And she wouldn't always have a stone statue within reach, either. She had to watch herself, be far more careful than she had ever been before.

Not just careful of the duke. She saw Calliope watching her, eyes narrowed in concern. Just as she had watched ever since the night of the masquerade ball. Not asking, not prying, for surely she knew Clio would never divulge all. Just watching. Had she been watching last night, too?

Clio sighed. How she hated deceiving Calliope, of all people! She loved her sister dearly, despite Calliope's managing tendencies, despite her need to make things *right*, even when that was clearly impossible. But it had to be done. Clio would never endanger Calliope, or any of her family.

She had chosen this path. She was willing to risk its dangers. Her sisters had not. In fact, Calliope was surely one of the very dangers she feared!

But no danger was greater than the Duke of Averton. He was like the hydra. Cut off one of his fearsome heads and another popped up in its place.

Clio waved to Calliope and shot her a bright smile. There was no fighting the hydra today. The sun was too warm, the air too sweet, rich with the scents of crystal water and mossy earth. A rare day of peace and accord. It shouldn't be squandered.

Chapter Eighteen

The village assembly rooms were surely not Almack's, just as Lady Kenleigh had said. But then, Calliope had always found Almack's vastly overrated—indifferent music, abysmal refreshments, and insipid conversation, not to mention arbitrary rules. Order was one thing; senseless silliness another.

This building was the largest in the village, long and low, sturdy local grey stone with high windows shining with welcoming light. She could hear the faint, lively strains of a reel as they alighted from the carriage. Music and laughter, brightly clad figures darting behind the old, wavy glass, beckoning her to join in the fun.

"At least we won't see any dukes here," Clio whispered, taking Calliope's arm as they climbed the shallow stone steps.

"We can always hope, anyway," Calliope answered.

"He does have the disconcerting habit of popping up wherever we are, lurking about behind trees and statues. I doubt he would want to bring such attention to himself by appearing at a village assembly, though." Clio handed her shawl to an attendant, pausing to smooth her upswept hair, the skirts of her apple-green gown. "Don't you think?"

Calliope straightened her own attire, pale blue on white embroidered muslin, and hoped that Clio was correct. It would indeed create a great stir for his Grace to show up here, but Averton never did shrink from attention.

And what of Clio's mysterious midnight visitor? Would *he* be here?

The main room was quite crowded, with the musicians, more enthusiastic than talented according to Thalia, playing away on a raised dais at one end. The dancers twirled and spun in the energetic reel, their feet tapping out a loud, staccato beat on the worn wooden floor. Refreshments were laid out on long tables under the windows, hearty sandwiches and pies, vast bowls of punch—very different from Almack's, indeed.

As they moved slowly through the thick crowd, Calliope carefully examined all the faces. A few of the men were tall, but not as much so as Clio's visitor. They were mostly large, red-faced country squires, as well as one elderly vicar and an extremely young curate.

She couldn't picture any of *them* donning hats and cloaks to go sneaking around at midnight! Nor did Clio react to any of them in any fashion other than distant politeness.

Calliope sighed as she took a seat near one of the windows. She was assuredly not cut out to be a sleuth! There was something below the surface, something just beyond reach, that she was missing.

"So very serious this evening, Miss Chase," Cameron commented lightly, dropping into the chair beside hers. "Do you not enjoy dancing?"

Calliope smiled at him, glad of the distraction from her labyrinthine thoughts. "Of course I enjoy dancing."

"Ah, yes, I remember. Athena was very light on her feet at the masquerade ball."

"And her dance with Hermes was surely the only bright spot of that dismal evening!"

"Well, we mustn't let this event turn sour, too. May I have the honour of the next dance?"

Calliope gazed out at the spinning dancers. They laughed and clapped, full of high spirits. "Perhaps later. Maybe we could walk for a bit? Take a turn about the room?"

"Whatever milady likes."

They made their way around the crowded room slowly, greeting people politely. Cameron leaned close to her as they skirted around the dance floor and murmured, "I think I may have found out something. Can you meet me tonight? In the garden, perhaps, near the ha-ha?"

Meet him? Calliope's stomach gave an excited lurch, and for a second she was actually frightened. Not of Cameron— of her own feelings. She longed to run away, back to her safe old practicality. But then she remembered the water-fall, the Greek bandits, and she knew she could not.

She just had to leap forward.

She only had time to nod as they came to a group of their own friends, Lady Kenleigh and Emmeline, Calliope's father and Lady Rushworth, and fell into conversation with them, an oasis of quiet familiarity. Cameron soon left them to procure glasses of punch, disappearing back into the crowd.

Calliope nibbled at a sandwich, feeling her own spirits rise to meet the lively music, the chatter and colour. How very excited she was—a midnight meeting! She was surely becoming just like the adventurous ladies of Lotty's books.

She laughed as Lady Kenleigh told a story about Emmeline's childhood, how she would play "antiquities hunting" with her brother by digging deep holes in the garden.

"…they were certain they would find a buried city, like Pompeii," she said. "The gardener was quite livid!"

"That sounds like something you and your sisters would have done, Calliope," Sir Walter said. "You were always so very—suggestible."

"I would prefer the word 'imaginative', Father," Calliope protested. "'Suggestible' makes us sound like little automatons. You always taught us to think for ourselves, to apply what we learned."

"And you girls always took that very much to heart!" Sir Walter said, chuckling. "Gave your dear mother fits. D'you remember when Thalia—?"

Sir Walter's tale was interrupted when the assembly room doors opened, as if brushed aside by a giant, invisible hand. Everyone turned to see who arrived so late; even the music seemed to slow. It could only be one person, of course.

"The Duke of Averton," Lady Kenleigh murmured. "Whatever would *he* be doing at a village assembly?"

Lady Rushworth lifted her lorgnette to peer at the new arrival. "And looking so positively restrained. For him, anyway. He always was such a peacock of a man."

"They say he keeps very much to himself at his castle," Emmeline said.

"Yet he deigns to come down among us peasants," Clio murmured. "How curious. Should we all bow and curtsy, do you think? Pretend we are being presented at Court? Too bad I forgot my plumes and train."

Indeed, it seemed that the crowd was quite unsure of what to do with such a personage in their midst. The press of revellers had grown so that there was hardly room to walk through the throng around the dance floor. Someone had opened the windows, but it was still warm and stuffy, heavy with the scents of perfumes and silks, woollens, wilting flowers. The music had grown more raucous, the dancing faster and less organised.

Now, it all seemed to slow, to grow muted and shadowed. The music did not cease—*that* would have been far too dramatic. But the focus of the room shifted, the lively conversation shading into whispers and murmurs.

Calliope turned towards the doorway, edging closer to Clio. The duke *was* looking rather restrained, just as Lady Rushworth said. No satin-lined cloaks or embroidered waistcoats, no leopard skins or chitons. He seemed a bit puritanical, even, in a black superfine coat and stark white cravat, simply tied and skewered with an antique cameo pin. His hair was tied back in an old-fashioned queue, and his face was serious but not haughty as he gazed out over the room.

Calliope glanced at Clio from the corner of her eye, to find that her sister gazed back at the duke with her own air of solemn serenity. The candlelight glinted on her spectacles, hiding her eyes.

Cameron was not yet back with their punch, and Calliope could not see him through the crowd.

"I do believe he's coming this way," Lady Kenleigh said, straightening the gauzy shawl over her shoulders.

Calliope's gaze snapped forward again to see that he really was "coming this way". The crowd parted for him, like an obedient little Red Sea. He nodded at the vicar and various other village worthies, but his progress was steady, his goal unmistakable.

Calliope caught a fold of Clio's green sash in her hand, as if *that* could hold her sister back if she really wanted to bolt or cause a scene. But it helped her feel connected to Clio in some way, anchored to the real world.

Scenes were never Clio's way, though. She watched the duke approach with a polite half-smile on her lips.

"Good evening, Lady Kenleigh. Lady Rushworth, Lady Emmeline. Sir Walter. Miss Chase. Miss Clio," he said, bowing his head to them. The shifting light caught on his brushed-back hair, turning it to burnished gold, like an antique mirror. "It is good to see you all. We have not met since Herr Mueller's talk at the Antiquities Society, I believe."

He was really quite handsome, Calliope thought with some surprise. Too bad he was also so very—strange.

"Good evening, your Grace," Lady Kenleigh replied, ever the gracious hostess even when taken by surprise. "What a pleasant surprise to see you here tonight."

"I am hoping to spend more time at Averton Castle in the future, Lady Kenleigh, so I thought I should get to know my neighbours better. I trust you are enjoying your holiday?" His inquiry was addressed to everyone, but his gaze was on Clio. As they watched each other, Calliope had a vision of two lions circling each other on the Delian shore.

Calliope tightened her grasp on Clio's sash, and said, "Indeed we are, your Grace. The landscape here is most intriguing. We took a walk to the falls a few days ago."

"And did you see the secret grotto?" the duke asked. "There are many fascinating tales of the water spirits who live there."

Water spirits like poor, trapped Daphne? Calliope wondered. Up close, she could see the red scar on his forehead, where his own fleeing Daphne had bashed him.

She also saw something else. The carving on his cameo pin was a tiny scroll. The symbol of Clio, Muse of History.

"Alas, most of us can't swim," Emmeline said brightly, cracking the tense mood. "We can only imagine the glories of the hidden grotto."

"Perhaps that is for the best, Lady Emmeline," the duke said. "It is probably just a cold, rocky cave."

"Or a place of hidden wonders," Clio said softly. "Which some fairy king wants to keep all to himself."

"Then it would be unfortunate for the fairy king that some of us mere mortals *do* know how to swim," the duke answered.

Lady Kenleigh, as if sensing the tension growing back, said quickly, "Have you had much time to explore the local landscape yourself, your Grace? The Roman fort, or some of the ancient barrows?"

"Not as of yet, Lady Kenleigh. I hope to remedy that very soon. And, in the service of getting to know my neighbours, I am having a small dinner party the day after tomorrow. I know it is shockingly short notice, but I hope you will all be able to attend. Your entire party, of course, Lady Kenleigh."

Lady Kenleigh and Lady Rushworth exchanged surprised glances. "Of course, your Grace," Lady Kenleigh said. "We have no fixed engagements. We would be honoured to attend."

"Excellent! I will see you then."

With one last bow, the duke strolled away, vanishing into the crowd.

"My goodness," Lady Kenleigh said weakly. "A dinner invitation to Averton Castle."

"Shall wonders never cease," Lady Rushworth answered. "Come, Sir Walter, I think I need to find some good, strong wine after such a shock to the system." She took his arm and they ambled off, chattering happily about the possible treasures to be seen at the duke's castle, and looking not in the least "shocked".

Clio, though, was rather pale. She tugged her sash free

of Calliope's clasp and snapped open her fan, ruffling her hair with a stiff breeze.

"I wonder if we'll see the Alabaster Goddess," Emmeline said. "They do say she is hidden away somewhere in those medieval passages!"

"It would not be worth going if we *didn't* see her," Clio said. "Along with whatever else he might have locked up in that fortress. Mummies, perhaps? Cursed jewels?"

Emmeline laughed. "Don't say that to Lotty! She will imagine mummies rising up out of their coffins at night and going lurching about in dark corridors, putting curses on all who dared invade their tombs."

"I wouldn't be surprised if they did resort to curses, finding themselves in the clutches of the duke," Clio said. "Ah, look, Emmeline, there is your handsome brother. I do believe I promised him the next dance."

Clio shut her fan and hurried over to Emmeline's brother, taking his arm to usher him into the forming set. Emmeline, too, set off to dance with Mr Smithson, leaving Calliope standing by herself.

Where on earth was Cameron?

Cameron made his slow way through the thick crowd, balancing delicate glasses of punch. The line at the refreshment tables had been quite lengthy, the punch and cakes growing sparse under the increasing demand. At last he claimed his prize and turned back to Calliope and their friends, only to be brought up short by the Duke of Averton.

So that was what the commotion at the door had been. Cameron should have guessed.

The duke stood directly in his path, a sombre statue in black and white. Those flat green eyes gave nothing away—no thoughts or memories, no anger or remorse.

Cameron felt himself go cold in response, an icy chill spreading to his very heart. His fists tightened on the glasses. It was a good thing he held them, solid impediments that prevented him from starting a brawl in the middle of a genteel assembly.

"Averton," he said coldly.

"Westwood," the duke answered quietly. "I am glad to see you here. I never had a chance to thank you."

"Thank me?"

"I was told you were the one who found me in my gallery, who summoned help."

Cameron nodded curtly. "I was."

"I'm grateful. You could have easily left me there."

"Abandoning wounded creatures is not my way."

A small, ironic smile touched the duke's serious expression. "What? The 'Greek god' is not given to careless cruelty?" He touched the side of his slightly crooked nose.

"Unlike some."

"Hmm. Well, whatever your motives, I'm grateful. My blasted carelessness! When I am near my antiquities I don't notice anything else."

"You needn't pretend, Averton. I know what happened. I know you were not alone in that gallery."

The duke's only reaction was a muscle that twitched along his jaw. His gaze shifted to the dance floor, where Clio promenaded with the Kenleighs' son. "Ah, yes. Our beauteous Muse of History, who has a temper to equal her loveliness."

"If you come near her again…" Cameron growled.

"So very protective, Westwood. But then they do say you cherish a *tendre* for the elder Muse. Perhaps you seek to impress her with your threats."

"It is no threat. Merely a warning."

"I remember your 'warnings' very well. In this case, they are quite unwarranted. I wish Miss Clio no harm; quite the contrary. You and I have no need to be enemies."

Averton gave him a nod and walked away. Cameron swallowed his cold anger, burying it deep in that ice, and went on his interrupted way.

No need to be enemies? Au contraire.

"What did the duke say to you?" Calliope asked when he reached her side, taking one of the glasses from him.

"Nothing of any consequence."

"Did he invite you to his dinner party?"

"No. Does the blasted man *have* parties? That seems far too normal a pastime."

"Very true. But you are invited to one. He has asked the whole house party. For some unfathomable reason, it seems he is newly determined to be sociable."

Cameron gave a derisive snort. "I doubt he'd want me in his precious castle."

"Perhaps not, but you have to come anyway. It may be our last chance to see the Alabaster Goddess."

"Or to corner a thief?"

Calliope frowned. "I'm not sure. Could the Lily Thief have followed us from town? Or be one of our own party after all?"

"Your friend Miss Price, perhaps."

"Lotty? She could assuredly think up such a dramatic scheme, but carrying it out would be something entirely different."

"The duke himself, then."

"I would like that. He is already a villain. Why not add one more black mark? But why would he? He has the Alabaster Goddess already."

Cameron shook his head. "I can't help but feel it has everything to do with that list. Why would he have it?"

"And hidden away like that." Calliope sipped at her punch. "Perhaps all will be revealed at the party!"

Chapter Nineteen

"Ouch!" Calliope gasped, as her elbow connected with the wall. Cradling the throbbing arm close to her side, she hurried down the narrow back staircase, holding her breath lest anyone hear her. At last she tumbled out into the midnight air, drawing the hood of her cloak up over her head.

She was glad of the aching elbow, though. It distracted her from her nagging doubts.

"What am I doing here?" she muttered, as she hurried across the garden. Shivering in the wind, running off to meet Cameron, like…

Like Clio and her mysterious night-time visitor.

This was not much like her, throwing caution to the winds, running off to meet a man in secret. But maybe that was the point. She no longer really felt like herself, like sensible Calliope. Not since she came to this place, felt its strange magic. Something new and frightening possessed her, and she just wanted to see him. Be close to him.

And here she was, slipping out of the house all alone. She laughed aloud at the deliciousness of it all! No wonder Thalia was so addicted to wild behaviour. It was wonderful.

But she was early to her rendezvous. Cameron was nowhere to be seen yet, and she was alone with the ancient ghosts. With the pile of old stones that led to those non-existent stairs.

Calliope drifted towards them, as towards an anchor in the wide sea of the night. They were still an oddity, so out of place in the neat bit of garden. She wondered that no one had dismantled them and carried the stones away for a wall or cottage. Perhaps this spot had some mysterious significance and therefore none dared touch it? A curse or spell?

Calliope tiptoed closer, her nervousness about meeting Cameron concealed by sudden curiosity. Yes, the stones *were* different from before. She was sure none had been loose when she and her sisters examined them when they arrived at the Abbey. She cautiously nudged one with the toe of her half-boot, but couldn't shift it.

She glanced back, making sure Cameron wasn't near, before she leaned over the low wall, peering down into what had been only a shallow pit and a couple of steps cut into the dirt. Though it was dark, lit only by the bright silver moon, it didn't seem so shallow now. The shadows extended on and on, like a corridor stretching away into the earth itself. She remembered her dream, a strange new world.

Calliope took a deep breath of the cold, peaty air. What *was* all this? Someone had surely been here since she last saw the stones, someone who had uncovered and opened an old trapdoor. Clio and her visitor? But why?

The gardens of Kenleigh Abbey were an absurdly busy place.

Calliope edged closer, taking a tentative step down into the pit. The dirt was spongey under her feet, but firm enough. She took another step and another, deeper into the shadows, hardly daring even to breathe…

"Well, and there you are, Miss Chase! Running away from our appointment?"

"Ack!" Calliope shrieked, her heart flying into her throat at the sudden sound. She lost her balance, sliding down on her backside and slipping down another step.

Gasping, she stared up to see Cameron staring down at her, outlined and shadowed by the moonlight so that he seemed an apparition. "Blast it, Cameron!" she cried, frightened into cursing. "You scared me."

"I'm sorry, Calliope. I thought you were expecting me," he said, scrambling down to her side. His boots knocked some pebbles loose, sending them skittering down into the abyss. "Are you all right?"

"Everything but my dignity," she muttered. She took his proffered hand and let him lift her to her feet. Their heads barely reached the top of the stairwell, and they were pressed close. Calliope clung to him, sure they balanced alone on the edge of a cold precipice—just like her dream.

"No bruises?" he asked gently.

"Not yet."

"I'm fairly sure I asked you to meet me near the ha-ha, not in a giant's grave," he teased.

"A grave!" she yelped. She hadn't thought of *that*. Could there really be bones under their feet?

"Not literally, I think. Still, these steps must lead somewhere. They do appear to go down a long way."

"That's the odd thing," Calliope said. "When my sisters and I first saw it, there seemed to be only one or two steps. Then just dirt."

He peered up at the opening above their heads. "It must have been blocked up."

"Why open it now? What is it?" *If not a grave.*

"If we knew that, my dear Calliope, I'm sure all our

questions would be answered. But then, sadly, we would have no need for secret meetings!" His hand tightened on hers, and he led her back up into the night air. "We'll have to come back when there is more light."

Calliope held on to his hand, feeling the warm safety of him envelop her until all the ghosts vanished and they were all there was in the darkness. As he drew her closer to him, his hands around her waist, she felt that excitement grow and expand, tingling and irresistible, like life itself.

She didn't want to let it go, ever. She didn't want to lose this fragile, beautiful spell.

She smiled up at him, winding her arms tightly about his neck so he could not fly away from her. His hair, too long, too curling, was like warm satin against her skin, his body so warm and solid and delicious against hers. How she yearned to stay here in his embrace all night—for ever! To kiss him, *feel* him, and forget about thieves and ghosts and families and everything.

"How beautiful you are, Cameron," she whispered.

His eyes widened in surprise, but before he could answer, she went up on tiptoe to kiss him, pressing one swift caress to his lips, then another and another, teasing him until he groaned and pulled her even closer, until there was not even a breath between them. He groaned, deepening the kiss, his tongue seeking hers, and she was lost in him. Of her need to be just this close to him, always, taste him, smell him, draw all he was into her until he was *hers*.

It wasn't like their first kiss, soft and tentative as they learned the taste of each other. It was fast and hungry, filled with the yearnings of their time together, the drive to be close and know that this was real.

Calliope didn't question herself, for once in her life.

She didn't know what all this fury of emotion meant; she only knew she had to be close to him. The muse united with the god.

Cameron drew back slowly, pressing tiny, fleeting kisses to her cheek, her jaw, the sensitive spot behind her ear. She trembled at the warm rush of his breath.

Calliope laughed, shivering, clinging to him as if she would never let go.

"Oh, Calliope," he groaned, resting his forehead against her hair. "We can't go on like this!"

She nodded, pressing her face to the curve of his neck, inhaling deeply the salty, heady scent of his skin. Yes—she saw now. *This* was the true thing she always sought, the eternal beauty. And she knew what she had to do.

She had to let go of her old self entirely, of her old inhibitions and fears. She had to be reborn—with Cameron.

She had to be bold.

"Come with me," she whispered. She clasped his hand in hers, leading him across the darkened garden, beyond the secret stairs. Her steps were shaky, weak with the force of their kiss, with what she was about to do. She could feel his puzzlement, yet he followed her without a word. Trust was one of the things they would have to find together.

She led him into the stand of trees, along a narrow, overgrown pathway until she found a small clearing, a ragged, enclosed circle. In the centre was an old ash pit, pale grey in the moonlight. A magical fairy circle, the perfect spot.

"Calliope…" he began, his voice hoarse.

"Shh." She pressed her fingers to his lips. Words would only shatter the spell. She was done with words, with worry and thought and always being proper. "Just follow me."

She stepped back from him to unfasten her cloak, letting it pool around her feet. As he watched her, his eyes narrowed, she drew down the deep, low neckline of her gown, revealing the curve of her bosom, the line of her pale shoulders. Calliope swallowed past a dry lump in her throat. What if she was doing this wrong? What if she wasn't pretty enough? What if…

No! She shoved away the fear. This was right. This was what she needed to do, to free herself—free *them*.

She pulled the pins from her hair, shaking the black curls free over her bare shoulders.

"You see, Cameron," she said, cursing the girlish tremor in her voice. She was trying to be *seductive!* "Surely I can be Aphrodite as well as Athena." She reached out and took his hand, urging him closer.

"Calliope!" he moaned. She felt his muscles tense, re-sisting her. "What are you thinking?"

"Please, Cameron." She shook her head, her hair spilling down her back so he could see her breasts in the moonlight. If only they were bigger! "It has to be here, now, in this place." She pressed against him, kissing his cheek, his neck, his jawline. His breath sucked in on a hiss. *Ah-ha!* She was getting somewhere.

"I want you, Cam," she whispered. "Don't you want me?"

"Of course I do, my beautiful Calliope. But…" His words were swallowed in her kiss, her lips soft and open on his, not to be denied. With a deep moan, he gave in, his touch seeking the bare skin of her shoulders.

It was as if Aphrodite *did* take over her soul, Calliope thought as she boldly untied his cravat, dropping it to the ground at their feet. The goddess guided her hands as she pushed his shirt away from his muscled chest, her mouth as she kissed the damp hollow of his throat, the curve of his shoulder. How smooth his skin was, hot under her caress. The feverish warmth seeped into her own soul, and she knew only him.

This *was* right.

Twined together, they fell to her cloak, the trees whirling dizzily over her head. Calliope landed on top, tossing away his shirt. He was exquisite, she thought in breathless awe. More glorious than any ancient statue, for he was alive, his skin glowing, vibrant with breath and desire and strength. Her trembling touch traced the light, coarse hair of his chest, the thin line that led tantalisingly to the band of his breeches. His stomach muscles tightened, his breath uneven as her touch brushed the tight press of fabric just below that line.

"Calliope," he gasped. "Be careful. If you are not sure…"

"I am Aphrodite, remember? I wouldn't be here if I was not sure." Exhilarated, bold, scared, she awkwardly opened his breeches and tugged them down over his lean hips. "Oh!" she whispered.

Cameron went very still, lying back on the cloak as he watched her warily.

"It is not very much like a herm, is it?" she said musingly. Those ancient talismans, tall, straight pillars with a startlingly large organ below, had thus far been her only experience of the male private parts. The reality was ever so much better. "Can I touch it?"

Cameron laughed roughly. "Only if you want all this to be over before it begins. Come here, my Aphrodite, and kiss me again before I go utterly insane."

Calliope fell happily back into his arms, their lips meeting, heartbeats melding. There was nothing at all careful about this kiss, it was all sun-hot desperation, urgent need that burst free like fireworks into the night sky.

Calliope felt the slide of his hands on her back as he released the last tapes of her gown. The breeze was cold on her skin, but she was hardly aware of it. Clothes were only a prison now, a barrier between her and the touch of his own bare flesh. She shrugged her gown away, rising above him as a naked goddess.

"Calliope," he groaned, his hands on her hips, holding her still for his starving gaze. "You are truly glorious."

"Not as glorious as you," she whispered. "My beautiful Greek god."

Still holding her tightly, he rolled her beneath him, on to the softest part of the cloak. Calliope laughed as her hair spilled all around them. She did feel glorious as he looked at her, felt free at last, as she knew she would! The past was gone. There was only now, this one moment, where she was one with the man she loved. He kissed her, and all thought vanished into sheer, undiluted sensation.

She closed her eyes, revelling in his caress, the press of his mouth on her breast, the curve of her ribs. Her palms slid over his back, so strong and young, so alive under her touch. Her legs parted as she felt his weight lower between them, the press of that hot, heavy organ she marvelled at.

She knew what would happen; she and Clio had once secretly peeked at some of her father's ancient sketches of Dionysian rituals and Pompeii bawdy houses. But those images never hinted at how it *felt*. Of the heady, dizzy sensation of falling, falling, lost in another person. Another world entirely.

"I don't want to hurt you," he gasped.

Calliope smiled, feeling the press of the tip of his penis against her, the way her whole body ached for that final union that meant he was hers. "You never could."

She spread her legs wider, invitingly, and he drove inside her. It *did* hurt; how could it not? A burning pain, but it was nothing to the way he filled her, joined with her at last. She arched her back against the pain, wrapping her arms and legs around him so tightly he could never escape her.

"You see? You didn't hurt me," she whispered. "I feel completely perfect."

Cameron laughed tightly. "Not half as 'perfect' as I do. My beautiful, wonderful Calliope."

Slowly, so slowly, he moved again within her, drawing back, lunging forward, just a little deeper, a little more intimate every time. Calliope squeezed her eyes closed, feeling the ache ebb away until there was only the pleasure. A tingling delight that grew and expanded inside, spreading through her arms and legs, her fingertips, out the top of her head like flames. Pleasure unlike any she had ever known or imagined.

She cried out at the wonder of it all, at the bursts of light behind her closed eyes, blue and white and red, like spinning Catherine wheels. The heat and pressure were too much, too much! How could she survive it without being burned up, consumed?

Above her, around her, she felt Cameron tense, his back arch. "Calliope!" he shouted out.

And she exploded, consumed by those lights. She clung to him, falling down into the fire.

After long moments—hours or days?—Calliope slowly opened her eyes, sure she had tumbled into a volcano. But it was the same forest clearing, the looming trees and pale moonlight of everyday life.

A life with a new sparkle.

Beside her, collapsed on to the cloak, his arms tight

around her waist, was Cameron. His eyes were tightly closed, his limbs sprawled out in exhaustion.

Calliope smiled, feeling herself ever so slowly floating back to earth. She felt the crackle of twigs and leaves beneath the fabric, the press of a stone against her hip. The soreness of her limbs, of her most secret places. It didn't matter, though. Nothing mattered but this time out of time. She had become Aphrodite, at least for a moment. Or perhaps she had just become truly herself.

Calliope half-drowsed, warm where her skin pressed to Cameron's, the night breeze playing over her body until she shivered. She felt sore and tired—and lighter than she had ever been before! Surely she could soar right up into the trees.

Cameron's arm was heavy over her waist, and she curled herself tighter into the haven of his body, feeling his breath on her shoulder, the uncoiled strength of his muscles under her touch as she lightly ran her fingertips to his elbow and down again to his wrist.

"Oh, Calliope," he murmured into her hair. "I can't pretend to understand you. But I do know one thing."

Calliope smiled. "And what might that be?"

"That you are truly magnificent."

She laughed, and rolled over to face him. The moonlight outlined his beautiful features, casting sharp angles, mysterious shadows across his eyes and brow. She traced his face carefully, all those commonplace things—nose, lips, cheekbones—that made up the wonderful thing he was. Cameron.

"I would have thought you would call me *bossy*," she said. "And managing…"

"Those things, too," he teased. He caught her hand in his, pressing her fingers to his lips, one after another.

Calliope trembled. "My darling, managing Athena. What made you what you are?"

"I wondered the same thing about you," she said. "You are so unlike anyone else I know. Have ever known."

He laid back on their cloak, his arms stretched under his head as Calliope sat up, gazing down at him. His expression was blank. "Me? I am the simplest of creatures, as easy to read as a book."

Calliope snorted. "A book in Latin, mayhap. I seldom understand you at all."

Cameron laughed, reaching out to catch her around the waist and drew her close again. "You surely understood me very well tonight!"

"Don't tease." Calliope slapped him lightly on the shoulder. "I want to understand your *mind,* too."

"Perhaps I just seem a puzzle because I did not grow up here, as your other suitors did. I often don't feel *English* at all."

Fascinated by this glimpse of his past, Calliope rested her head on his shoulder. "Do you feel Greek, then?"

"Not that, either. Perhaps I don't really belong anywhere."

A cold sadness touched Calliope's heart. As vexing as her family could be, as maddening as their squabbles and disorderly ways were, she did know she belonged with them. That they were a part of her, whether she liked it or not. "What was your childhood like, Cameron?"

He shrugged, and she felt the smooth ripple of his muscles beneath her. His fingers moved gently in her hair. "Perfectly ordinary, I would have said. I knew nothing else. I thought everyone spent their lives moving from Florence to Naples, Lake Geneva to Rome to Vienna. I loved seeing new places, learning new ways of life."

New ways of life. And Calliope had only ever known

one. "Why did your parents choose such a nomadic existence? Your father's studies?"

"That, of course. He was always in search of new *objets*, new curiosities. Just as so many of our friends do. But also…"

"Also what?"

"My mother was not truly—comfortable in England."

Calliope realised she knew little about the late Lady Westwood, except that she had been Greek. And, from the one or two times Calliope had glimpsed her, very beautiful, with the same sculpted features and cognac-coloured eyes as her son. "She was homesick?"

"Probably. And she had a natural melancholy, too. She never showed that to me, of course. With me, she was always cheerful and smiling, always telling me tales of her own childhood or one of the Greek gods. Artemis was her favourite. But even as a child I could see the sadness in her eyes. The loneliness of having left her home for a place where she could never be fully accepted."

"But she was a countess!" Calliope cried, aching for the unhappiness of a woman she had never known.

"A countess who was the daughter of a Greek scholar. Oh, she was invited places, of course, and a few people— like your parents—were her friends. Yet I think she always missed the warmth of her homeland, the spirit of her own people. She especially missed the island of Delos, the birthplace of Artemis and Apollo, where her father often took her in his studies."

"Was she happy when your father took her to the Continent?"

"Happier, I think. It was sunnier there, the people more open. She never went back to Greece, though. She died in Naples when I was still very young, and I was sent back to England to school."

"So, you went to Greece for her."

Cameron laughed. "I suppose I did, though I never thought of it like that! I wanted to see if her tales were true."

"And were they?"

"Oh, yes. True—and more. It was her finest gift to me."

Calliope gazed up at him, at the wistful glint in his eyes. "She gave you your freedom."

"My freedom?"

"It's what I've always admired, and envied, in you. The way you care for no one's opinion—the way you follow your own path in life."

"It's not true that I care for no one's opinion, Calliope. I cannot really be a part of a society that treated my mother unkindly, so I do care little for their rules and strictures. But I very much care what some people think of me, like the Saunders. Like you."

"Me?"

"Especially you. Your disapproval has cut me to the quick in the past, Athena."

Calliope gave a startled laugh. "I would never have imagined my opinions would be taken in such a way! And anyway, I feel so very different now."

"You envy freedom? Care-for-nothingness?"

"Sometimes."

"And here I have always envied your family."

"My family? My wild, quarrelsome family?"

"Of course. The way you and your sisters are bonded so tightly together that no one could ever separate you. That is so alluring, you see, to someone with no family at all."

"I do love them very much. I could never do without them. But sometimes I just want…"

"What is it you want, Calliope?"

She propped herself up on her elbow, swallowing hard. Could she say it? Tell him? She had never spoken of it before, even to Clio. His face was so open as he gazed up at her.

"When my mother was dying," she said slowly, "I sat beside her and held her hand as the fever raged. And she made me promise to always take care of my father and sisters. She said I had always been so careful of them, so responsible, she could die in peace knowing that they were safe in my hands. That I would always see to their welfare. That I would be their new mother."

Cameron took her hand in his, twining his fingers with hers. "Such delicate hands for such a great task."

Calliope tried to shrug it away, as she always had. She was a dutiful daughter, or she tried to be. But how could she convey the heavy feeling that came over her then, like a loop of chains, binding her for ever? "I was the eldest, and I always did feel responsible for my sisters anyway. Ever since Clio was born."

Cameron wouldn't let her dismiss those chains so easily, though. His clasp tightened over her hand. "My dear, managing Athena. Of course you care about your family, you want them to be well and happy. But it doesn't have to be a burden only for your shoulders."

"What do you mean?"

"I mean—I have too much freedom, and you have too many charges. We should share what we have."

Calliope sat up straight, staring down at him in wary surprise. Did he mean… "What are you saying?"

He drew her down on to his chest, stroking the tangled length of her hair as one would soothe a startled bird. "We work well together, do we not?"

Calliope sucked in a shaky breath. "We argue. All the time."

"Not *all* the time. We didn't quarrel for, oh, at least two hours tonight, did we not?"

She had to laugh. "Our mouths were too busy."

"Ah, you see! You made a joke. You must feel freer already." He cradled her closer, as if he would not let her go. "Just rest now. We have a few hours until daybreak."

And a few hours to change her very life....

Chapter Twenty

"Since the ladies have gone into the village to do some shopping, I thought you gentlemen might like to peruse these," Lord Kenleigh said, unlocking a hidden safe in his library and drawing forth a silk-bound album. "Lady Kenleigh doesn't know I have them, of course. I bought them in Italy years ago, when I was on the Grand Tour."

Cameron was only half-attending to Lord Kenleigh and his album, predictably filled with erotic etchings of various goddesses and mythological figures. His mind kept turning on the night before, and Calliope and their burst of irresistible passion.

He was truly bewitched by her fathomless dark eyes. How else to explain why he got involved in her harebrained scheme to somehow find the Lily Thief? Anyone clever enough to snatch that diadem would easily elude their fumbling detective work. And Cameron could rather see the thief's point—Averton, Lady Tenbray and their ilk were hardly responsible stewards of ancient culture.

But he had come to see Calliope's view, too. Theft, no matter the artistic motives, was not a solution. This was not

Greece, where banditry ruled. Theft was quickly and sternly dealt with in England. And Cameron was beginning to fear that the thief was closer than Calliope thought. Perhaps even one of the members of her beloved Ladies Society.

He never wanted to see Calliope hurt, never wanted to see those beautiful eyes clouded with pain, that wonderful confidence falter. Especially after last night. Nothing was the same now.

"Ah, now, this one is delightful," Herr Mueller said. Cameron glanced up to see that the professor had abandoned the naughty etchings of Leda and the swan, Danae and the shower of gold, to examine the more conventional paintings displayed on the walls.

Cameron strolled over to peer closer at the canvas. It was "Cupid Blindfolding Youth", a tiny pink-and-white cherub laughing and tying a scarf over the eyes of a young woman. Glossy dark curls draped over her bare shoulders as her white silk gown slipped off, and she, too, was laughing, one hand outstretched as if reaching for the viewer.

She looked like Calliope, in those rare moments when she forgot herself in merriness. The curve of her lips, the faint rosy flush on her cheeks.

"Delightful, indeed," Cameron said.

"This one, too, is very fine," Herr Mueller said, pointing out a scene of Socrates lecturing to his followers in the marketplace. Unlike Calliope-Youth, it invoked no emotions in Cameron, but he had to admit that the details were beautifully wrought, the fallen ruins of Greece brought back to vivid life.

"Yes, the columns here and here, the steps Socrates sits on, the colours," Herr Mueller said. "It evokes what we love about the classical world, *ja*? Order and symmetry."

Cameron smiled. "Some would claim 'order and symmetry' are cold."

"But you and I know that is not true, Lord Westwood! The Greek forms can be rigorous and mathematical, yet also full of life."

Cameron looked back at the raven-haired Youth. "A harmony between passion and order?"

"Exactly so, Lord Westwood. They say you have travelled in Greece?"

"I have. My mother was Greek, I was raised on tales of the gods and goddesses who lived under its hot sky and sun."

"Then you must understand this dichotomy between rationality and emotion better than most Englishmen. And far better than us Germans! I have studied the order all my life. I cannot seem to grasp the passion. Perhaps I ought to travel to Greece myself, *ja*?"

"I would definitely recommend it," Cameron said. "I never really understood the stories myself, until I stood on the land where they originated."

In truth, he had never fully understood until he met Calliope. Never saw how cool order and hot passion could unite so perfectly.

"Then I will go. Just like all your English poets! How they flock across the Mediterranean. Ah, and here is a painting of the Muses at Helicon!" Herr Mueller pointed out a large scene of the nine Muses, gathered around their sacred spring with their various symbols and accoutrements. "Just like the young *fräuleins*, the Chases."

Cameron's gaze went to the figure in the middle, set slightly higher than the others. Calliope, eldest of the Muses, patron of epic poetry, holding her writing tablet. Unlike the real Calliope, she had golden blonde hair, but her expression was much the same. Steady and serious as she peered out at the viewer.

"Perhaps not *exactly* like the Misses Chase," he said.

"Ah, no! For you see, this Clio does not have the red hair. And this Thalia is, how do you say, not so *exuberant*."

Cameron glanced at the Thalia, her face half-hidden by the mask of comedy she held up. Beside her sat Clio, light brown hair braided into a neat coronet. She held a scroll and a pile of books. Beside her sandalled foot, springing from the dark green grass, was a single purple hyacinth.

"The artist has made fine use of symbolism," Herr Mueller said, gesturing to the flower.

"Indeed. For Clio was the mother of Hyacinth..." Cameron's voice trailed away as he remembered that blasted list. *The Grey Dove, the Golden Falcon, the Purple Hyacinth...*

The Purple Hyacinth. It couldn't be. And yet—it made a strange sense.

"...and here we see the Oracle at Delphi," Herr Mueller said, having moved on to the next painting as Cameron still stared at Clio and her purple flower. Her painted gaze seemed direct, mocking, as if she dared him to say it aloud. "Surely you have been to Delphi, Lord Westwood?"

Cameron shook away the cold sensation of surprise, or dawning realisation. Of the knowledge that he had been very, very foolish. There was no time for that now. He could hardly just run off and accuse her, the sister of the woman he loved! He wasn't even fully certain. He had little to go on besides a flower and his gut instincts. He had to move softly, carefully.

And how, blast it all, *how* was he to tell Calliope?

"Yes," he said, turning his back to the Muses. "Though Delphi is just a dusty little village called Kastri now. There is nothing of the Pythia to be found there, just some broken columns and overgrown thistle."

"Very sad. None the less, it must be exhilarating to stand exactly where such great prophecies arose!"

Cameron continued his conversation with Herr Mueller, examining the paintings, the artefacts displayed in Lord Kenleigh's glass cases. He must have made a credible job of it, too, for Herr Mueller seemed to find nothing amiss. But his thoughts were focused on that one little flower.

Calliope sat back on the carriage seat, peering out at the road as they bounced along on their way back to the Abbey. Thalia and Emmeline chatted happily about the new bonnets they had bought in the village, while Lotty buried herself in a volume acquired from the small bookshop, occasionally exclaiming over an especially dramatic passage. Only Calliope and Clio, seated next to each other, were quiet.

Calliope could not fathom her sister's thoughts, but she herself remembered only the night before. Her body joined with Cameron's, their kisses and moans in the darkness, the humid blurriness when they lost themselves completely. The confidences she had never shared with anyone

He was—well, he was wonderful. But what would happen now?

Calliope slumped back on the seat, having thoroughly confused herself. She had surely got no closer to answers of any sort since coming to Yorkshire! Not about the Lily Thief, about Cameron. About herself.

They turned down a different lane and the duke's castle came into view, pale grey and hulking against the blue sky. The first time Calliope saw it, she had thought it needed only pennants to make the picture complete, fabric snapping in the wind to welcome warriors to the joust. Those pennants were there today, bright rectangles of green, white and gold.

"Do you think it's meant to be a new Camelot, Cal?" Clio said.

Calliope turned to find her sister's gaze on the castle, opaque behind her spectacles. "Perhaps it's to welcome us to his party. A theme gathering."

"Medieval days? I must find my wimple and surcoat, then, and hope torture is not among the scheduled festivities."

"Hmm, yes. Shall he toss us in the dungeon, do you think?"

Clio smiled wryly. "*You* needn't fear such a fate, Cal. Lord Westwood would surely ride up on his white charger and rescue you from the beast."

Calliope took her sister's hand. "You needn't fear the duke, either, Clio. You needn't even go to the party at all! I don't understand why he invited us. I thought he came to his fortress to shut himself and the Alabaster Goddess away from the world."

Clio squeezed her hand. "I don't understand, either, yet I somehow feel I must go."

"To protect the goddess?"

"Yes, to protect the goddess. And…"

"And what?"

Clio shrugged. "What else is there?"

Chapter Twenty-One

❧❧❧❧❧❧

Camelot, indeed, Calliope thought the next night, as their carriage turned through ornate iron gates and rolled up a steep incline towards the duke's castle. If it hadn't actually been built in the Middle Ages, it was a superb imitation, an impenetrable keep set atop a craggy hill, surrounded by a now-dry moat. The narrow windows were ablaze with light, a vivid glow that softened the harsh edges of the stonework. Those pennants snapped from the corner towers. Calliope half expected armoured knights to come galloping out to meet them as they entered the inner courtyard.

It was an austere, gravelled square of a space, with walls looming high all around, but torches flared in a straight line leading to the doors. An old well in the centre bubbled away, transformed into a modern fountain.

"I told you I should have worn my wimple," Clio said.

Calliope laughed. Even without a wimple, Clio had a vaguely antique look about her tonight, in a dark amber-coloured gown with long, draped sleeves and a wide sash embroidered with dragons and flowers. And her eyes seemed clear for the first time in days, her laughter unforced.

Calliope had her doubts about coming here tonight. Look what happened the last time they accepted an invitation from the duke! Strangely, though, it seemed to have done Clio some good.

"You would have ruined your coiffure with a wimple," she said, alighting from the carriage.

"Perhaps I would have felt less out of place." Clio stepped down beside Calliope, straightening her spectacles on her nose. "One almost expects William the Conqueror to come riding in. Do you think we will be served roast boar, to be eaten with our fingers?"

"Nothing so amusing as that, I fear," Thalia said, joining them as they went up the steps and through the open doors. "Just more lectures from Herr Mueller."

"Oh, I doubt his Grace will allow himself to be upstaged in his own house, especially by a mere scholar," Clio said. "But I don't think you need to be worried about being bored, Thalia."

"If I am, I'll just go and search for dungeons and secret passages," Thalia answered airily. "There are bound to be some. How else could one escape the siege?"

"How else, indeed?" Clio murmured. They followed the rest of the party out of the tiny, cold foyer into the drawing room.

If it could be called a "drawing room", Calliope thought. "Solar" was more like it. A long, rectangular space with fireplaces at each end, massive enough to roast oxen for the feast. Their great, crackling flames banished every bit of chill even from this room made of stone—stone floor, stone walls soaring up to timber rafters. The furnishings, too, seemed ancient, large, dark pieces carved with forest scenes and gargoyle faces. The chairs were strewn with gold velvet cushions; tapestries of knights and their ladies hung on the rough walls.

"His Grace will be with you shortly," the footman announced. Then he left them, closing the door behind him as if to shut them all up in this medieval prison. Laughter and conversation burst out as soon as the portal closed, exclamations over the house, over this chair or that painting.

"They do say Averton is a great eccentric, even worse than his grandfather. And they called *him* The Mad Duke!" Lady Kenleigh said, seating herself by one of the fires. "I certainly do believe it. Did you see his house in town? A veritable warehouse…"

Calliope watched as Thalia found an old set of virginals in the corner, and Clio wandered off to examine a tapestry. Her father was conversing with Lady Rushworth. Assured that her family was fully occupied, she looked around for Cameron.

They had not been able to talk alone since their tryst in the woods. It was probably just as well, since her cheeks turned hot every time she remembered how boldly she had lured him into lovemaking! Could she talk about such serious matters as thieves and codes without grabbing him, kissing him?

Yet she always seemed to know where he was in every room. Always sensed when he was near. Things just always seemed brighter when he walked in. As if he brought the Greek sun wherever he went.

Now he stood by a glass case near the other fireplace, far down the vast chamber, studying a cluster of Greek vases. With one more glance to be sure her family and friends were all busy, Calliope slipped to his side.

He didn't look at her, but he also seemed to know when

she was near. A smile touched the corner of his lips as the fringe of her shawl brushed his hand.

"Extraordinary, are they not?" he said, gesturing to the vases.

Calliope stared at them. They were a surprisingly small collection for a man as rapacious as the duke. No doubt the rest were stored elsewhere, and these were just the choice bits. And "choice" they were, glossy and perfect. She recognised a red-figure piece by the Andokides Painter, coppery red against velvety black. And an amphora depicting a party scene, drunken dancers turning and twisting in a way that suggested extraordinary mobility.

Calliope leaned closer to see an inscription in Greek, etched near the bottom of the amphora. "'Euphronios never did anything like it,'" she read aloud. "These pieces are incredible. They look like new! Wherever did the duke find them?"

"Straight from the ground in Greece, or maybe Italy," Cameron said tightly. "They must have been buried for centuries in their original homes to be in such condition."

Standing close to him, Calliope could feel the coiled tension of his muscles, the curl of his fists. She knew his body well now. That anger was there again, the white-hot glow she sensed when they saw the duke's gallery in London. When he spoke of the women Averton had taken cruel advantage of in his youth. She didn't think a fight here, tonight, would do any good. Not when they were so close to their goal of finding the thief, and yet still so far away! She laughed and tugged at his arm, turning him towards another krater.

"This one puts me in mind of you and the duke," she said teasingly. It was a scene of two men, Herakles and Antaios, wrestling, while two goddesses on either side watched dispassionately. The delineation of the musculature was extraordinary, two straining, powerful men locked in mortal combat. It was obvious Antaios was losing. His face was white with the pallor of impending death.

Hmm, Calliope thought. Perhaps this particular vase was not such a fine distraction after all.

Cameron did laugh, though. "Ah, Calliope," he said quietly. "If only."

"I hope you don't decide to recreate this scene tonight. This is meant to be a party, you know."

"A party with no host, it would seem."

"The duke does seem to enjoy being fashionably late, even to his own events," Calliope said. "I can't help but feel this is not just a simple dinner party, though."

"Not just a newfound sociability on his part? I fear you are probably right."

Calliope turned away from the vases, from white-faced Antaios, to look at a tapestry, a faded scene of a medieval harvest. The castle in the background was much like this one. "Have you thought more about the list?" she asked.

A shadow seemed to pass over his face, erasing that smile. He still examined the krater, not looking at her. "I have. In fact, Calliope, I may have discovered something."

"You have?" Calliope cried in fresh excitement. *At last!* "How clever you are. I can't decipher it at all, no matter how long I look at it."

"It was hardly cleverness. Just sheer luck."

"What is it? What did you discover?"

Cameron glanced over his shoulder at the group crowded around the fireplace, far from them. They were all there now, except Clio, who stood on tiptoe to peer out of one of the narrow windows, as if she would fly away. "We can't talk here."

"But they are so far away, surely they can't hear," Calliope began. Her protests faded as he shot her a sharp look. His smiles, his light humour, were all quite gone. He was as hard and unemotional as one of the duke's statues. Whatever he had found must be terribly serious, then.

Did she really, truly want to know?

Suddenly, Calliope realised that this search for the thief had, up until now, been something of a game. Oh, not the antiquities part—that she cared about deeply. But the thief himself had somehow been abstract, a symbol for the evils of illegal artwork being shuffled about, not cared for, not studied. It wasn't real people. Now it was, all too much.

But she had come too far to give up, no matter what.

"Do you know who it is?" she whispered.

"I might. Or at least know what is part of it all," he answered. "We can talk later. For now, I think we should join the others to wait for our host."

"Yes, of course," Calliope said, her stomach queasy.

"And, Calliope, I think you should keep a close eye on your Ladies Society tonight. Just to be sure."

"My friends?" Her stomach gave another sick lurch, and she pressed her hands tight to the pain. "Are they in some danger?"

"Please, Calliope, just stay near them."

Cameron walked away towards the fireplace. Calliope took one halting step after him, determined to make him tell her what he knew. Discretion to blazes, if her friends and sisters were in danger!

She halted suddenly as she felt a cool burst of air against her ankle. The rest of the room was so warm, so muffled; she couldn't believe a draught would dare invade the duke's domain. But a small breeze stirred the hem of her white muslin gown, and it seemed to come from beneath the tapestry.

Calliope turned back the edge of the cloth, just enough to see a small crack where a door was hidden. The breeze came from just below, where the door would end, leaving a half-inch gap. A secret entrance to the outside, then? How was that possible?

She remembered the earthen steps at the Abbey. This place was more crowded with hidden portals than any of Lotty's novels!

She reached out cautiously, touching the crack with her gloved fingertips. The wood fit very tightly with the wall, painted grey to match the stone, but she could feel the metallic bump of a hinge.

The drawing-room door—the legitimate one—opened, and Calliope jumped back, letting the tapestry fall back into place. Their host appeared at last, no Dionysus or Celtic king tonight, but a stylish gentleman in dark burgundy superfine, his hair tied back. His gaze, green as sea glass, was as penetrating as ever, though, sweeping over his gathered guests. Calliope folded her hands together tightly to still their trembling, feeling like a child caught pilfering sweets.

"Good evening, everyone," Averton said. "Forgive my lack of punctuality, there was business that could not wait."

"Not at all, your Grace," Lady Kenleigh answered. "We were just admiring your very unusual arrangements."

"Ah, yes, my medieval castle." The duke strolled into the room to stand beside the fireplace, resting one hand on the massive mantelpiece. The rings he wore, emeralds and rubies, gleamed in the flames. "A weakness, I fear, stemming from the King Arthur tales I relished as a boy. The round table, the tournaments, the holy quests…"

"The code of chivalry?" Clio said. "Knights paying gentle court to their ladies fair?"

The duke turned towards her, his face expressionless. Calliope edged closer, mindful of Cameron's request that she stay close to her friends. Averton just smiled. "You have been reading *The Romance of the Rose* in addition to Plato, Miss Chase?"

"I am not a medieval scholar," Clio said. "But surely every lady must know the benefits—and the drawbacks—of being the object of chivalrous intentions."

"Is *The Romance of the Rose* like *Lady Edwina's Destiny*?" Lotty interrupted. "There is this curse, you see, and it can only be broken by true love's gift. A magical rose, of course…"

"Miss Price is a true romantic," Clio said, giving Lotty a gentle smile.

"How fortunate you are, then, Miss Price," the duke said. "Most of us no longer have that luxury, and must balance the romance of Arthur with the pragmatism of Charlemagne." *Charlemagne.*

A bell rang in the distance, cutting through the tension that hung in the firelit air. "Dinner is ready. Lady Kenleigh, may I escort you into the dining room? I fear I go against the convention with no hostess tonight, but my cook has been hard at work all day preparing a fine repast. I seldom entertain, you see, and the servants feel their talents go to waste."

Calliope looked about for Cameron, only to find that he had quite vanished in the crowd.

They were not served boar to be eaten by hand, of course, but a sumptuous feast that would put any London house to shame. Vol-au-vents, mackeral *à la* Stewart, duck and chicken pie, stewed vegetables, raspberry Charlotte. All of it perfectly prepared and delicious.

The conversation naturally turned on the duke's collections, descriptions of his favourite pieces, questions from Herr Mueller, everyone's travel narratives.

Calliope listened to it with half an ear, nibbling at the delicacies on her plate as she watched Clio, seated across the table from Calliope and fortunately far from the duke. Clio's face showed no reaction as she listened to tales of statues rescued from crumbling temples, fished out of the sea. Calliope noticed, though, that Clio ate little and seemed to imbibe more wine than usual.

Cameron, too, behaved oddly, slipping into the dining room as the soup was being served. He shot Calliope a quick smile, but was quiet. Most unusual indeed.

Calliope sipped at her own wine, wondering if she had tumbled into another dream. A strange blend of ancient, medieval, and modern where familiar faces were suspect and she suddenly understood nothing at all. The names on that list could surely apply to all of them, for they were not themselves any more. They were falcons, flowers, doves. Cicero. Charlemagne.

Calliope finally set her wineglass back down on the table. She had surely had enough! The conversation, the laughter, was like a clamour in her ears, the delicious food tasteless. She longed to jump up from her velvet chair and run away! To run all the way home to London and pull the bedclothes up over her head. To turn the clock back before she ever heard of the Lily Thief. Ever made love with Cameron.

But that could never be. The Calliope of that time was gone, everything was different. Her family, her feelings for Cameron, her whole way of seeing the world. She couldn't go back. Did she even want to? No.

She looked down the table towards Cameron, who was chatting with Lotty as if he hadn't a care in the world. How beautiful he was, her reckless Greek god. How she longed for him, despite how easily he could shatter her world.

He was loathe to tell her whatever it was he had found, because he didn't seem to want to hurt her. She knew him quite well now, knew his real kindness and compassion, and she could see it in his eyes. She loved that, but feared it, too. If the duke was the Lily Thief, or some stranger, or someone like Mr Smithson or Freddie Mountbank, it would not hurt her. So, it must mean it was not one of them. It must mean...

"...do you not agree, Miss Chase?" Herr Mueller suddenly said.

Calliope glanced towards him, startled. Which Miss Chase did he mean? Hopefully not her, as she had not been attending the conversation at all! But he watched her expectantly. "Oh, yes, quite," she said, hoping she had not agreed to something idiotic.

"There you see, your Grace, the word of a Muse," Herr Mueller said.

The duke smiled. His sea-glass gaze went to Clio, who was busily cutting a piece of lamb into ridiculously tiny bites. "Muses are notoriously fickle, Herr Mueller, as you must know. They withdraw their favour in an instant, heartlessly leaving a man bereft."

"Not *my* Muses," Sir Walter said stoutly. "Perfect ladies, just like their mother."

"Certainly, Sir Walter," the duke answered. "I meant no disrespect to your daughters. They are a credit to their upbringing."

"Lady Chase and I certainly shared similar views on the education of daughters," Lady Kenleigh said. "When my Emmeline was a child..."

* * *

The rest of the meal passed in talk of education, of exposing children at a very young age to the glories of art and history. Calliope's reverie was not disturbed again until the ladies returned to the drawing room, leaving the men to their brandy and tales of ancient battles. Clio excused herself to retrieve her shawl from the footman.

"What a charming man the duke is," Lady Kenleigh commented, as she settled again by the fireplace. A servant brought in the tea tray. "I always thought him rather cold before."

"Are not most dukes rather cold, Mama?" Emmeline asked. "It seems to be something they inherit along with the title—ineffable haughtiness."

The others laughed, but Lady Kenleigh said, "Not at all! Your father was great friends with the Duke of Rothheil, and he was not cold at all. Averton, though, is something different."

Once some time had passed and everyone was very distracted by the conversation, Calliope excused herself to find the ladies' withdrawing room and wandered back to the hidden door, far at the other end of the room. It was still there; she had not imagined it. Slipping behind the tapestry, she groped along the stout wood until she found a handle. It shifted under her slight pressure, sliding inward.

A rush of cold air brushed over her face, making her gasp and fall back a step into the heavy tapestry. Behind her were the muffled, reassuring voices of her friends. Ahead of her—she had no idea. Chilliness. Darkness, broken only by a faint gleam far ahead.

Calliope was a sensible girl, or so she had always imagined. Surely the sensible thing would be to turn back, to shut the door and forget it existed. But had she not decided she was no longer the old Calliope? That she could not go back?

She couldn't burst into the dining room and insist Cameron come with her. If she wanted to see what was up there she had to go alone, while she had the chance.

Just one quick look, she decided. Then she could tell Cameron what she found, in exchange for his own news. Now resolute, Calliope stepped on to the first stone stair, drawing the door closed behind her.

The staircase was steep, leading up to that faint light she saw ahead. It was very cold. She drew her shawl close, hurrying upwards. She was beginning to have second thoughts, yet it was too late now. She had to go forward. She *was* a Muse, after all, and Muses might be fickle, but they were surely brave.

The light was a lantern, hung at the mouth of a corridor. She must be deep in the castle, she thought, for there were no windows here, no arrow slits. Just bare stone walls. The corridor was narrow and disappointingly empty.

Calliope sighed. What had she been expecting? Casks of jewels? A letter saying "I am really the Lily Thief, signed the Duke of Averton"? Feeling foolish, she started to turn back to the stairs, when a hollow clunking sound stopped her short.

She spun around, her stomach tight. "Who is there?" she called.

A figure emerged from the shadows at the entrance. "I should have known you would appear," a familiar voice said wryly.

"Cameron!" Calliope cried. She dashed back down the corridor, throwing her arms around his neck. He caught her close, lifting her from her feet. How warm he was, how solid and safe! "What are you doing here? Aren't you meant to be in the dining room?"

"I told them I had to, er, answer nature's call," he said. "What about you?"

"The same, of course. I just had to see what that door was."

"That's my Athena." He pressed a kiss to her hair and let her go, keeping her hand in his. "I should have known you couldn't stay away once you realised there was a hidden portal."

"It doesn't seem to go anywhere, though, does it?"

"There's another door at the end. Come, I'll show you." He unhooked the lantern, using its glow to lead them to the far corner of the empty corridor. Calliope held tightly to his hand. With him, these strange, cold halls were more an adventure than a fright. She peered eagerly over his shoulder as he opened that second door.

"More stairs?" she said.

"These go down."

"Into the bowels of the earth?"

"Just like those in the garden at Kenleigh Abbey. Do you want to turn back?"

Calliope stared doubtfully down those stairs. It was even colder here, darker, even more narrow. Of course she wanted to go back! She was no fool. Not usually, anyway.

But when would they have a chance to explore this place again? They would probably never even come back to Averton Castle. And she had vowed to finish this, no matter what it took.

Be Athena, she told herself sternly. No fear. "I want to go on. We have to take this chance while we have it."

He grinned at her. "Then on we go. Just don't step on any rats."

Rats! Calliope lifted the hem of her gown, tiptoeing down the steps behind Cameron. "Athena never faced rats," she muttered.

"Just Trojans," he answered.

"And Persians."

At the foot of the steps was yet another door. "We won't get lost?" she asked.

"And wander beneath the duke's castle for ever? Never fear, we'll remember the way back. See, another door."

This door led not to an empty corridor but to a small room. As Cameron lifted the lantern high, Calliope gasped. Surely *this* was what she had hoped for!

The room was a jumble of treasures. Some, like the sarcophagus, she remembered from Acropolis House, but many she had never seen before. A bare-breasted snake goddess and inlaid bronze dagger from Knossos. Golden Laconian goblets. A headless marble Aphrodite, and a bodyless warrior's head. A bronze, engraved mirror.

And, at the far end, like a queen reigning over her disorganised kingdom, was the Alabaster Goddess. Her stand now repaired, she stood proudly, her bow ever poised in defence.

She was not alone, though. Like worshipping acolytes, two people hovered at that base. They spun around, startled, when the light from Cameron's lantern touched them. The rays glinted on a pair of spectacles.

"Clio!" Calliope cried. "What are you doing here? And what…?" Her shocked gaze swept over the scene, over her sister and the man who was with her. He looked like a gypsy, with long, raven-black hair, a golden hoop glittering in one ear. He was tall and very lean, even slimmer without the greatcoat and hat he had worn in the garden. His black eyes watched Calliope warily, silently.

An open box of tools lay at Clio's feet, hammers and

slender chisels. Clio held a long metal bar in her hands, wedged beneath the goddess's repaired base.

"No," Calliope breathed. "It can't be."

Clio dropped the bar with a clang, holding out her hands. "Cal, I'm so sorry! I never meant that this—"

"Well, well. If it isn't the Purple Hyacinth," the Duke of Averton said from the doorway. "And let me guess. The Golden Falcon? At last we meet." He smiled at them all, a cold, tight grin that made Calliope shiver. "And Westwood, too. I shouldn't really be surprised. My, my. Such a very cosy scene."

The only sound was the rush of wind down the steps, the steady drip of water from somewhere above. Until Clio picked up the bar, its metallic scrape against the floor abnormally loud.

"Oh, no, my dear," Averton said, his voice sad. "That is not a good idea."

Chapter Twenty-Two

That bizarre dreamlike quality that had overlaid the whole evening intensified, closing in around Calliope like a fog. She pressed her fingers to her pounding temples, watching through the haze as Clio's companion edged closer to her protectively, silent, glowering.

Cameron took her arm gently, as if he feared she might crack like a piece of porcelain. She half-feared she might, for she felt as brittle and delicate as the framed papyrus hanging on the wall.

Calliope stared at that scene, at the shifting blues and reds of the paint. Thoth watching as souls were weighed, carefully recording on his scroll whether they were saved or damned.

The duke hovered in the doorway like a judgemental spirit himself, watching them with those flat green eyes, tense and unpredictable. Calliope was hardly aware of him, though, or of Cameron's touch on her arm. She could only think of one thing.

It was Clio all along. Clio, her sister, who was the Lily Thief, who snatched those antiquities away so they were never seen again. Clio, who had listened to Calliope's worries and plans, who showed her that list. Clio, who she had loved and trusted above all others, ever since the day she was led into the nursery and shown her new baby sister, red-haired and solemn in her beribboned cradle.

Clio, who had been scheming to steal the Alabaster Goddess all this time.

"How could you?" Calliope said, hating herself for the hurt and tears so thick in her voice. She didn't *want* to be hurt, to be vulnerable, ever again! "How could you do this, Clio?"

"Cal, please," Clio pleaded. She edged around her companion, her hand held out to Calliope, but she went still when Calliope gave her a freezing glance. "I never meant to hurt you, never wanted to lie to you. I would have told you everything, once it was all over."

"Once you had stolen every antiquity in England?"

Clio shook her head, her eyes diamond-bright. "It's not like that!"

"Is it not, Miss Chase?" the duke asked conversationally, as if they were sipping tea in a drawing room and he inquired about the weather. "How interesting. We see you here, prying my Artemis from her base, the trapdoor to the secret passage open. Tell us, then—how is it? And do be thorough. I told the others I was going to show all of you some special artefacts. They won't miss us for quite a while."

Clio swung towards him, her hands curled into tight fists. "I will tell *you* how it is, your Grace. Duke of Avarice. You took all these things from their rightful homes, the places where they belonged, and piled them up here to moulder away. To wither away to dust just to satisfy your pride and conceit. I know how you came by these items, how you yanked them from the dirt, from their altars. Or, no, you wouldn't soil your bejewelled hands! You paid lowly *tombaroli*, men who would do anything to feed their families, to snatch them for you. That is how it is."

The duke suddenly lunged forward, quick as a snake, to seize Clio's wrists and drag her close to him. Their gazes locked, and though only their hands touched, the air crackled with the tension of mortal combat. Combat Calliope was paralysed to stop.

"You think you know everything, don't you, Clio, the great Muse of History?" the duke said softly. "You think you are the champion of the ancient world, the storied heroine rescuing sacred treasures from the evil, rapacious dragon."

"I am not a heroine," Clio answered, staring up at him. "I am just a mortal woman who is trying to do what's right, to save what I can. You don't deserve the Alabaster Goddess. She is meant to…"

"To be yours?"

"To go home. She cannot be possessed by anyone, let alone you. A man so full of greed…"

"Careful, Clio." He drew her an inch closer, her hands tense in his clasp as she strained away. "You don't know everything."

"I know *you*! I know men like you. You think you can own things, own people, that you are entitled to imprison whatever you desire."

His gaze narrowed. "Is this because I kissed you in the gallery? Because you——"

"Let me go!" Clio cried, suddenly lashing out, kicking him in the leg. But her silk evening slippers were thin, and he didn't even wince.

Cameron let go of Calliope, pushing her towards the goddess as he tackled the duke. Averton, distracted by Clio, had obviously forgotten the rest of them were even in the room. He fell to the hard floor with a surprised shout, quickly strangled when Cameron's fists closed around his coat collar.

"I will not let you abuse another woman," Cameron growled, pinning the duke down.

Averton laughed breathlessly. "Are you going to break my nose again, Westwood?"

"No less than you deserve. I told you to stay far away from the Chases."

"True. And you are quite right—it's no less than I deserve. I *did* kiss her. Old habits and all that. I think you'll agree with me that the Chase Muses are quite irresistible. Why else would you follow Miss Calliope all over England on such a fruitless errand?"

Cameron's face went white with inexpressible anger, and he lifted the duke's head as if to bash it to the floor. Calliope, cold with fear, cried out, "No!" But she tripped and fell against the Alabaster Goddess, helpless to run to him—just like in a nightmare. Clio's gypsy companion helped her to her feet, saying, "Steady, *signorina*," as he held her upright. Perhaps, then, he was not a gypsy after all, for his accent was pure patrician Venetian.

"Oh, let him go," Clio said, burying her face in her hands. "Much as I would like to see his pretty nose bashed in, it would solve nothing. We're already caught. No doubt his exalted Grace will see Marco and me hanged."

Hanged? The vision of her sister mounting the scaffold was more than Calliope could bear. She pulled away from the patrician gypsy—Marco?—and stumbled to Clio's side, catching her sister's arm in a tight clasp.

Clio said nothing, but leaned into Calliope, boneless and exhausted.

"You see, Miss Chase, that is yet another thing you don't know," the duke said affably. Cameron had reluctantly stepped away at Clio's words, and now Averton rose stiffly to his feet, brushing the dust from his coat. "It's true that you must cease your Lily Thief activities at once, but I think means less than a rope would be sufficient."

"And you think *you* could be those means?" Clio said.

"Oh, I doubt that I personally—or any mere mortal man—could stop you from doing anything. But perhaps you could be persuaded." The duke reached inside his coat and withdrew a folded sheet of parchment.

"What is that?" Clio asked. "Some sort of arrest warrant?"

"Clio," Calliope murmured. She glanced towards the trapdoor Averton had mentioned earlier, a shadow of beckoning freedom in the dark corner. Could they run fast enough?

"Hardly a warrant. It is a letter from the director of the Antiquities Society, Lord Knowleton. I believe he is a friend of your father?"

"What could Lord Knowleton have to say in this matter?" Calliope asked, puzzled.

"A great deal, as it happens. He and the other members of the Society, including Sir Walter, are deeply concerned about the theft of such precious objects as that sarcophagus over there. Or Artemis, who everyone seems so interested in right now. They knew of the tales of my rather reckless youth." The duke glanced at Cameron, who stood silently glowering next to Calliope, whip-tense and ready to pounce again at an instant's notice. "I sometimes consorted then with elements less than worthy of a duke's heir, and have a few connections still. They also knew I am rather interested in collecting."

Clio snorted. "*Rather?* Half of Greece and Egypt sits rotting in your house."

"You forget Assyria, my dear. I do have some rather fine lion figures, plus one or two steles."

"But what does this have to do with the Antiquities Society?" Clio interrupted. Clearly her shock was wearing off. Calliope held her hand tightly so she could not fly at the duke and scratch his eyes out.

"So impatient. But I will tell you. Knowing all this, Lord Knowleton and the Society came to me and asked me to use some of my old connections to discover who was carrying out these thefts. Those of the Lily Thief, and many others, less publicised. Not just here, you see, but in Italy and France. I track them down by whatever means possible, and eventually I see to it that the items return to their owners." Averton laid a gentle hand on the goddess's alabaster sandal. "So, you see, though these objects are exquisite, and I have loved having them for a time, they are not mine."

Clio drew away from Calliope, standing stiff and pale. "I don't believe you."

"Of course you don't." The duke handed her the letter. "Perhaps you recognise the signatures? Or the Antiquities Society seal? The document lays out my task. I insisted on such a thing in case an occasion for explanation arose, which of course it has."

Clio read the letter, her lips pressed together. Calliope peered over her shoulder, searching the neatly penned words until she came to the signatures at the bottom. "It appears to be legitimate," she said slowly.

"How did you find out it was me?" Clio asked, neatly refolding the paper.

"You should be very proud of yourself," the duke said. "You were quite evasive. It wasn't until luck sent me in the direction of your list of contacts that I was able to make the last connections. I knew the Alabaster Goddess was just the bait I needed to draw you out of hiding. She is exactly the sort of antiquity that you like, is she not? Beautiful, special, taken from a temple or sacred site."

"She was merely bait to you?"

"Not merely, my dear. Such a rare object could never be merely anything. My father bought her many years ago, but the selfish old monster never wanted to share her. I didn't even know she existed until I inherited the title."

Clio stared at Artemis. "So she…"

"Is the only thing in this room that is entirely mine." The duke's gaze lingered on the curve of Clio's cheek for a long moment before he turned away. "We should return to the party, I think. We have given them quite enough time to gossip about us."

"No hanging, then?" Clio said, her tone suspicious and tense.

The duke did not look back, as if he couldn't bear to see Clio's face again. "I think we've had quite enough drama for one night, don't you? It should be enough for the Lily Thief to vanish from the scene. And be sure to take your tools when you leave. This place is cluttered enough as it is."

He departed, his footsteps echoing away up the stone steps. The silence in the room was thick, as muffling as wool batting. Calliope hardly knew what to say, what to do. For one of the few times in her life, her practicality, her precious good sense, was of absolutely no use. All she had believed she was working towards was gone.

"Do you hate me, Cal?" Clio said quietly.

Calliope shook her head, closing her eyes as if she could blot out the whole night. "Why would you steal those things, Clio? We don't need money! And we hardly need to add to our collection."

"Cal, surely you know me better than to think I could do this for money?"

"I thought I knew you. But how could I? You hid this from me. You knew how I hated the Lily Thief, how I hated the disappearance of these antiquities and how they were lost to scholars for ever. Yet you said nothing. You let me play the fool!"

"How could I say anything? For those very reasons I had to hide it all from you. But every moment of secrecy was agony. You're my sister, I longed to tell you! To confess everything."

"Then why didn't you?"

"Because the work was too important. I couldn't let my personal feelings get in the way." Clio's sharp, tear-filled gaze shifted over Calliope's shoulder, to Cameron. "*You* understand, don't you, Lord Westwood? After all, you sent your own father's collection back to Greece."

"I did," he said. "But they were mine to send."

Clio lifted her chin. "The people who held those objects were not their true owners. They stole them from their real homes."

"Clio, did you not think of—of *us*, of Father and the girls when you did this?" Calliope asked, suddenly so deeply sad and tired. Exhausted to her very bones. "What if you had been caught?"

"Caught by someone other than the enigmatic duke, you mean? Of course I thought about it. I left letters for you hidden in my room, explaining everything. But I was good at what I did, and I have—had—an excellent network of associates." She smiled at her gypsy aristocrat. "Is that not so, Marco?"

He grinned, and for the first time Calliope saw how very beautiful he was, her sister's silent accomplice. "*Sì, signorina.* Your sister, Signorina Calliope, she is the best smuggler in all England."

"Such a thing to boast of at Almack's," Calliope muttered.

"I am truly sorry I hurt you, Cal," Clio said. "Please, please believe me. But it had to be done." She turned away, going to help Marco pack up their tools.

"Come with me, Calliope," Cameron said gently, taking her arm. "It's cold here, and you look as if you could use a warm cup of strong tea."

"My mother always believed tea could cure anything," Calliope said, letting him lead her towards the door.

"Perhaps she was right, if the tea happens to have a measure of brandy stirred in."

They retraced their steps, climbing up the steps and turning back down the empty corridor. When they first traversed this path half an hour—or was it a hundred years?—ago, she had been full of tense, cold anticipation. Now she was just tired. Stunned.

"It was my own sister all along," she said. "How could I not have seen it? How could I have been so blind?"

"You probably did see it, but denied it. Even to yourself. It's hard to admit the faults of the ones we love. Almost as hard as admitting our own."

Calliope remembered her sister burning her Medusa costume, showing her the list of names. So quiet, so serious, so deeply wary of the duke. *Had* she seen? Had she simply refused to acknowledge the fact that the thief was right in front of her? "I don't know. I just don't understand. And I don't want to see her hurt."

"Of course not. She's your sister. She certainly went about things the wrong way."

"I should say so!"

"But she had reasons for what she did. She told you, she thought she was doing what was right."

Calliope paused, studying Cameron in the faint light. He

gazed back steadily, his cognac-coloured eyes full of concern, and—and pity. He pitied her, and thought Clio was right.

Suddenly, his very calmness, his compassion, infuriated her. She resisted the strange, primitive urge to hit him, to lash out and knock him down as he had the duke. "You don't seem very surprised by what has happened tonight," she said. "By Clio's confession."

His gaze turned wary. "Calliope, listen to me. I meant to tell you, later. Remember?"

"You did know, then? You knew about Clio?"

"Not for long. It was that name, the Purple Hyacinth."

"And that was what you said you had to tell me earlier?"

"Yes."

"So, why didn't you tell me *then*? You let me flounder around in my ignorance, until we were faced with that awful room, with Clio and her gypsy. You let me…" Let her have sex with him. Suddenly it was all far too much. The whole evening crashed down on her, and she wanted to cry, to wail, to beat her fists against the stone wall. To match childish actions to wild, childish emotions.

Everyone she loved the most, relied on the most, had lied to her. Hidden things from her for *her own good*.

"I want to go home," she said, spinning away from Cameron. "I'm tired. Tired of everything, everyone."

"Calliope, please, listen to me!" Cameron said urgently. But she hurried away from him, racing towards the light and noise of the party. If she could just be among people again, back in the real world, escape from cold caves full of anti-quities and lies, she could be herself again. Find her way.

But she knew, even as she ran, that nothing could be the same again.

Cameron watched Calliope flee, her white dress fading away like a ghost in the shadows. Every fibre of his being urged him to run after her, to catch her in his arms and hold her until she listened to him, until she heard him and understood. To *make* her understand.

But he knew Calliope well by now, too well to think that such tactics could ever work on her. He remembered the duke holding Clio, his stare burning into her as she resisted hearing him. The Chases were stubborn and wilful, set on their own course, and force would never change them. Only gentle, rational persuasion had even a chance. Something Averton couldn't understand, but Cameron was beginning to.

It was that very stubbornness, that strong will, that made him love Calliope so very much. That certainty, that passion for a cause, for *right*—even when her "right" wasn't his own. She had a fire she thought well hidden behind her cool good manners, her stylish white gowns, but which she could never extinguish from her eyes. Her laughter. He craved the blazing heat of that fire. He had been wandering in the cold world alone for too long.

He needed Calliope by his side for the rest of his life, to quarrel with, be exasperated by, to kiss and love. If only he could earn her love in return, to set that flame free once and for all!

But, blast it, that *stubbornness*! Cameron kicked at the wall, barely feeling the impact of the stone. She just wouldn't listen.

"Where is Calliope?" he heard Clio say. He glanced up to find her coming down the corridor towards him, holding a lantern. One would never guess she had just spent the evening trying to dislodge an alabaster statue from its base. Every auburn hair was in place, her amber-coloured gown impeccable. Cool and elegant.

And her very composure, oddly, gave him hope. For

another quality Muses possessed was changeability. Perhaps Calliope would not stay angry for long.

"She has returned to the party," he said.

"Without you?"

"She insisted rather, ah, forcefully that she wanted to be alone."

"Threw a bit of a tantrum, did she? That is not much like Cal. But then, who could blame her? It has been a trying evening, and all my fault."

"So it was, Purple Hyacinth. Lily Thief. Whoever you are tonight."

"Clio will do, since I am sure you will soon be my brother."

"If your sister can forgive me."

"Forgive *you*, Lord Westwood? Whatever for? You didn't try to steal the Alabaster Goddess. Is it because you defended my motives?"

"That, and the fact that I discovered your identity earlier and had not yet told her."

"Ah, I see," Clio said. "How did you guess?"

"I should have known even earlier, considering that we all live in such a classical world. I saw a painting of the Muses in Lord Kenleigh's library. Clio, the mother of Hyacinth."

"It was a mistake. I should have chosen a less obvious moniker. They're meant to be somewhat recognisable, though, at least by the people in the network."

"Like your friend Marco?"

"Marco. The Golden Falcon." She smiled. "He is so very dramatic. Most Venetians are, you know."

"Dramatic and gone, I hope."

"Of course. He left by the tunnel. It eventually comes out near Kenleigh Abbey."

"The steps in the garden."

"This house party was a godsend. Yorkshire is riddled with hidden tunnels and passages. Left over from smuggling days, of course."

"And the goddess?"

"Still here. I am not such a fool as to take her when I'm caught. I know when to admit defeat. For now."

As Cameron studied the hard glint in her green eyes, he could almost, *almost*, pity the duke. Desiring a Muse was never an easy thing.

"Come, Lord Westwood, you can escort me back to the party," Clio said, taking his arm. "And don't worry about Calliope. It is me she is truly angry with, not you. Her storms never last long." She paused. "Not usually, anyway."

It was that "not usually" that concerned him.

Chapter Twenty-Three

"Soon it will be time to return to town," Emmeline said, digging along the river's edge, looking for water flowers.

"Oh, yes," Calliope answered, distracted. Her sketch-book was open on her lap, but only a few rough lines began to denote the nearby bridge. "For your betrothal ball."

"Yes. At least one good thing came of this holiday, even if we didn't end up catching the Lily Thief. My parents quite gave up the idea of Freddie Mountbank as a good match!"

"Shall you be happy with Mr Smithson?"

"Oh, yes, I think so. He is very kind-hearted, you know, so I am sure of always getting my own way." Emmeline laid out her plants in a basket, brushing off her hands as she peered closely at Calliope. "Will we soon have news of your own engagement?"

"Mine?" Calliope ducked her head over her sketch-book, her face warm despite the cool, overcast day. "What would make you think that?"

Emmeline shrugged. "You were absent from the duke's party for quite a while last night."

"The duke was showing off his collection. Lord Westwood and I were with him and Clio, quite well chaperoned."

"I just thought you looked a bit pale and surprised when you came back to the drawing room. As if something had happened."

Pale and surprised? Calliope sighed. That was the very least of it. Those few moments in Averton's hidden room were the most surreal, the most difficult she had ever known. Even now, after a night of fitful sleep, she hardly knew what to think. What to feel. She had loathed the Lily Thief for so long, but she loved her sister.

She looked over at where Clio sat on a large, flat rock below the bridge with Thalia, the two of them dangling their booted feet above the rushing water. Clio was quiet today, and she had tried to catch Calliope's eye over breakfast and on the walk here. She wouldn't press, though, Calliope knew that. She would let Calliope talk to her in her own time.

If only Calliope knew what to say.

"I just think one person has no need of so many riches," Calliope said. "So selfishly hidden away."

Emmeline laughed. "What he puts on open display is quite astonishing enough. I can't imagine what he might hide."

Calliope hadn't imagined, either. "Averton is rather—surprising."

"To say the least." Mr Smithson called Emmeline's name and she turned towards him, leaving Calliope alone with her sketches.

She drew in a deep breath, closing her eyes. Despite everything that had happened here, she would miss this place. Its solitude, its quiet, silvery magic. Something about it had surely changed her, unlocked something deep inside so that, for a while at least, she felt lighter. Free.

Was it really this place? Or was it someone? Someone who had made her see things differently. See a new way.

Calliope saw a vision of Cameron's handsome face, his laughing eyes, as he held her close in the moonlight. As he kissed her until the whole world spun dizzily around them and she could hardly remember even her own name. She knew only him, wanted only him!

She also saw him as he had been last night, his face set in hard, angry stone, so white-hot with fury as he knocked the duke to the ground. All to protect Clio, to protect *them*. Yet he had known even then that she was the thief. Had known, and hadn't told Calliope.

Calliope pressed her hands to her aching temples. Nothing was what she had thought, nothing and no one—Cameron, Averton, Clio. She had built her whole life on a foundation of certainty as strong as granite. On beliefs she thought unshakeable. As fierce and permanent as the Alabaster Goddess herself, with her bow and her crescent moon.

That foundation proved to be ephemeral as sand. What would now replace it?

What could she be sure of?

"May I sit with you for a while?" she heard Clio say softly. She opened her eyes to find her sister standing next to her. Clio was as lovely as ever, every hair in place, her spectacles on her nose. But she looked worried, lightly poised as if to dash away at a sign of rebuff.

She had always been thus, Calliope thought, remembering when they were children running round the gardens. Calliope always the organiser of their games, Clio following, but as self-contained as a cat. As a goddess. Her thoughts and motives always her own.

"Of course," Calliope said. She slid over on her fallen log, making room for her sister.

Clio settled next to her, wrapped tightly in her cloak. They sat in silence for a moment, listening to the splash of the water, the distant laughter of their friends. Finally, Clio said, "I truly am sorry for deceiving you, Cal. I never wanted to hurt you."

Calliope bit her lip. "What if you had been caught? Did you think of that?"

Clio gave a humourless laugh. "Every day. I was quite terrified. Especially of you."

"Me?"

"You were so very determined to find the Lily Thief. I knew it was only a matter of time."

"You had nothing to fear. I wasn't clever enough to see what was right in front of me."

"You didn't *want* to see. And neither did I."

"What do you mean?"

"The duke, of course." Clio shook her head. "There was always something not right about that man. I thought he was just insane. And obsessed. Instead, he had a purpose I never even suspected. I was a fool."

Calliope remembered the duke's eyes as he watched Clio. "We were all fools."

"I had to do what I thought was right, Cal. To protect something precious and irreplaceable. I see I never should have concealed it from you, for we both want the same thing."

Calliope laughed. "I could never be brave enough to take up smuggling, like you! Or consort with people like that Marco. He seemed rather fearsome."

Clio laughed, too, a faint blush touching her pale cheeks. "Marco is all right. He has a soft heart under that impenetrable Venetian hide, and he loves art as we do. I don't mean that you would ever lose your good sense, as it appears I have. I mean we both wanted to protect the Alabaster Goddess and all she stands for."

"True." A silence fell over them again, but it was lighter, easier, touched with their old sisterly comfort. Eventually, Calliope held out her hand and Clio took it, holding it tightly. "You can tell me anything from now on, Clio. I have learned not to judge, not to make pronouncements. At least not until I've heard all explanations! Just promise me something."

"What?"

"That you will not take such risks in the future. We Muses have to stay together, all of us."

Clio didn't reply. Instead, her gaze narrowed as a large, glossy black carriage rolled into view. It dashed up over the bridge, and for one instant the window lowered to a glimpse of bright hair, a hand laden with emerald and ruby rings. Then it was gone, followed by a wagon filled with trunks and cases. In the centre, covered in heavy canvas and bound by thick ropes, was Artemis, her bow tightly swathed.

Clio watched the procession until even its dust was no longer seen. "I promise no more Lily Thief," she said quietly, reaching inside her cloak. She withdrew a white lily, wilted, brown at the edges of its satiny petals. No doubt it had been meant to be left in place of the goddess last night. She tossed it into the river.

Calliope had certainly noticed Clio hadn't promised to take no more chances. But the end of the Lily Thief was a place to start.

"What about Lord Westwood?" Clio said.

"I don't think he'll turn you in."

"That's not what I mean, Cal. I mean, what about *you* and Lord Westwood?"

Cameron and her? Before last night, she had begun to hope. To maybe think that her long-ago dreams of a man who could understand her were real. He did understand her, as she did him, for their hopes and ideals were much the same. With him, perhaps, she could at last be free. Free of being the eldest Muse, the one in control, the one who always knew the answers. With him, she could just be *Calliope*. Could begin to learn who Calliope was.

But then she had behaved so childishly last night. Refused to listen to him. And right when their quarrels at last seemed finished!

"Lord Westwood and me?" she said. "I don't think there is any such thing now."

Clio frowned. "Do you still argue with him, then?"

"No. Not like we used to, anyway. He is probably tired of me, of my silly schemes."

"Oh, Cal. What other man would have spent all this time helping you with your 'silly schemes'? Following you through secret tunnels? You just have to face facts, my dearest sister. He is meant for you, and you for him. There can be no one else for either of you, because you would make any other mate quite unhappy with your respective eccentricities." Clio gave a theatrical sigh. "It is the curse of being a Chase Muse. We're never happy with ordinary life. At least *you* have found someone who shares your oddity. The rest of us seem destined for solitude."

Thalia chose that moment to let out an Amazonian shout, standing up on her rock with her arms flung wide. She twirled around, her hair a golden flame.

"Especially Thalia, I think," Clio murmured. "Only Apollo himself could ever be *her* match."

Calliope laughed, suddenly feeling so light she could surely float away! Clio was right, and Calliope had been a fool to ever doubt it. She was fortunate to find her match, to find a man like Cameron—kind, funny, handsome, infused with the same love of history as the Muses. A man who could show her a new world.

Was it too late?

"I have to go," she said, jumping to her feet. Now, before one more minute was wasted, she had to find Cameron and tell him her feelings. Her yearnings.

"Yes, go, go," Clio urged, laughing as Calliope ran up the slippery riverbank.

Calliope soon left behind the voices of her friends, the river and the bank, as she dashed down the overcast lane. The wind was colder here, and she drew her cloak close, as if to shut away the outer chill—and her own inner doubts. When she was with her sisters, listening to Clio talk, it was easy to believe all would be well in the end. Now, alone, doubts always crept in. Old, plaguing doubts.

She remembered Cameron's face, the veiled hurt in his eyes, when she stormed away from him, refusing to listen to him. Was it all too late? Or, despite his kisses, had he really never cared for her at all?

She wished she could truly call on an ancient goddess, one who could banish all self-doubt, all fears. But all she truly had was herself, and that had to be enough.

"You have to tell him how you feel," she told herself as she turned through the gates of Kenleigh Abbey. "If you don't, you will surely regret it for the rest of your life."

And turn into a bitter old Muse, lecturing her bored nieces and nephews on the glories of the classical world.

She found him in the garden. He stood on the lower step of the terrace, staring out at the hidden passageway, now blocked up again. His hands were locked behind his back, his face expressionless, as if carved in marble. The wind curled his hair over his brow in that poetic tangle she loved so much. Her beautiful Greek god, staring into a world only he could see, a reality only he could know.

Would he share that world with her? Was it possible now?

"'How shall I receive the god, the proud one,'" she said softly, walking down the terrace steps to his side, "'the arrogant one who stands in the highest place, above all the gods and people of the teeming earth'?"

He glanced at her, his face unchanging. But she thought, hoped, she saw a gleam deep in his eyes.

"Are you back from your walk already?" he said.

"I am. The others are still at the river."

"Why did you return alone?"

"To find you, of course."

He brow arched in surprise. "To find me?" he said warily. Perhaps he thought she meant to berate him again.

"It was so very late when we returned to the Abbey last night, we never had another chance to talk."

"Ah, yes. Last night." He unclasped his hands, crossing his arms over his chest as he nudged at the grass with his boot. "Quite an adventure, was it not?"

"You could call it that. Who would have thought the duke could be on the side of good, for once? *Good* as he sees it, anyway. As for Clio…"

"I never meant to conceal the truth from you," Cameron said gently. "I just did not want to see you hurt."

"I know. If there is a god who is the protector of women, he is surely your patron! You would have told me, and in a far more gentle way than what happened last night."

"I only discovered the truth when I saw that painting in the library. Even then I wasn't sure. Not until we saw her with the Alabaster Goddess."

Calliope nodded. "I talked with Clio. She has vowed

there will be no more Lily Thief. But when I think of the danger she put herself in…!"

"That is just the way you Muses are. You care so deeply. Passionately."

Calliope laughed. "I never realised I had 'passion' at all! I just thought I had certainty. The knowledge of what is right and wrong. Until…"

"Until what?"

"Until you. Your passion, your daring—it ignited my own. You helped me discover things about myself, about the world, that I never imagined. *You* are the Muse, I think."

His mask finally cracked, and he turned to her with hope, fear, desire in his eyes. Emotions that matched her own. "Calliope, I never—"

"No." She pressed her finger to his lips, just as she had last time they stood on this terrace. "I have to say this before I lose my nerve. I was wrong not to stay and listen to you last night. Not to trust. It—well, it's not an easy thing for me to trust. But I know now I can always rely on you to tell me the truth, whether I want to hear it or not. I can rely on you to protect me and my family, to support me even when you think I'm wrong. Like when you agreed to help me find the Lily Thief in the first place."

He grinned at her, catching her hand in his. He kissed her fingers, sliding them down to press over his heart. Through the soft wool and linen, the trappings of civilisation, she felt the strong pulse of sheer, primitive life. "Calliope. I only agreed to help you catch the Lily Thief because I wanted to spend time with you."

Calliope laughed, thrilled at the admission. "You wanted to spend time with me? Even after I had argued with you, berated you?"

"It seemed the only way you would associate with me.

And you see the lengths I would go to in order to be close to you? Running down secret passages. Associating with thieves and false gypsies and even dukes. Horrid stuff."

"But why did you *want* to be close to me?"

"Because you are beautiful, of course," he teased. He caught her around the waist, twirling her off her feet in a heady whirl of laughter. "And because of that passion you deny possessing. I could sense it inside of you, like a flame burning in your eyes. It drew me in; I couldn't stay away. Surely you are more siren than muse."

"A stubborn siren?"

"I adore your stubbornness. I adore how you defend the ones you love, the ideas you hold so fiercely true."

Calliope laughed again, breathless, winding her arms tightly about his neck to hold him captive. "No one has ever loved my stubbornness before. And you think I'm beautiful? Really?"

"The most beautiful woman in all England."

"But not Greece? I'm sure you saw some *very* beautiful women there. Veritable goddesses."

"None to rival you, chief of the Muses. *You* are what I always sought. What I travelled the world seeking, and here you were all the time. My fierce Athena."

"I think we need to invoke another goddess right now," she whispered.

She felt the curl of his smile. "And who would that be?"

"Aphrodite. Did she not serve us well before?" Smiling, she took his hand in hers and led him again towards the trees. Only there, in their secret spot, could she truly show him what was in her heart.

He followed, unresisting but silent. Was this declaration going to be even harder than she feared?

She turned to him when they reached the clearing, her

heart in her throat. Balanced on her hand as she offered it
to him. "Cam, I must say—"

But his lips swooped down on hers, swallowing her
tentative words, catching her breath, her senses, her very
balance, and sending them spinning away. She was surrounded entirely by *him*.

Her own fierce desire, awakened in this very spot, rose
up to meet his, equal—no, surely greater! With a groan,
she wrapped her arms tightly him as he lowered her to the
ground. His weight was heavy and sweet, their bodies
fitting perfectly as if always meant to be. How she had tried
to push away her feelings for him, to deny what was in her
heart! But those feelings were stubborn, and would not be
banished. They burst free now, an explosion of sparks,
bright colours, wild excitement.

She needed him, loved him, and that was all.

Calliope shoved his coat from his shoulders with impatient hands, fumbling with his cravat, his shirt and waistcoat, until she had what she wanted—his bare, warm skin
under her touch. She scored her nails lightly along the long
groove of his spine, almost to his taut buttocks, and then
back up again to plunge into the satiny curls that tumbled
over his neck. Her beautiful Greek god.

Cameron growled, low and rough, his tongue seeking
hers in a kiss not practised and seductive, but blurry and
needful. Calliope's skirts seemed too heavy, abrading her
sensitive skin, and she reached down with one hand to pull
at them. Not even breaking their kiss, he helped her, strip-
ping away her cloak and gown until she lay beneath him
in her chemise.

Calliope wrapped her legs around him, holding him so
close he could never escape. Here, in their forest grove,
entwined with him, she was finally free.

* * *

The grey-yellow light was hazy above them when Calliope opened her eyes. It grew late in the day, yet she could not shed her lazy, delicious heaviness. Couldn't bring herself to even move.

Their clothes were scattered about the clearing, little piles and tufts of wool and linen, stirring in the breeze. She kicked at a stray stocking, and Cameron's arms tightened around her. Calliope rolled over to find him with his eyes closed, a half smile on his lips. How lovely he was, so free of cares! So relaxed, like Apollo after his task of summoning the sun was finished. So irresistible.

Calliope arched into the curve of his body, pressing a soft kiss to his cheek. He smiled without opening his eyes, drawing her even closer.

"Thank you," she whispered.

"Shouldn't I be the one thanking you, Aphrodite?" he said hoarsely.

"Will you be thanking me when they read the banns and you cannot escape?"

"Or *you* can't escape. Muses are notoriously changeable. I think I should apply for a special licence. Less time for you to fly away."

"I shall never want to fly away. I'm going to follow you wherever you go, you know."

"Good. Then I'll always be aware of when you're chasing after thieves, putting yourself in danger."

Calliope ran her fingertips along his arm, feeling the tense strength of his muscles, his leashed power. He shivered under her touch. "My thief-chasing days are done. I don't always like what I find at the end of the chase, you see."

"I'm glad to hear it."

She propped herself up on her elbow, gazing down at his face, that lazy half smile she loved so much. "That doesn't mean I want our adventures to be over! I've just found that part of myself, after all. I'm not ready to go back to being staid and sedate."

He twined one of her long, black curls around his finger. "Were you ever staid and sedate? I must have missed it. But I am an old stay-at-home now. An old earl, soon to be an old, married earl. My gallivanting days are over."

"They had best not be over quite yet! For mine are just beginning. If I have to go adventuring by myself—"

"Never!" He stopped her words with a laughing kiss. "Very well, then, my Muse. What do you say to a wedding trip to Greece?"

"That will do—for a start."

"And when we return, we can start our own band of Muses. Of little goddesses and godlings."

Calliope laughed. "Do you really want that many daughters? It is no easy task, I can tell you. Especially when they possess the Chase wilfulness."

"Of course I do, if they all look like their mother. I would be the happiest man in the world."

"In that case…" Calliope pushed him on to his back, her hand lingering on his naked chest, trailing downward. "We had best get started."

Epilogue

As the boat drew nearer to the island of Delos, gliding leisurely through the azure water, Calliope saw it was just as her husband had described. Grey with morning mist, damp, shapeless, with no mountains or valleys to delineate it. A desert in the sea. How Apollo's mother Leto must have despaired when she was set down amid such barrenness to birth her sacred twins!

Calliope felt no despair, though, only a fluttering excitement as they drew closer, the mists parting. How long she had waited for this! Ever since the day she had sat by a Yorkshire stream and listened to Cameron tell her of this mystical place. Back then she could never have imagined she would see it for herself. That Cameron would be her husband.

She held tightly to his hand, watching the sun appear through the greyness, as if Apollo's chariot pierced the fog.

"Shall we see the gods today, then?" she whispered. "I fear the clouds will keep them away."

"Have patience, my love," Cameron said, smiling at her. "You should know the gods never appear on demand. They are as fickle as Muses. Almost."

She leaned closer, pressing a light, tickling kiss to his neck, bare without a cravat. "Was I so *fickle* last night?"

He laughed. "Not in the least."

Calliope smoothed back the tangle of hair from his brow. How very handsome her husband was, as if Apollo himself had alighted in their boat! Once she would have said he could not be more beautiful than he was on their wedding day, standing before a flower-bedecked altar in her father's drawing room and vowing to love her for the rest of their lives. But she would have been wrong, for he belonged *here*. In this ancient, wild, dangerous land, full of sunlight and sea air, he came completely alive.

And so did she. Never had she seen colours so vivid, heard laughter so clear and true. The sharp, briny taste of olives and new wine; the heat of the sun on her bare skin as she lay in bed with Cameron, lazy afternoons full of lovemaking; the cool, green smell of the night. The brilliant stars overhead. It was *life*, real life, as she had never even imagined it before.

"There was once a bridge between Delos and Rheneia," their boatman said, his oars sounding hollow in the waves as they entered shallower water. "Built by the rich and very vain Nicias. They say it was a golden creation, lined with fine tapestries and garlands. Worshippers could march right across with their offerings, no fussing with boats and such."

Cameron laughed. "No doubt Nicias was an orderly sort of man! My mother once told me a tale of earlier processions here. Everyone haphazardly leaping ashore in no particular order, singing, tossing garlands about. No order or ritual. Most shocking."

"I'm glad his 'orderly' bridge has vanished, then," Calliope said. "I like the idea of jumping ashore, singing and strewing flowers."

"Calliope de Vere! How shocking," Cameron said, his arm going around her waist to hold her close. "Where is my practical, orderly bride?"

"Left behind in London, of course."

Their boat at last touched the rocky beach, and Cameron leaped out, reaching back to swing her up into his arms.

Calliope protested, laughing. "I can walk, you know!"

"You don't want to get your shoes wet, do you? Besides, this is far more fun."

Once they left the narrow beach, he set her on her feet and they turned down a narrow, overgrown pathway, hand in hand. The landscape was thick with thistle and barley grass, blasted and brown. It appeared the only living beings besides themselves were lizards, brown and black, darting into the meagre shade of twisted trees and old boulders. The sun crawled up overhead, spreading white-hot rays until it seemed to come in pulsating waves, burning into the dusty earth.

Calliope shed her shawl, letting the light fall on her arms and shoulders, bared in a light muslin gown. This place, so barren and empty, hardly seemed a fit home for gods, not like better-preserved temples and theatres they had visited on the mainland and on Mykonos. Yet she could feel its magic. It was as real, as palpable, as that sun overhead. This was a place truly out of time. All her reading and study could never have prepared her for this reality.

If only her sisters could see it, too, she thought. How they would love it.

Finally, they emerged into a wide clearing, a ring guarded by the lionesses of Artemis. Weathered now, worn away by the centuries, diminished in their number, they still stood vigil. Ever young and fierce, poised to pounce on heretical intruders and tear them to bits.

Calliope was glad of her offering, then, a bouquet of bright flowers she laid at the feet of the first lioness.

"This was once the Sanctuary of Apollo," Cameron said.

Calliope gazed around at the littered ruins, the tumble of broken columns, steps leading to vanished portals, pieces of the colonnades that once guarded the sacred statue of Apollo, which was only a portion of torso now, but had once loomed tall. The marble, a silvery-white colour, sparkled in the heat.

"They say Apollo spent his summers here," Calliope said, adjusting the tilt of her straw hat. "One would have thought the winters would have been more practical."

He laughed. "You see, you *are* still my sensible bride. Come, I'll show you something else."

Calliope followed him to the far end of the sanctuary site, where the now-dry pool of Apollo stood, surrounded by the remains of his sacred swans. They were overlooked by a low, flat base of the same silver-coloured marble.

"This is where your Alabaster Goddess once stood," he said quietly. "Or so they say."

"Oh!" Calliope gasped. She knew that Artemis had originally come from Delos, long before she fell into the Duke of Averton's possession. Yet to see where she had once stood vigil, guarding the placid swans with her steady bow, was overwhelming. Calliope laid her hand on the base, feeling the heat baked into the stone rising up inside her like the power of the goddess herself.

And, for the first time, she understood what Clio must have really felt. Her despair at leaving the Alabaster Goddess in the clutches of the duke, when this was her home.

But Clio was on her own path now, gone on a tour of Italy with their father and Thalia. Perhaps one day she would come to this place, too, and would understand things that had been hidden for so long.

Calliope stared up at where the goddess once stood. All she saw was the clear turquoise blue of the sky, the dazzle of the light. In the distance, she thought she could hear music, young voices lifted to the Delian Apollo.

"I heard a tale once," she said. "Apollo and Calliope, chief of the Muses, once came to Delos together, and here they conceived Orpheus, the greatest of all musicians." She took one of Cameron's hands, pressing the palm flat to her stomach. "Will we be blessed with a new Orpheus, do you think, in about, oh, eight months' time?"

Cameron's gaze shot to hers, filled with doubt, wonder, and—and joy. Joy to rival the sun, to rival any god's greatest triumph.

And they kissed under the wide Greek sky, celebrating a new life blessed by the protection of the Alabaster Goddess.

* * * * *

Author's Note

The trade in illegal antiquities is nothing new, of course. It has probably been going on ever since one caveman envied another's wall art! But in recent years, with the rise of the internet and the development of more sophisticated equipment, it has become a huge global industry. Every day countries are stripped of their irreplaceable cultural heritage, and the study of the past is obstructed.

Two fascinating sources on this important subject are: *The Medici Conspiracy: The Illicit Journey of Looted Antiquities From Italy's Tomb Raiders to the World's Greatest Museums* by Peter Watson and Cecilia Todeschini; and *Stealing History: Tomb Raiders, Smugglers, and the Looting of the Ancient World* by Roger Atwood.

Harlequin Intrigue top author Delores Fossen presents
a brand-new series of breathtaking romantic suspense!
TEXAS MATERNITY: HOSTAGES
The first installment available May 2010:
THE BABY'S GUARDIAN

Shaw cursed and hooked his arm around Sabrina.

Despite the urgency that the deadly gunfire created, he tried to be careful with her, and he took the brunt of the fall when he pulled her to the ground. His shoulder hit hard, but he held on tight to his gun so that it wouldn't be jarred from his hand.

Shaw didn't stop there. He crawled over Sabrina, sheltering her pregnant belly with his body, and he came up ready to return fire.

This was obviously a situation he'd wanted to avoid at all cost. He didn't want his baby in the middle of a fight with these armed fugitives, but when they fired that shot, they'd left him no choice. Now, the trick was to get Sabrina safely out of there.

"Get down," someone on the SWAT team yelled from the roof of the adjacent building.

Shaw did. He dropped lower, covering Sabrina as best he could.

There was another shot, but this one came from a rifleman on the SWAT team. Shaw didn't look up, but he heard the sound of glass being blown apart.

The shots continued, all coming from his men, which meant it might be time to try to get Sabrina to better cover. Shaw glanced at the front of the building.

So that Sabrina's pregnant belly wouldn't be smashed against the ground, Shaw eased off her and moved her to a sitting position so that her back was against the brick wall. They were close. Too close. And face-to-face.

He found himself staring right into those sea-green eyes.

How will Shaw get Sabrina out?
Follow the daring rescue and the heartbreaking
aftermath in THE BABY'S GUARDIAN
by Delores Fossen,
available May 2010 from Harlequin Intrigue.

Bestselling Harlequin Presents® author

Lynne Graham

introduces

VIRGIN ON HER WEDDING NIGHT

Valente Lorenzatto never forgave Caroline Hales's
abandonment of him at the altar. But now he's
made millions and claimed his aristocratic Venetian
birthright—and he's poised to get his revenge.
He'll ruin Caroline's family by buying out their
company and throwing them out of their mansion...
unless she agrees to give him the wedding night
she denied him five years ago....

**Available May 2010
from Harlequin Presents!**

HARLEQUIN® *Blaze*™

is proud to introduce...

New York Times bestselling author

Brenda Jackson

with
SPONTANEOUS

Kim Cannon and Duan Jeffries have a great thing going.
Whenever they meet up, the passion between them
is hot, intense…spontaneous. And things really heat
up when Duan agrees to accompany her to her
mother's wedding. Too bad there's something
he's not telling her….

Don't miss the fireworks!

*Available in May 2010
wherever Harlequin Blaze books are sold.*

red-hot reads

www.eHarlequin.com

HB79542

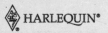

HARLEQUIN®

INTRIGUE

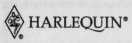

HARLEQUIN®

LAURA MARIE ALTOM

The Baby Twins

Stephanie Olmstead has her hands full raising her twin baby girls on her own. When she runs into old friend Brady Flynn, she's shocked to find herself suddenly attracted to the handsome airline pilot! Will this flyboy be the perfect daddy— or will he crash and burn?

Babies & Bachelors USA

"LOVE, HOME & HAPPINESS"

Former bad boy Sloan Hawkins is back in
Redemption, Oklahoma, to help keep his aunt's
cherished garden thriving and to reconnect with the
girl he left behind, Annie Markham. But when he
discovers his secret child—and that single mother
Annie never stopped loving him—he's determined
that a wedding will take place in the garden
nurtured by faith and love.

REDEMPTION
·RIVER·

Where healing flows...

Look for

The Wedding Garden
by Linda Goodnight

*Available May 2010
wherever you buy books.*

Introducing

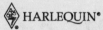
HARLEQUIN®

Showcase

Reader favorites
from the most talented voices in romance

Two titles
available monthly
beginning May 2010

HSCIBC0410

REQUEST YOUR FREE BOOKS!

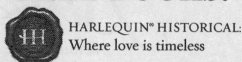

HARLEQUIN® HISTORICAL:
Where love is timeless

2 FREE NOVELS PLUS 2 **FREE GIFTS!**

YES! Please send me 2 FREE Harlequin® Historical novels and my 2 FREE gifts (gifts are worth about $10). After receiving them, if I don't wish to receive any more books, I can return the shipping statement marked "cancel." If I don't cancel, I will receive 6 brand-new novels every month and be billed just $4.94 per book in the U.S. or $5.49 per book in Canada. That's a saving of 20% off the cover price! It's quite a bargain! Shipping and handling is just 50¢ per book.* I understand that accepting the 2 free books and gifts places me under no obligation to buy anything. I can always return a shipment and cancel at any time. Even if I never buy another book from Harlequin, the two free books and gifts are mine to keep forever.

246/349 HDN E5L4

Name _____ (PLEASE PRINT)

Address _____ Apt. #

City _____ State/Prov. _____ Zip/Postal Code

Signature (if under 18, a parent or guardian must sign)

Mail to the **Harlequin Reader Service:**
IN U.S.A.: P.O. Box 1867, Buffalo, NY 14240-1867
IN CANADA: P.O. Box 609, Fort Erie, Ontario L2A 5X3

Not valid for current subscribers to Harlequin Historical books.

Want to try two free books from another line?
Call 1-800-873-8635 or visit www.morefreebooks.com.

* Terms and prices subject to change without notice. Prices do not include applicable taxes. N.Y. residents add applicable sales tax. Canadian residents will be charged applicable provincial taxes and GST. Offer not valid in Quebec. This offer is limited to one order per household. All orders subject to approval. Credit or debit balances in a customer's account(s) may be offset by any other outstanding balance owed by or to the customer. Please allow 4 to 6 weeks for delivery. Offer available while quantities last.

Your Privacy: Harlequin Books is committed to protecting your privacy. Our Privacy Policy is available online at www.eHarlequin.com or upon request from the Reader Service. From time to time we make our lists of customers available to reputable third parties who may have a product or service of interest to you. If you would prefer we not share your name and address, please check here. ☐

Help us get it right—We strive for accurate, respectful and relevant communications. To clarify or modify your communication preferences, visit us at www.ReaderService.com/consumerschoice.

HH10R

HARLEQUIN® *Blaze*™

is proud to present

New York Times bestselling author

Vicki Lewis Thompson

with a brand-new trilogy,
SONS OF CHANCE
where three sexy brothers
meet three irresistible women.

Look for the first book

WANTED!

*Available beginning in June 2010
wherever books are sold.*

---

red-hot reads

www.eHarlequin.com